EYE
OF THE
SWORD

ANGELAEON CIRCLE
BOOK TWO

EYE
OF THE
SWORD

A NOVEL

KARYN
HENLEY

*Wishing you joy
in your journey!*
Karyn Henley

WATERBROOK
PRESS

EYE OF THE SWORD
PUBLISHED BY WATERBROOK PRESS
12265 Oracle Boulevard, Suite 200
Colorado Springs, Colorado 80921

ISBN 978-0-307-73014-5
ISBN 978-0-307-73015-2 (electronic)

Cover design by Kristopher K. Orr; cover photography by Joel Strayer

Published in the United States by WaterBrook Multnomah, an imprint of the Crown
Publishing Group, a division of Random House Inc., New York.

WATERBROOK and its deer colophon are registered trademarks of Random House Inc.

Library of Congress Cataloging-in-Publication Data
Henley, Karyn.
   Eye of the sword / Karyn Henley. — 1st ed.
      p. cm. — (Angelaeon circle ; bk. 2)
   Summary: Trevin is forced to leave Melaia alone to battle with the advances of a
swaggering Dregmoorian prince while he undertakes the king's quest to solve the mystery
of the missing comains and find the harps that will restore the angels' stairway to heaven.
   ISBN 978-0-307-73014-5 — ISBN 978-0-307-73015-2 (electronic)
   [1. Angels—Fiction. 2. Fantasy.] I. Title.
   PZ7.H3895Ey 2012
   [Fic]—dc23

                          2011039623

Printed in the United States of America
2012—First Edition

10 9 8 7 6 5 4 3 2 1

To Raygan and Heath,
excellent brothers and two of the finest men I know

The Three Kingdoms

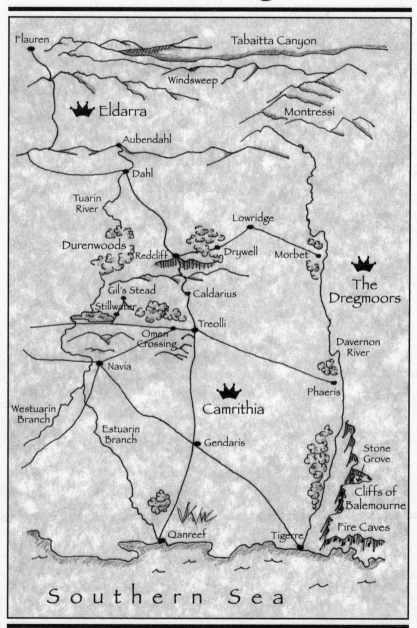

Cast of Characters

Ambria: Queen of Eldarra; mother of Resarian.

Arelin: Angelaeon; a warrior angel.

the Asp: A spy for the Angelaeon; lives in the Dregmoors.

Lord Beker: King Laetham's advisor.

Benasin: The Second-born immortal; father of Jarrod.

Catellus: One of the missing comains of Camrithia.

Cilla: Serving woman at the palace in Qanreef; wife of Paullus.

Dio: A bard for the court of Eldarra.

Dreia: One of the Archae. Guardian of plant life and the Wisdom Tree.

Dwin: Sixteen-year-old brother of Trevin.

Earthbearer: One of the Archae. Guardian of ground and under-ground; also known as Lord of the Under-Realm.

Flametender: One of the Archae. Guardian of fire.

Fornian: One of Prince Varic's men; Dregmoorian.

Haden: Brother of King Kedemeth; a horseman of Eldarra.

Hanni (Hanamel): High priestess of the city of Navia.

Hesel: One of Prince Varic's men; Dregmoorian.

Iona: Fifteen-year-old priestess of Navia.

Jarrod: Nephili; half brother of Melaia; admitted to the ranks of Angelaeon as Exousia.

Lady Jayde: A noblewoman from the southern isles.

Kedemeth: King of Eldarra; father of Resarian; brother of Haden.

Laetham: King of Camrithia; Melaia's father.

Livia: A servant-messenger of the lower order of angels.

Melaia: Seventeen-year-old princess of Camrithia; Nephili.

Nash: King Laetham's personal servant.

Nuri: Thirteen-year-old novice priestess of Navia.

Ollena: Expert swordswoman; Angelaeon of the rank of Exousia.

Paullus: Angelaeon; tavern-keeper at the Full Sail in Qanreef.

Peron: Novice priestess at Navia; turned into a drak at the age of six.

Pym (Pymbric): Armsman to Trevin.

Lord Rejius: Firstborn immortal; ruler of the Dregmoors.

Resarian: Fifteen-year-old prince of Eldarra.

Seaspinner: One of the Archae. Guardian of water.

Serai: Angelaeon; Melaia's handmaid.

Stalia: Immortal daughter of the Firstborn; queen of the Dregmoors.

Trevin: Twenty-one-year-old comain of Camrithia; brother of Dwin.

Varic: Dregmoorian prince.

Windweaver: One of the Archae. Guardian of wind.

THE ANGELAEON

FIRST SPHERE: The three highest ranks are not strictly angels but
　　winged heavenly beings who serve in the presence of the Most High.

CHERUBIM	SERAPHIM	OPHANIM
Guard light and sound (music)	Personal servants of the Most High	Guard celestial travel

SECOND SPHERE:

KURIOTES	ARCHAE	THRONOS
Regulate duties of lower angels and govern worlds	Guardians of the world's elements: wind, fire, water, plant life, and earth	Negotiators and justice-bearers

THIRD SPHERE:

EXOUSIA	ARCHANGELS	ANGELS
Warriors and keepers of history	Guardians of people groups; influential in politics and commerce	Messengers

WORLD SPHERE:

<u>NEPHILI</u>
The "clouded ones"; half-angel, half-human

<u>SYLVANS</u>
Elflike earth-angels; inhabit forests and woodlands

<u>WINDWINGS</u>
Winged horses

EYE OF THE
SWORD
OF THE

As Trevin stepped into the seedy tavern at Drywell, his hand instinctively slid toward his dagger. Not that he was daft enough to challenge the three well-muscled strangers who had cornered his younger brother. Nor did Dwin look as if he wanted to be rescued. He laughed like a madman, his dark curls matted to his forehead, his hands around a mug. One of the three men pushed another mug his way.

A stringy-haired tavern maid sidled up to Trevin. He shook his head and watched her swish away. Maybe he was the mad one, tracking Dwin to Drywell when he should be at Redcliff preparing for the banquet being given in his honor that night. He fought the urge to throttle his little brother.

Melaia's name blurted from Dwin's mouth. His shoulders bounced as he chuckled.

"Dwin!" barked Trevin, striding to the table. His brother spewed barley beer, guffawing as if "Dwin" were the funniest name he had ever heard.

The three strangers eyed Trevin with expressions ranging from amusement to disdain. They appeared to be his age, maybe a few years older. One had a crooked nose. Another was wiry, and a scar ran across his temple. The third wore a close-cut beard, dark as charred wood. A crimson band spanned his forehead and disappeared beneath wavy locks.

At first Trevin thought they might be malevolent angels, but he sensed no aura, pure or impure. By their appearance they were Dregmoorian. Raiders and refugees entered Camrithia from the Dregmoors these days, but the men sitting with Dwin fit neither description. They were too richly dressed. Merchants? Or spies passing themselves off as merchants?

Dwin saluted Trevin with his mug. "My eshteemed brother," he slurred.

Trevin deliberately moved his hand away from his dagger. "Let's go, Dwin."

"I was just getting shhtarted." Dwin grinned.

"It's time you finished," said Trevin.

"I believe the young man wishes to stay," said the Dregmoorian with wavy hair. His eyes were as black as stag beetles. "Join us." He signaled to the tavern maid. "More beer!"

Trevin was tempted. The midsummer day was warm, he was sweaty, and the stone-walled tavern was cool. But he didn't want to drink with Dregmoorians. Besides, he hoped to get to the great hall early and perhaps spend some time with Melaia before the banquet started. He relished the thought of seeing her dressed in her royal best. Even in her priestess's garb, she was beautiful, but seeing her in a gown stole his breath and rushed his pulse.

Trevin started for the door. "Let's go, Dwin."

Dwin stood, wobbling, and the three Dregmoorians smugly rose to let him out. If they were spies, Trevin could only guess what information they had floated out of Dwin, who would say anything to keep the drinks coming and the air jovial.

Dwin swayed toward Trevin. "I musht show you the gash pits. Gash spits. Pit spits." He doubled over in laughter. "Gashpitspits."

"Show me, then." Trevin offered a hand to his brother, who shook it off and weaved toward the door. Benches scraped back up to the table behind him as the Dregmoorians returned to their drinks.

"Gash pits. Spits," murmured Dwin, stepping outside. He squinted in the bright afternoon light, then pointed to a path leading through the woods. "That way."

"Show me the pits another time," said Trevin. "Where's your mount?" He eyed the tethered horses that stood beside his borrowed roan. The three finely groomed and blanketed mounts no doubt belonged to the Dregmoorians.

"Follow me." Dwin wove down the path.

"Your mount?"

"At the gash pits. They stink. You'll see." He giggled. "No, you'll smell." He pinched his nose and weaved ahead.

Trevin followed him to a clearing, barren except for Dwin's gray donkey,

Persephone, and the dry well from which the village took its name. He frowned at the well. Steam writhed out of it, along with a burbling sound.

"Obviously no longer dry," he muttered.

"You think the town'll change its name?" asked Dwin. "Mistwell. Fogwell. Hellwell." He chortled.

Trevin peered over the crumbling rim of rock into the well. At the bottom of the shaft, a dun-colored muck belched bubbles of hot vapor, its stench not unlike eggs gone to rot. "You're right," he murmured. "It's gash." The stuff was touted as a drink to restore youth, but it was dangerous. He had seen gash-drunks, youthful but foggy eyed and dull minded, dying from their addiction to it.

"Over here." Dwin crouched beyond the well. Muck oozed from a rift in the ground, and steam curled into the air.

"Looks like the Under-Realm is vomiting its own bile," said Trevin.

Already a greenish hue, Dwin turned away and lost his stomachful of beer.

Trevin shook his head in disgust and knelt to examine the rift, which was as wide as his thumb. Its length he couldn't judge, for it snaked into the woods east of the clearing.

"It's a landgash, Dwin. Lord Beker sent a dispatch about them, but I thought landgashes were closer to the Dregmoors. The blight must be growing worse." Killing crops and parching rivers, the blight that had started in the Dregmoors was slowly creeping across Camrithia. Stinking rifts would not help matters.

Hoofbeats sounded behind them. Trevin rose. Dwin turned, lost his balance, and sat hard on his rump.

The three Dregmoorians reined their mounts to a halt four paces away, followed by a tan wolf dog with one black leg and gray eyes. At the edge of the clearing, Dwin's donkey backed into the shadows, pulling her tethering rope taut, her ears laid back.

The man with wavy hair and the crimson band across his forehead, clearly their leader, nodded at Dwin. "You said you're a friend of the court and can get us into Redcliff. Or was that a child's boast?"

"It doesn't always pay to listen to my brother," said Trevin.

"It could pay today." The man rattled a coin purse at his belt. "We're looking for a forerunner. Someone to ease the way."

"You're best advised to go back to where you came from," said Trevin.

The man with the crooked nose flexed his hand around the handle of his sheathed dagger. "I fancy your tongue as a souvenir, comely boy." He turned to their leader. "What do you think, Varic? We could add that to our gifts for Redcliff."

"Not today, Hesel." Varic laughed. "I wish to impress the princess, and I hear Camrithian ladies turn their heads at the sight of blood."

Trevin clenched his jaw. Why did this jackal wish to impress Melaia?

"Let's try again." Varic eyed Dwin and fingered the free end of his waist sash, a fine silver mesh. "You promised to introduce us at Redcliff. Do you mean to go back on your word?"

Dwin rose, pale.

Trevin folded his arms. "What's your business at Redcliff?"

"Are you the gatekeeper?" asked Varic. "The constable?"

"He's a dung digger." The wiry one wrinkled his nose. "Can't you smell him?"

"Ah, Fornian, always a good judge of character." Varic grinned at Trevin. "Ever tried gash?" He tossed a gourd ladle at Trevin's feet. "Drink some. It's free."

Gash merchants, Trevin thought as he picked up the gourd. No doubt they had an eye on the profit to be made from newfound rifts and a tavern nearby. He turned the gourd in his hands, admiring the delicate black designs etched into it. "If you and your friends drink gash, you've less wit than your dog."

Varic narrowed his eyes and pointed at the ladle. "Drink up."

"We always let guests go first." Trevin tossed the gourd back to Varic.

Startled by the gourd's return, Varic was slow to the catch. It struck his knuckles with a loud crack. "Scum," he snarled.

The wolf dog bared its teeth. Hesel and Fornian dismounted and drew their daggers.

Trevin tensed. He had expected Varic to catch the ladle and respond to the sarcasm with a few choice words. Trevin shot Dwin a glare, warning him to keep quiet. Dwin's tongue could be sharper than his own. As long as the daggers were not aimed his direction or Dwin's, the threats were just bravado. Let the bullies strut and swagger, and they'd be on their way.

Trevin drew his own blade but kept the tip up, unmenacing, warily watching the Dregmoorians' movements.

"A cripple's grip," Hesel crowed. "The dung digger is missing a finger."

Varic rubbed his knuckles, his stare boring into Trevin. "Which one?"

"Little one."

"He can handle a dagger better than you," said Dwin.

Trevin groaned inwardly. Out of the corner of his eye, he saw Fornian edge closer to Dwin. Trevin hoped his brother had his knife with him—and that he was sober enough to use it.

"What's your name, dung digger?" Varic leaned forward in his saddle, studying Trevin. "Where do you come from? How did you lose your finger?"

Trevin glared. "You tell me your business, and I may tell you mine."

"My business?" Varic gave a sharp laugh. "We hear your king is short of royal defenders—comains, I believe you call them—so we've come to help clean up the Camrithian countryside. I think we'll start by giving a couple of dung diggers a much-needed bath. Nice and warm—in gash. Off with your sandals, boys."

Trevin seethed. Now twenty-one, he had lost his boyhood long ago. Daggers, swords, fists—one-on-one he would take this jackal. His muscles burned with coiled energy. He locked eyes with Hesel, who pointed his dagger at Trevin's feet.

"I'll have your sandals, boy," said Hesel.

Trevin raised his dagger. "And I'll have your crooked nose."

Each eased into a fighter's stance, assessing the other. Trevin knew he had the advantage of height and reach, but Hesel was all muscle and would be a goring bull if he found an opening. Fornian's dagger was a concern as well. Trevin glanced at Dwin, who clutched his knife but still looked unsteady on his feet.

Swift as a snake, Hesel struck, slashing toward Trevin's face and growling, "*Your* nose, lowlife."

Trevin ducked and cut toward Hesel's shins.

Hesel dodged, and their daggers met with a clang.

Back and forth they attacked and parried, Trevin trying to prevent Hesel from slipping in close enough to lunge at him. At the same time, he tried to keep track of Fornian and Dwin, who circled each other warily but had not engaged.

Trevin evaded a cut and struck back, scoring Hesel's left arm. Hesel lashed out in retaliation. As Trevin jumped back, he saw Dwin twist away from Fornian, throwing the wiry man off balance.

Fornian stumbled, Varic whistled, and the wolf dog charged Dwin.

Trevin swerved from Hesel and dived in front of his brother.

At Varic's sharp command, the dog froze, his fangs a handbreadth from Trevin's wrist. Fornian bounded up and knocked away Dwin's knife, and Hesel grabbed Trevin's dagger.

"You want into Redcliff, I'll get you in," said Dwin.

"You will not," Trevin huffed.

The dog growled.

"Get up!" snapped Varic.

Trevin edged away from the dog and stood, panting.

Hesel pointed his dagger at Trevin's feet. "I'll have your sandals."

Trevin removed his sandals. At least Hesel wasn't demanding his nose.

"Tunic too," ordered Varic as the wolf dog ambled back to his side.

At sword point Trevin stripped to his leggings.

Varic motioned to Trevin. "Into the well."

"You're mad," said Trevin. Hesel prodded him toward the steaming pit.

"Salaciously sane," said Varic. "In fact, I feel like doing you a favor. You lack balance. Make his hands match, Hesel. A small finger is just the token I need to impress a certain lady."

"But you said Camrithian ladies shrink back at blood," said Dwin.

Varic grinned. "I was not speaking of a Camrithian lady. Shall we have a finger, Hesel?"

As Hesel swaggered toward him, Trevin grabbed the man's wrist and knocked his dagger hand on the ragged edge of the well, sending the blade tumbling into the darkness. Before Hesel could recover, Trevin hooked his leg behind the man's knees. The brawny Dregmoorian hit the ground, and Trevin laid into him, fast and furious. Hesel was strong, but Trevin was enraged. He punched and pummeled, twisted and turned until he had Hesel pinned.

Varic applauded. Panting, Trevin looked up to see the wolf dog crouched, poised to leap at him, and Fornian holding his dagger at Dwin's throat.

"I would recruit you for my guard, dung digger," said Varic, "but you have more courage than common sense. One word from me, my dog is on you, and your brother will be something the countryfolk gawk at for years to come." He stroked his mesh sash. "But I'll be fair. You release my man, and I'll release your brother."

Trevin slowly loosed his grip on Hesel and stood, his back to the well, watching Fornian. He wanted to tell Dwin to take the blasted devils to Redcliff and be done with their bullying, but the oath he would take on the morrow loomed over him. A comain—pledged to defend king and kingdom—dared not provide a way for no-goods like these to enter the royal city.

Hesel rose, wiping his bloody mouth. But Fornian kept his dagger at Dwin's throat.

Trevin flexed his fists and growled, "Release my brother."

"Now!" commanded Varic. The wolf dog shot toward Trevin.

Fangs rushing toward him, the well at his back, Trevin didn't hesitate. Before the dog could leap, Trevin grabbed the sharp, crumbling ledge of the well and hurdled over it, hoping to find the inner wall with the balls of his feet. As the mongrel clawed at the ledge, he lowered himself, grabbing at chinks in the stone, trying to hug the wall, but it was slick with slime. Before he could gain a hold, he slid within an arm's length of the bubbling ooze.

Trevin heard Varic's whistle and Dwin's strained voice talking fast. He wedged his feet and hands in the widest cracks he could find and felt his way around until he straddled the well. His eyes stung from the steam, and he swallowed to keep from retching at the stench.

Hesel peered down, one eye swollen. "How long can you hold on, dung digger?"

Dirt and rocks, leaves and sticks showered down on him. Trevin turned his head, closed his eyes, and clenched his teeth. Moments later hoofbeats faded into the woods.

Trevin listened for Dwin, then called to him. No answer. He shook the dirt and twigs from his hair and studied the shaft above him. He had scaled walls before but with hooks, never barehanded. The crevices that pocked the sides of the well might serve as handholds if they were not too slick. He reached up and grabbed a protruding rock with his right hand.

As the rock touched the place where his small finger was missing, a mist descended over his mind. Within the mist stood the cloaked figure that haunted his terror-dreams. Never had he fallen into his dream in the daytime.

Gripping the rock, he fought back the image, ignored the flashing pain in his hand, and swallowed his screams.

A stinging sensation on his feet pulled him from the dream and brought him fully back to the danger of his situation. Hot muck spat on him with each thick belch of gash below.

"Climb," Trevin muttered to himself. "Climb or boil."

CHAPTER 2

Scraped, bruised, and sore, Trevin headed through the woods toward Redcliff astride Dwin's donkey. He had returned to the tavern for his mount only to find the horse missing. He suspected Dwin had filched the roan from the tavern post so he could lead the Dregmoorians to Redcliff in style. The dolt.

On the other hand, maybe Dwin knew exactly what he was doing. Maybe he had met with the Dregmoorians before. In that case he was no dolt; he was a traitor. Trevin broke into a cold sweat and nudged Persephone with his heel.

Persey picked up her pace, then settled back into a walk.

Trevin growled. "I can go faster barefoot." He slid off the donkey's back and onto a pine cone. "Blast!" he yelled, hopping on one foot, rubbing the other. He was already sore from brawling; he didn't need a pierced foot as well.

A flutter sounded overhead, followed by a sharp chirp.

Trevin squinted into the treetops. A drak clung to a bobbing branch with its taloned human hands. Not long ago he had aspired to be a talonmaster to the falconlike spy-birds. But then he had seen the shock in Melaia's eyes when she learned each drak held a captive human soul. Worse, Lord Rejius had kidnapped Peron, a child Melaia loved like a sister, and bound her in a drak's body. Now Trevin loathed the whole business of mastering draks.

He grabbed a pine cone and drew back to heave it at the bird. Then he froze. Most draks were large and traveled in pairs. This bird was small and alone.

"Peron?" He dropped the pine cone. He had no meat to offer, no glove to protect himself, but he held out his hand and whistled.

A breeze shuddered through the leaves, rippling the drak's dull black feathers, and the bird flapped away.

Trevin turned back to Persey and yanked her forward. "Come on, beast. You'll make me late to the feast laid in my honor."

Persey plodded through the dim woods as if she had all year to get back.

Trevin groaned. The new comain, valiant horseman of the king, was now a shirtless, shoeless donkey drover. "I hope no one sees me entering Redcliff," he mumbled.

The wind gusted. Leaves danced. A whisper swirled through the air. *Seeeeeker.*

Persey's ears twitched. Her nostrils flared.

Trevin jerked around but saw no one.

Seeeeeker.

A shiver snaked up his spine. The same flesh-prickling voice had come to him twice before, both times in the tower aerie.

Seeeeeker.

Both times he had dashed out of the aerie as quickly as he could. He didn't hesitate to make a quick escape again.

Seeeeeker.

Persephone obviously agreed. Trevin barely made it onto her back before she broke into a ragged gallop.

⇜❧⇝

By the time Trevin approached the east wall of Redcliff, the tallest tower of the palace stood dark against the sunset sky, its stately silhouette interrupted only by the form of a body suspended from the parapet. Presumably another overlord who had supported the recent coup attempt. Trevin knew that if Melaia hadn't captured his heart, he might be hanging from the wall himself. Even now his loyalty to the king was largely unproven. His being late to dinner would not add to the king's trust. And Dwin... If he had told the Dregmoorians anything traitorous...

Trevin thrust away the thought and headed for the stable gate, which was cloaked in shadows. He pushed on the massive wooden door. It didn't budge. He pounded on it.

The peephole slid open, and then the barred inner gate grated through its track, and the bolt scraped aside. Pym, a stout, bandy-legged armsman, swung open the door.

"What are you doing outside?" Pym asked. "You're supposed to be at dinner."

Persephone nudged her way into the stable, and Trevin ducked in behind her.

Pym chuckled as he ran a hand through his shock of unruly hair. "Did the lady keep your tunic?"

"It was no lady."

"I guess not." Pym wrinkled his nose. "You smell overripe. And your cheek is bruised."

"I ran into Dregmoorians intent on drowning me in landgash. They were headed here."

"Must be the ones who arrived this afternoon. They caused quite a stir at the gates, they did."

"Did Dwin get them in?"

"As I heard it, guards detained them while Dwin took their message to the king. They've come to propose a peace treaty, they say. Between Camrithia and the Dregmoors. One of them is Prince Varic."

"*Prince* Varic," Trevin muttered.

Pym spread hay in a stall for Persephone. "They left their horses here only awhile ago. As for your brother—" He nodded toward the door to the court-yard, where Dwin sat on an upturned keg, grinning.

Trevin clenched his fists and stomped over to his brother.

Dwin eyed Trevin through his black curls. "I knew you'd bring Persey back."

Trevin stifled the impulse to cuff him. "You made a regal fool of yourself. You led the enemy straight to our gates while, for all you knew, I lay dead at the bottom of a well."

Dwin waved his hand as if brushing away gnats. "I sent Jarrod for you. Didn't he find you?"

"I rescued myself, no thanks to you. I could have boiled to death in gash."

"You think *I* could have pulled you out? That's why I sent Jarrod. Or is a warrior angel not good enough for you?" Dwin looked around and lowered his voice. "Besides, I was spying."

"For whom? The Dregmoorians?"

"For Camrithia. And don't get all hot about it. You used to spy for Rejius."

"And I despise myself for it," said Trevin. "Besides, a spy *gathers* information. He doesn't get drunk and tell all he knows."

Dwin shrugged, a sheepish look in his eyes. "I drank one too many."

"And then led the enemy straight to the king. What if they're assassins?"

"They're here for peace."

"Right. And I'm here to learn basket weaving." Trevin shoved the door open. "I'm late for dinner. I trust you can find my dagger among your new friends' belongings."

"I already have it." Dwin smirked. "I suggest you don a tunic before you prance in for dinner."

Trevin slammed the door and headed across the courtyard to the temple, where he and Dwin had rooms. Passersby looked askance at him. The odor of gash hung about him like an aura. He would need more than a fresh tunic.

⸙

By the time Trevin reached the palace, torches lit the darkening courtyard. He quickly made his way inside, loped down the corridors, and elbowed through the back-room bustle of attendants laden with baskets of bread, trays of meat, and jugs of ale and wine. He huffed. Feasting seemed a foolish extravagance when the countryfolk could hardly grow enough for their own bellies.

At the serving entrance to the great hall, he paused. Extravagant or not, this feast was for him, and he intended to enter with the assured demeanor of a comain. He calmed his breath and surveyed the room. Lampstands flanked the hall and sent a flickering glow onto the walls. The fragrance of spiced wine, fresh bread, and roasted meats drifted through the air as servants placed heaping trays before nobles and their ladies at tables running the length of the hall. Trevin recognized some of the guests as Angelaeon. Jarrod wasn't among them. He was no doubt searching Drywell.

King Laetham, garbed in purple, presided over the feast from his usual place at the center of the head table. Melaia sat to his right.

Trevin didn't have to see her to know she was there. He sensed her as shimmering silver light. But to see her was pure pleasure, and he let his gaze linger. Her loose braid, the color of dark honey, fell over her shoulder as she leaned toward her copper-haired handmaid, Serai, and spoke intently. The gleam in her rich brown eyes rivaled the gold medallion suspended on a chain at her throat.

A barking call for ale rose from the other end of the table. To the left of the king, Varic held his goblet toward a servant. Trevin swallowed dryly. The seat of honor at the king's left hand was meant for him tonight, not for this wretch. He took a deep breath and strode into the hall, hoping he was rid of the smell of gash. He couldn't hide the bruise on his cheek.

Melaia looked up, her smile stunning.

Trevin wished the moment would freeze with her gaze locked on his. Never mind his hunger for food.

He smiled back and nodded. "My lady." As he passed, he let his hand brush her shoulder.

"I see Jarrod found you," she said. "Your cheek—"

Before Trevin could explain, the king turned his way, his eyes questioning Trevin's late arrival.

Trevin went down on one knee and briefly bowed his head. "Your Majesty."

King Laetham nodded, his thick, graying hair oiled and glinting in the lamplight.

"My apologies for being late." Trevin folded his hands to hide his scraped fingers and angled his head, hoping the bruise would seem a shadow. "I was detained by the discovery of landgash emerging at Drywell."

The king's eyebrows arched. "Landgash? So close? I must ride out and see these oddities. I hear they're strange to behold."

"They are, sire."

"You must meet our guest." King Laetham turned to the Dregmoorian. "Prince Varic, this is Trevin, the young man who will be appointed comain tomorrow. Perhaps you would attend the ceremony with us?"

Varic leaned back in his chair, goblet in one hand, pheasant leg in the other. His face stiffened momentarily, but then he flashed a haughty grin.

Trevin tried to breathe normally and keep the color from rising to his face. He would not bow his head to this Dregmoorian, even if he was a prince.

"Appointing this one?" asked Varic. "I wouldn't miss it." He went back to his meal. "Congratulations, sire. He's a fine figure of a youth."

Trevin's muscles ached with the urge to lunge at the prince. No doubt Varic would welcome the fight. Nothing would make a comain look more foolish than assailing a royal guest in front of the entire assembly.

King Laetham clapped Trevin on the shoulder. "I accept your apology for being late. Find me after the entertainment tonight. I have a task in mind for my new comain, but for now my orders are to enjoy your feast."

As the king waved a hand toward the vacant chair beyond Serai, lamplight glinted from a ring on his forefinger. Trevin couldn't help staring at the ruby the size of an acorn that adorned the ring.

The king posed his hand regally. "A gift from the Dregmoors. A peace offering."

"Wonderful, sire."

Trevin strode to his seat, plopped down, and stabbed a stuffed breast of dove.

❧

After dinner King Laetham rose. A hush drifted over the hall. "Our festivities have only begun," he said. "We have feasted on fine food and shall soon feast on fine music. But first I present our guests: Prince Varic of the Dregmoors, Lord Hesel, and Lord Fornian."

Trevin wished he could get a good look at Hesel. The cur was hiding his black eye behind a raised goblet.

The king continued, "This noble delegation has come to propose a peace treaty with Camrithia."

Murmurs rippled through the audience.

"Tomorrow you shall all be my guests for the appointing ceremony for Main Trevin." King Laetham swept his ringed hand toward Trevin, introduced him, and gave a glowing account of how, only a few months earlier, this new comain had rescued him and his daughter from the sorceries of Lord Rejius and his attempted coup.

Trevin thought the king's story a bit exaggerated. Certainly he hadn't rescued the king single-handedly. Even so, he basked in the praise, glad for the Dregmoorian prince to hear the king's version.

"Our kingdom grows stronger," proclaimed King Laetham. "I am confident we are on the verge of an era of great prosperity. Let us drink to our future!" The king himself filled the prince's goblet.

Prince Varic rose, lofted his goblet high, then gulped down its contents without pausing. He saluted the king with his empty cup, and the court minstrels leaped into a rollicking tune with lyre, pipe, and tabor.

As the guests clapped and sang, Melaia carried her kyparis harp to the side of the hall. Trevin shifted uncomfortably in his seat. He supposed the harp was safe with her, but he hated to see it displayed before the Dregmoorians.

He was hazy about the details, but somehow Melaia's harp and two others like it had to be united in order to restore the angels' stairway to heaven, which had been destroyed by Lord Rejius, the immortal Firstborn and ruler of the Dregmoors. Rejius had arranged for the murder of the angel Dreia, Melaia's mother, in order to steal just such a harp from her. The memory curdled Trevin's stomach. He didn't doubt that Rejius would kill for the other two harps as well. With all three the Firstborn could lord himself over the angels by controlling their path home.

Was that why the prince had weaseled his way into Redcliff? Was he here to steal Melaia's harp?

Trevin touched his bruised cheek. He knew firsthand how Lord Rejius used underlings to reach his goals. Guilt still ate at his conscience for having once served the Firstborn.

He looked down the table at the prince. Varic ran his finger around the rim of his goblet as he studied Melaia, and Trevin's skin crawled. He drank the last of his fruited wine and turned his gaze back to her. He had never lacked attention from young women, but this one, the one he wanted, was out of reach, and there was no remedy for it. She was a princess, and he could never be more than a lowly comain.

"If only she were a normal maiden," he murmured.

"What's normal?" asked Serai, amusement dancing in her green-flecked eyes.

Trevin smiled sheepishly, raising his hands in surrender. For an Erielyon like Serai, normal was hiding her wings securely beneath her cloak. "Maybe 'normal' is not the right word," he said.

Serai frowned. "Your fingers are scratched. The bruise, I noticed earlier. Did you and Dwin have at it?"

"I leaped into a well, then climbed out."

Her eyebrows rose. "Why did you leap into a well? Demonstrating your rock-climbing ability?"

"You might say that."

She rolled her eyes. "My brother, Sergai, was always pulling stunts like that." Her smile trembled, and she murmured, "I should be ready to help Melaia when she's done."

Trevin scooted aside to give her room to leave the table. Her twin brother had died a vicious death the previous fall at the hands of Lord Rejius. The past was slow to let go of its choke hold.

Applause erupted. As the minstrels took their final bows and filed to the side of the room, Melaia made her way to a stool in the center of the hall. She bowed to the king, then sat down elegantly with the harp in her lap, her palms to the strings, her eyes closed.

Trevin drifted with the guests into a suspended silence. Then Melaia plucked a simple tune that gradually unfolded and fanned into an intricate melody that danced around the great hall.

Usually Melaia's music entranced Trevin, but tonight his thoughts kept straying to the gold medallion at her throat. Was it a gift from Prince Varic, a peace offering like the king's ruby? "I wish to impress the princess," Varic had said. Why?

More important, had he succeeded?

CHAPTER 3

Soon after King Laetham retired to his chamber, Melaia and Serai slipped out the back door of the great hall. Trevin caught up with them in the torchlit corridor.

"I think I saw Peron today," he said.

Melaia turned to him, wide eyed, the harp in one arm. "Where?"

Trevin grinned. He loved having answers for her questions. "She was in the woods between here and Drywell."

A shuffle echoed in the corridor behind them. He peered into the shadows where Melaia's bodyguards were stationing themselves.

"Is that where you got this?" She gingerly touched his bruised cheek.

"Near the woods." He turned his head so she could see the bruise better— and keep her hand on his face a little longer.

Melaia handed her harp to Serai. "Return this to my room, please. I want Trevin to take me to the aerie to look for Peron."

Serai hesitated. "You're going to the aerie? Now?"

"Yes," said Melaia. "And when you get to my room, see if you can find menthia ointment for Trevin's bruise."

"The ointment I'll take," said Trevin, remembering how Melaia had spread it over his bruised stomach the previous fall, "but I cleaned out the aerie. The cages are gone."

"I wouldn't cage Peron," said Melaia, "but she might look for us in the aerie. At the least we might glimpse her from the tower."

"Excuse me," said Serai. "But—"

"Spotting Peron is best done in daylight," said Trevin.

"Not for you," said Melaia. "You can see in the dark."

Trevin sighed. He would like nothing better than to spend time with Melaia in the dark aerie. "I can't go right now. Your father's expecting me."

"He's expecting you, too, Melaia," Serai pointed out. "Or are you conveniently forgetting?"

Melaia pursed her lips. Then her eyes brightened. "If we go to the aerie first, maybe he'll be asleep by the time we reach his room."

"You don't want to see your father?" asked Trevin.

"I was in and out of meetings with him all day."

Serai narrowed her eyes. "My lady, *you* may be able to put off your father, but Trevin would be wise to respect the king's wishes."

Melaia groaned. "Why are you always right?"

"It's my job," said Serai. "Shall I assume Trevin will see you safely back to your chamber tonight?"

Melaia nodded toward the bodyguards. "Grim and Glum will make sure I get back."

Serai rolled her eyes. "You're in a mood. Khareet and Dano are doing their jobs as well. Be grateful."

Trevin bit his lip to keep from smiling as Melaia and Serai put their heads together, sharing sharp words. He stepped back and feigned interest in a torch bracket. Serai bore the same direct, no-nonsense authority as her mother, Livia, knowing what to say and when to say it. Her calm confidence had held Melaia steady more than once as she learned the role of princess.

As the ladies' discussion quieted, Trevin stepped forward. "I'll gladly accompany Melaia back to her chamber. And perhaps, Serai, you might ask Khareet or Dano to see you back safely."

"You don't think I can take care of myself?" Serai asked.

Trevin had seen Livia wield a sword with deadly results and had no doubt that Serai could do the same. "I'm more worried about the harp."

Serai hugged the harp and lowered her voice. "It's the Dregmoorians, isn't it? Is there something I should know?"

"Just be wary," said Trevin.

Serai nodded and approached Dano, the leaner of the two bodyguards. As he accompanied her down an adjacent hallway, Trevin hoped he had not overstepped his bounds to suggest protection for Serai. He was not a comain yet.

Melaia headed up a short flight of stairs toward the west breezeway. As

Trevin hurried to catch up, he laughed to himself. Never would he have imagined that he would befriend a princess who happened to be the daughter of Dreia, the angel who once guarded the Wisdom Tree and the angels' stairway to heaven. He tried to picture Melaia escorting spirits of the dying across the stairway and nodding to angels as they ascended and descended, but the picture was ludicrous. He couldn't see Melaia confined to the interior of a tree, even the Wisdom Tree.

A cool night breeze drifted through the arches of the breezeway, riffling Melaia's hair. Trevin matched her stride. "Is that a new necklace?" he asked.

"It's much too large, don't you think?"

"Was it a peace offering from Prince Varic? Like your father's ring?"

"How did you guess?"

He shrugged and glanced behind them. Khareet followed at a respectful distance. Trevin lowered his voice. "What do you think of the prince and his friends?"

"What do *I* think? Which I? I, heir to the throne? I, Dreia's daughter?" She looked at Trevin, her eyes pained. "Or I, Melaia?"

He rubbed the corners of his mouth, wishing he could kiss away her pain. If she were not a princess, he would try.

She sighed. "I, heir to the throne, say a peace treaty is appealing, no matter who proposes it. I, Dreia's daughter, suppose peace is best, because Father will be more likely to allow me to search for the harps I need to restore the Tree. The task is never far from my mind."

"As Melaia—simply yourself—what do you think of the Dregmoorians?"

"Arrogant and sly, all three. I wish they had stayed in the Dregmoors, but that's my heart speaking, not my head."

Trevin's spirits rose. "I say trust your heart."

"You should have heard their boasting."

"I can imagine."

"Prince Varic is the son of Queen Stalia of the Dregmoors." Melaia fingered her necklace. "She's Lord Rejius's daughter, isn't she? He and Benasin spoke of her in the aerie."

"Yes. I remember." Trevin glanced through one of the wide arched windows at the aerie tower, rust red in the wash of moonlight. The day Rejius and Benasin fought there, he had been on the wrong side. He wished he could expunge from his past his years of servitude to the Firstborn.

"The prince's mother may be queen," said Trevin, "but you can be sure it's Lord Rejius who reigns. No good can come of a visit from the Firstborn's grandson."

"But you have to admit, the offer of peace sounds good," said Melaia.

"Coming from a braggart who would serve gash in jeweled goblets, an offer of peace is hardly worth the time it takes to turn it down," said Trevin.

"You're ruthless." Melaia grinned, an admiring glint in her eye. "Prince Varic probably does have jeweled goblets. According to him, gold and jewels are as abundant in the Dregmoors as rocks on their shore. He's building an opulent palace for himself. If Father signs a peace treaty, Camrithia will share in their riches."

"We don't need jewels; we need a good harvest, an end to the blight."

For a moment they fell silent, the only sound their footsteps on the marble floor as they entered the antechamber that led to the king's stairway.

"What do the Dregmoorians get in return for their peace offer?" asked Trevin.

"I don't know," said Melaia as they ascended the stairs. "I didn't stay for the entire meeting. Maybe the Dregmoorians finally realize it's better to be our allies than our enemies."

"I doubt it," grumbled Trevin. "I wager they're here to clean up the Camrithian countryside."

"Meaning what?"

Trevin tramped up the stairs, refusing to groan at the aches in his fight-sore legs. "Meaning they're here to take all they can," he said. "And they'll give us nothing good in return."

❧

When Trevin and Melaia entered the king's chamber, they found him draped over a great padded chair, his eyes closed. His personal servant, Nash, cleared away scrolls scattered across a table.

"Father?" said Melaia.

Without opening his eyes King Laetham extended his right hand, ruby ring gleaming. Melaia kissed his hand.

The king opened his eyes and looked at Trevin, who bowed. "I did summon each of you, didn't I? I didn't expect both of you at once."

"Shall I wait outside, sire?" asked Trevin.

"That won't be necessary. As comain, you may be privy to the news."

"What news?" asked Melaia.

King Laetham frowned at Trevin. "You've been in a fight?"

"I encountered ruffians."

"I trust you prevailed."

Trevin nodded, considering. He was alive and had full, if not comfortable, use of all his limbs. "I prevailed, sire," he said. He just wished he had blackened Varic's eye as well as Hesel's.

Melaia put her hands on her hips. "What's the news?"

King Laetham motioned Trevin to a padded bench by the far wall. "Pull over a seat."

Trevin strode to the bench as Nash slipped the royal sandals off the royal feet.

"Ah!" The king smiled and eased back in his chair.

"Is it news about the peace treaty?" asked Melaia.

"Your music sounded divine tonight, my dear," said the king. "Whenever I see you play your harp, it takes my mind back to your mother. She had such talent."

"Gifting," said Melaia.

The king chuckled. "Call it what you will; you didn't inherit it from me."

"What's the news?" asked Melaia.

Trevin tugged the bench across the room. Nash trotted over and lifted the other end.

"Prince Varic remarked on your beauty, you know," said the king.

Trevin wanted to slam the bench to the floor. Instead, he clenched it so hard his fingernails dug into the wood. He and Nash gently set the bench in front of the king.

Melaia sat on it and motioned for Trevin to take the place beside her. "I think, Father, that Prince Varic is inclined to remark on the beauty of every woman he sees."

"He wouldn't be wrong, eh, Trevin?" The king winked.

"No, sire." It galled Trevin to agree with Varic, but he would not disagree with the king.

"What's the news?" Melaia asked again.

The king nodded at Trevin. "Tell me about the landgash you discovered."

Melaia leaned forward, gripping the edge of the bench.

Trevin ached for her, but being king, her father could ignore her as long as he wished, which was obviously his point. Although Trevin felt for Melaia, he admired the stately calm and unruffled manner of the stubborn king.

"Dwin found two rifts of landgash at Drywell," said Trevin. "I've seen them myself. One has contaminated the well. The other is near the east edge of the clearing."

The king rubbed his forehead. "Lord Beker has seen similar rifts in his travels. He says they produce a foul odor."

"Like eggs gone to rot," said Trevin.

"Beker tells me the Dregmoors are full of these dreadful rifts spewing hot mud," said the king. "They make the soil barren and worthless—but I don't suppose you've been to the Dregmoors."

"No, sire, but I know they turn gash into a drink."

"The stuff that's touted to restore youth. If that's true, a well full of it might be to our gain."

"I wouldn't want anyone to drink gash," said Melaia. "I once saw a man addicted to it. His skin was as smooth as a baby's, but he was in a stupor, dying from the inside out."

Trevin nodded. He and Melaia had once camped near a gash-drunk and his family. The memory was warm, and Trevin found himself wishing Melaia was still that naive priestess.

The king tapped the arms of his chair. "When Beker returns, I'll look to his counsel on the matter. We've problems enough without the earth turning against us, but I suspect we can do nothing to fight this sort of invasion."

Nash set a basin of water on the floor in front of King Laetham. The king sank further into his chair as Nash eased the royal feet into the water. "Now for more pleasant thoughts. My news." He smiled at Melaia. "Prince Varic has proposed a marriage."

Trevin tensed.

Melaia's hand drifted to the gold medallion at her throat. "To whom?"

The king laughed. "You, my dear."

Melaia squeezed her eyes shut. "Surely you're not considering his proposal."

"Of course I am. It's part of his peace offer."

Melaia's voice trembled. "You would sell your daughter to a Dregmoorian brute?"

"A Dregmoorian prince." King Laetham's voice rose. "May I remind you, Daughter, he will one day be king of the Dregmoors?"

Trevin cleared his throat. "He will one day be king of Camrithia if he marries Melaia."

The king glowered at him. Nash massaged the king's left foot.

Trevin looked from Melaia to the king, both faces set in stubborn willfulness. "I beg your pardon, sire," he said. "If Varic marries Melaia, Camrithia may gain peace, but the Dregmoorians will gain Camrithia."

"Melaia gets Camrithia." The king eased his left foot back into the water and held his right toward Nash. "And not until I die."

Melaia's face turned ash white. "Prince Varic's grandfather tried to murder you and take the throne. How do you know Lord Rejius isn't now trying to gain control through his grandson?"

"Lord Rejius was defeated," said the king. "He seeks an alliance of peace."

"And the price is your kingdom?" asked Melaia.

The question hung in the air like mist before a downpour.

The king's fist thundered down on the arm of his chair. "Curses!" he bellowed. "Daily I'm besieged by landowners, town councilmen, merchants, farmers—all wailing about raiders from the Dregmoors who sweep in and steal their goods, their crops, their cattle. Even children. Children, Melaia! 'Stop the raids!' my people demand. But how? Tell me that. My comains abandoned their posts and disappeared. Their men-at-arms returned home to protect their families but still demand that I stop the raids! I can no more stop raids than I can stop the sun rising in the morning. Unless…"

The king leaned forward, his gaze boring into Melaia. "Unless I can establish an alliance with the Dregmoors. Then the raids will stop, and we'll have some hope of making our enemies our allies. You, Melaia, will be an envoy of peace between our kingdoms."

Melaia met the king's glare with her own. Her words marched out. "I have vowed to marry no one but Trevin."

The king jerked back as if she had slapped him.

Trevin gaped at her. Marry? His mind buzzed. When had she made that vow? How had she come to have such strong feelings? Had she hinted? Had he been too dull minded to understand? He wanted to take her in his arms and let her breathe out the news gasp by gasp. He felt as strong as a mountain stag leaping from ridge to ridge, as brilliant as thunderlight jagging from cloud to cloud, as reckless as a shooting star hurtling across the boundless heavens. He could hardly stay seated.

And he didn't. The king rose, grabbed the neck of Trevin's tunic, and wrenched him to his feet. "I thought you had changed, thief."

"I have," Trevin garbled.

"You think you can steal my daughter?"

"Father!" Melaia tugged at the king's arm. "I said *I* vowed. Trevin didn't know."

"Swear it." The king's breath fumed hot in Trevin's face. "Swear by the crown that you didn't know."

"I swear," choked Trevin. "I swear by the crown. By the throne. By the scepter—"

The king shoved him onto the bench and glared at him. "You don't have to invoke the whole palace."

Trevin rubbed his throat.

The king stomped through spilled water to his chair and turned his glare to Melaia. "I'm not so daft that I don't have a healthy suspicion of Prince Varic, but I also have a healthy suspicion of my new comain. I even have a healthy suspicion of my own daughter." He squinted at Melaia as Nash toweled the floor. "It was your vow and yours alone?"

She set her jaw and nodded.

"Then you will unvow it. Trevin has no rank."

"After tomorrow he'll be a comain," said Melaia.

"A comain is the king's rider, not a prince, not a future king. It's in Camrithia's best interest to become an ally of the Dregmoors. This is about stopping the raids."

Trevin's hopes died like a doused campfire. He bit his lip to stay out of the argument.

Melaia knelt, nudged Nash aside, and dried the king's feet. "Father, all I ask is a little time. You're suspicious of Prince Varic. Give us time to test his sincerity. Tell him to stop the raids while we consider his proposal. Meanwhile, let me find the two other harps. If I can unite all three, I can restore the stairway and—"

"That priestess who raised you stuffed your head full of nonsense, girl," said the king. "I cannot allow you to leave Redcliff. For your own good."

"In that case send Trevin on my behalf."

"He'll be occupied."

"But—"

"I'm sorry, Melaia." The king stroked her hair, and his face softened. "I know this is hard for you to understand, but you are our hope."

"I can't—"

The king raised his hand. "Hear me out, both of you. Lord Beker will soon return to his post as my advisor, which he can do only because you, Trevin, will take over the task of finding my missing comains. I sent Beker south. He found no comains, but he did fully man Fort Tigerre at the mouth of the Davernon. However, I can spare him no longer. I've recalled him, and I'm sending you on the search north. I want you to consult the Oracle."

Trevin glanced at Melaia. She looked as surprised as he felt.

"I know," said the king. "I've never placed faith in anything beyond the natural. But I'm at my wit's end. It can't hurt to consult the Oracle, ask for a prophecy or sign. If along the way you discover the whereabouts of these harps Melaia wants, by all means send them to her."

An energy stirred in Trevin, not like the jolt moments earlier, but like the muscles of a horse beneath him, measured and steady. With this challenge he could prove himself worthy, both to the king and to Melaia.

"No marriage to Prince Varic," said Melaia.

"I promise you nothing." King Laetham rubbed his furrowed brow. "You ask for time. I grant you one season. I dare not delay the prince longer than that. Trevin must return with my comains, or news of them, by harvest moon. That will give us time to settle this issue before we move to the winter castle at Qanreef." Nash wriggled slippers onto the king's feet.

Melaia rose, her fists clenched.

Trevin stood as well. "You can depend on me, sire," he said. "I'll ride north as soon as I can."

"While you're there," said the king, "you might as well inform King

Kedemeth of the Dregmoorian threat. The Eldarrans have been allies in the past, and it cannot hurt to renew the goodwill between our kingdoms. If the Dregmoorians grow impatient, we may need our neighbor's aid. Now, a good night to both of you."

Trevin and Melaia rose from the bench, and Nash opened the door for them. Prince Varic stood in the hallway, a flask in one hand, awaiting his turn with the king.

Varic shot a look of disdain at Trevin, who met it with a smug smile as he brushed past. The prince slipped in front of Melaia. Trevin turned to see him adjust her necklace, allowing his fingers to run across her throat.

"My gold looks striking on you," said the prince.

"Withdraw, Varic," Trevin muttered through his teeth.

Melaia gently pushed aside the prince's hand. "What's in the flask?" she asked.

"Dregmoorian beer," said Varic. "I thought your father might like a taste." He leaned toward her, his voice soft but clear enough that Trevin knew he was meant to hear. "A friendly warning, my lady. In our country losing a finger is the penalty for thievery. A man missing a finger is in no way trustworthy."

Trevin clenched his fists but stood steady.

Melaia shouldered past Varic. "Main Trevin, escort me to my chamber."

"Gladly, lady." Trevin hurried after her, followed by Dano, who had returned from escorting Serai, and Khareet.

They didn't speak until they reached the bottom of the stairwell and turned down an adjoining corridor toward Melaia's quarters in the northeast tower. A cool breeze drifted through unshuttered windows.

Trevin huffed. It would take more than a breeze to cool his steaming anger. "Dregmoorian beer. Would Varic try to poison your father? Tonight?"

Melaia stormed ahead. "He wouldn't dare. Besides, Nash will taste the beer first."

"What is the prince doing with your father at this time of the evening, anyway? Haven't they both drunk enough?"

"Perhaps my father summoned the prince, hoping he would arrive when I did," Melaia fumed. "My father has become quite the matchmaker."

Trevin glanced out a window as they passed. The moon had gone behind clouds, leaving the aerie tower blood dark.

Melaia's steps slowed. "Trevin, I can't marry Lord Rejius's grandson. I have to admit he's handsome, but he's—"

"Handsome? Like a venom-spitting puff adder."

The corners of Melaia's mouth twitched toward a smile. "At least he doesn't look like a warty bullfrog."

"He will when he grows old," said Trevin. "He'll be bulbous and jowly."

Melaia raised one eyebrow. "You can tell that? What about me?"

"Elegant and kind."

"And you?"

He smiled. "Dashing and assured, of course. Like your father but more—"

"More balanced." Melaia sighed. "I don't know if I truly love my father or if I just feel sorry for him. When he's hopeful, he's delightful company. When he's in despair, his presence is as heavy as a millstone."

"You care," said Trevin.

"I do care," said Melaia. "I guess that's love. I admire my father's desire for peace, and I love the concern he carries for his people."

"No one can fault him for that," said Trevin. "But he should be more concerned about your well-being."

"He tries. But he's losing hope. He falls into melancholy more often these days. I hope I didn't send him into the depths tonight."

"Why would he despair? He has the upper hand."

"I don't know how far to push him. If one of us doesn't bend, one of us will break."

A gust of wind fluttered the torch flames, making shadows dance in the stairwell to Melaia's rooms.

"Have you ever heard a voice when no one was around?" asked Trevin.

"I hear voices from the trees. It's a gift I inherited from my mother."

"What do the voices say?"

"Sometimes they echo my thoughts. Sometimes I hear theirs. Usually they say, 'Save us' or 'We die,' because of the blight." She shivered.

Trevin wished he could put his arm around her, but with Khareet and Dano following, he didn't want to try.

"I've heard one voice," he said as they headed up the stairs, "but I've heard it three times."

"From the trees?"

"I think not. I heard it twice in the aerie."

"What does it say?"

"Seeker," he whispered.

Melaia pursed her lips. "Tomorrow we'll go to the aerie," she said. "We'll watch for Peron and listen for your voice."

As they neared the top of the stairs, Trevin rubbed his right hand. Now was the time. "You surprised me tonight with your vow," he said softly.

"I meant to keep it a secret, but after hearing my father's news, I couldn't stay quiet. I hope you're not offended."

He laughed. "Just surprised. I didn't know you had such feelings. Lately we've spent only snatches of time together." He glanced over his shoulder at the bodyguards. "And never alone."

"So you're not offended?" She looked sideways at him. "I'm relieved. I was an awful shrew last fall, terribly angry with you. It's a wonder you're still willing to abide my presence."

He started to reach for her but stopped himself. "Melaia, you're all I could want."

She grinned. "You *are* a thief. You stole the very words I was going to say." She dashed up the last two steps and across the landing to her door, where she paused. "I can sense you, Trevin. I couldn't before, because I couldn't still my mind when you were near. But I've begun to sense you. You're the most tantalizing shade of gold."

She swept into her room, calling, "Serai, did you find the ointment?"

Trevin stared after her. Angels couldn't sense him, but Melaia could. That must mean he was Nephili, half-angel as she was. Livia had suspected as much, but neither of his parents had claimed to be an angel. Then again, both had died before he knew to ask.

Melaia sensed him. Proof enough.

He stood taller. Gold. He was tantalizing gold.

Melaia appeared with a lidded jar and handed it to him. "Don't slather it on." Her soft fingers gently stroked his bruised cheek. "Just rub in a small amount until the ointment disappears."

"Won't you show me how?" he asked. "I have a bruise on my upper arm too. One on my chest. My thigh—"

She swatted his arm. "Begone before I give you another one."

CHAPTER 4

Trevin sat on his pallet, smearing menthia ointment on his bruised cheek. The sharp scent took him back to a night by a hearth fire in a cottage near Stillwater when the priestess Melaia had spread salve over his bruised belly. That night she had asked him who he was, and he had told her he didn't know. He had acted the part of a confident kingsman, but his deeds had shown him a coward, a thief, an informant. Even now he didn't dare tell Melaia the extent of his guilt for fear she would reject him.

He inspected his arms for bruises and wished there was a salve for his conscience. Even knowing he was Nephili didn't assuage his guilt. Perhaps after the king officially proclaimed him a comain, he could finally put aside his past and start anew.

Jarrod, in his priestly blue robe, leaned his lanky frame against the doorjamb. "So you were feasting in Redcliff while I dredged a reeking well for your body."

Trevin chided himself for being too preoccupied to sense Jarrod's presence. He usually felt angels before he saw them. He tugged off his tunic. "You would prefer to have found a body?"

"I'm relieved to see the body alive." Jarrod retied his long hair. "Though how you kept yourself from drowning, I'll never know. I guess your scratches tell the story."

Trevin dipped into the ointment again, grateful that Jarrod was not upset with him. As Dreia's son and Melaia's half brother, Jarrod had a strong sense of destiny, and he could snarl like a lion when he was angry—another reason to keep parts of the past well hidden.

"I'm sorry you missed dinner." Trevin rubbed ointment on his upper arm.

"I don't regret missing the king's excesses," said Jarrod, "but I do regret losing an opportunity to study our three guests."

"You'll have your chance. Unfortunately, they may be here a while."

Dwin ducked into the room. "They're lodging at the palace. With their dog."

"And you procured them the best rooms, didn't you?" Trevin put the lid on the ointment and wiped his hands. "No doubt you played nursemaid and told them a bedtime story."

"I did not. I saw only where they're staying."

"So you can join them for ale in the morning?" asked Trevin.

"Cork the venom," said Jarrod. "You know what feuding between brothers leads to. You've seen Rejius and Benasin fight."

"They're immortal," said Trevin.

"Which only means that if you two feud, you'll have less time to make it right before the end." Jarrod gave them a stern look and headed down the hall.

Dwin pulled an amphora from a trunk and unplugged it. "A little wine? As a peace offering?"

Trevin snatched the amphora and plug from Dwin's hands. "I've had my fill of peace offerings." He replaced the stopper, but his anger was not as easily bottled. He shook the amphora at Dwin. "You cloud your mind with this stuff."

"No I don't. It makes me feel good."

"Can't you feel good without a drink? Too much of this stuff numbs you."

"It makes me happy." Dwin rolled out his mat.

"Has it ever occurred to you that Rejius supplied you with strong drink to keep you happily in his control?"

"He provided you with drink too. And women. He never brought me women."

"Rejius never controlled me that way."

"No?" Dwin snorted. "You did everything he asked of you."

"Because of *you*, Dwin. Lord Rejius knew I'd do anything to safeguard you. He threatened your life to control me."

"Don't tell me you weren't in it for yourself as well." Dwin plopped onto his mat.

Trevin huffed. His brother would never know the compromises made for his sake. "At least we had the sense to get out before the king hanged us."

"*You* had the sense, and I went along. Now you're to be a comain. As for me—"

"You'll stand up for yourself and become something more than a drunkard, I hope." Trevin slipped the amphora back into the trunk.

"It's settled, then," said Dwin. "You'll be a comain, and I'll be a spy. Like the Asp."

"The Asp lives in the Dregmoors. No one knows who he is. You've no notion of what his life is like or what danger he faces to send information to the Angelaeon."

"Exactly." Dwin lay down. "I'll be a spy. I'm practicing already." He yanked his cloak over his head.

Trevin yanked it off. "What do you mean you're practicing already?"

"I'm spying on the Dregmoorians. When they walked into the tavern at Drywell, I recognized the skinny one."

"Fornian."

"Dagger devil." Dwin rubbed his throat. "I saw him in Redcliff over a year ago. About the time Lord Rejius became the king's physician."

"Then why didn't Fornian lead them to Redcliff?"

"They'd still have been stopped at the gate. Varic wanted someone to get them inside without a confrontation. I told them I could take them straight to the palace."

Trevin threw Dwin's cloak at him. "You should have stopped drinking one beer before that. Give it up, Dwin, before you're as burdened with regrets as I am. No more spying."

"Too late." Dwin dug into his waist sash and brought out a small scroll. "You're not the only one who can pinch a pouch."

"Whose pouch?"

"Hesel's." Dwin tossed the scroll to Trevin.

"Hangman's noose, Dwin! Sometimes I think you have no more sense than your donkey."

"Don't insult Persephone. She got you home, didn't she?"

Trevin unrolled the scroll and scanned it. "It's a list of accounts."

"Written in Dreg," said Dwin.

"You noticed. Did you read it?"

"Enough to know Hesel's a gash runner. Some accounts are obviously paid in coin. Other payments I can't make out. You're better at Dreg than I am."

Trevin read aloud, "Sheep. Goats." He frowned at the next word. *Tohdlit.* He read it again to be certain. *Tohdlit.* The hair on his neck prickled. "Children." He scanned the scroll a third time. "They're trading gash for children."

Dwin rose to one elbow, frowning. "You sure?"

Trevin shook the scroll at him. "You tell no one but Jarrod about this until I can show it to the king. The fewer who know what you've been up to, the better."

⌛

Trevin had hoped to go to the aerie with Melaia the next morning and put the Dregmoorians out of his mind and hers, but the information in the scroll could not wait. Hesel had to be exposed. No doubt Varic would claim he knew nothing about gash running, but Hesel's guilt would stain the prince's credibility.

Trevin requested an audience with King Laetham. When the king put him off, he requested a meeting with Melaia. When she finally sent word that she was not free to see him, he trudged to the stable yard and concentrated on his original task for the day—appraising three horses.

He watched them browse. A feisty carob-brown mare. A fine black gelding. A gaunt-shouldered white stallion.

Comains usually knew their mounts long before they were appointed to their posts. Trevin knew as well, but Pym had questioned his choice, as had Dwin, Jarrod, and even Melaia. So Trevin studied the horses once more. His choice was the same.

Pym ambled up. "You've decided. I can see it in your eyes."

"The white," said Trevin. "Almaron."

"I could see that too."

As if in agreement, the stallion approached Trevin.

"For a stallion he's more agreeable than most," said Pym. "I'll see that he's ready for you this afternoon."

Trevin ran his hand along Almaron's neck. Pym had found him half-starved with two slash wounds, one on each shoulder. Although Pym had nursed the horse back to health, the scars gave him an odd look.

"We've both seen our share of trials," said Trevin. "You've proved your worth." He patted Almaron. At least one of them wouldn't need to prove himself.

⟶⊰⊱⟵

In midafternoon, from the arched entrance of Redcliff, Trevin surveyed the valley that spread out below the city. Gray banners with the king's white lion emblem billowed atop poles that bordered the main road across the bridge and into the valley beyond. A crowd swarmed the path and encircled the field where the appointing would take place.

Trevin recognized the long spiral of two dark birds riding the wind above the distant hills. Draks. He looked toward the aerie and regretted not being able to meet Melaia there. Maybe tomorrow.

Sensing the warm brown presence of Jarrod, Trevin turned. "Draks are back."

Jarrod shaded his eyes and studied the sky. "Not surprising, I suppose, since the Dregmoorians are here."

"Does Rejius scry through the birds' eyes?"

"Or one of his lackeys does. The Firstborn no doubt licks his wounds while he prepares another attack."

And the Second-born? Trevin wondered. "What about Benasin? Where is he?"

"My father's whereabouts are anyone's guess, but he'll rise again as well. The feud is far from over." Jarrod eyed Trevin. "Did you and Dwin settle accounts?"

"Dwin and I have a truce of sorts," said Trevin, "but he worries me."

"Where is he now?"

"At the field. He's determined to play the spy. He thinks it's all excitement and glory. He has no idea of the risks involved."

Jarrod chuckled and headed to the field. "I'll speak to him."

"Your mount, Main Trevin," called Pym, leading Almaron to the archway.

Trevin laughed at Pym's wet hair, spiked in all directions like weeds in the woods. "Don't tell me you took a bath for this occasion."

"As much of a bath as I could stand." Pym handed Trevin the reins. "I can abide the water. It's the soap I don't take kindly to." He scratched his scalp. "Flustrations! Makes me itch, it does."

Trevin stroked Almaron's broad, smooth forehead. "Here's one who enjoys being cleaned and curried."

"I might enjoy it too if someone gave me a rubdown after." Pym took a pack from the stableboy, who led Pym's roan.

"We'll beg for baths after a fortnight of traveling the roads," said Trevin. "Lord Beker will be here within the week. I intend to leave as soon as we get his counsel."

"Then you have a week to accustom yourself to carrying this." Pym slid an oval shield out of the pack.

Trevin squinted at the black-and-gold design painted on it. Each comain had carried a shield adorned with an animal—a leaping white stag, a proud ram, a regal osprey. "What is this symbol?" he asked.

Pym scratched his head. "The painter said the princess chose it. He claims it's an eagle."

Trevin turned the shield this way and that. "The painter must have been in a hurry."

Pym took the reins of the roan. "I wasn't lucky enough to see my old master Undrian appointed comain. I'm pleased to serve you, Trevin, but once we find Main Undrian…" He heaved himself onto the horse.

Trevin mounted Almaron, impressed that Pym had not given up hope of finding his comain alive and well. "When you serve Undrian as armsman again, I'll have Dwin at my side," he said. "If he can avoid getting himself hanged before then."

Trumpets blared, and Trevin urged Almaron through the archway. As he and Pym cantered over the bridge and down the crowd-lined path, cheers filled the air.

Across the field Melaia and King Laetham stepped onto the platform where two thrones stood. Prince Varic and his cronies had seats of honor in the stands on the right. Dwin was all smiles in the crowd to the left, standing between Iona, the lovely raven-haired priestess, and Nuri, the dimpled novice. Hanni, the high priestess of Navia, looked on, her almond eyes attentive to her charges, who served with her at Redcliff until the Navian temple could be repaired from the damage it had received during a raid the previous fall.

Trevin and Pym dismounted within the broad ring of spectators. Trevin handed his shield and Almaron's reins to Pym, then strode with a confident air toward the platform, where he bowed on one knee. He smiled to himself. Melaia was not wearing the gold medallion today.

King Laetham rose and welcomed the crowd, gesturing broadly with the hand that wore the ruby ring. This was the demeanor Trevin admired in the king, the calm manner that inspired confidence. No one would know that the monarch held "healthy suspicions" of the Dregmoorian peace delegation—or of his new comain.

A bard flamboyantly readied his lyre. As the music began, Prince Varic leaned over and, with a look of amused disdain, spoke to Hesel and Fornian. They laughed.

Trevin clenched his teeth and swore to do everything in his power to make certain the king did not pawn off Melaia to this gash breath.

As the last strains of the ballad drifted away on the breeze, King Laetham stood and fixed his dark gaze on Trevin. His deep voice rang out. "Trevin, you have been chosen as comain because of your courage defending this kingdom and this crown." His eyebrows met in a frown. "Do you pledge to faithfully serve Camrithia?"

"I do," said Trevin.

"Do you *vow* to aid those who support this realm and oppose those who threaten it?"

Trevin felt Varic's gaze. "I do."

King Laetham nodded. "I therefore grant you the favor and authority of the king's house." He took Melaia's hand, and they descended to the field, where Melaia lifted a sword from a purple cloth.

The king placed his hand firmly on top of Trevin's head. "It is my privilege"—he paused as the suspense gathered—"to appoint you…and proclaim that you will henceforth be known as…Main Trevin, comain of the kingdom of Camrithia. You may rise."

The crowd applauded as Trevin stood and Melaia placed the sword across the king's outstretched hands. When the people quieted, King Laetham said, "Main Trevin, receive your sword."

Trevin raised the sword high. Sunlight glinted off the highly polished blade. Though not ornate, the weapon was solid. Pym strapped the scabbard belt around Trevin's waist.

As Trevin turned, sword raised, to face the crowd, a grand cheer exploded. He felt his soul ignite with a fire of purpose, courage, and destiny. He slipped the blade into the scabbard, strode back to Almaron, and mounted. Then he rode slowly back to the gates of Redcliff, weaving from one side of the road to the other and leaning down to shake hands with well-wishers.

"Main Trevin!" the crowd shouted. "Main Trevin!"

He nodded at their greetings and grinned at young boys in whose eyes he could see dreams of someday riding for the king. As a boy, he had joined throngs that greeted comains as they rode forth, but he had used those occasions to pick a few pouches. Never did he imagine he would one day be a comain.

When Trevin reached the city gates, he looked back, then wished he hadn't. Varic strolled across the field with Melaia and King Laetham.

"Main Trevin!" cried those who waited in the streets of Redcliff.

Trevin sat tall and turned his eyes to the road ahead while both his love and his loathing walked the fields behind him.

CHAPTER 5

Stars speckled the late-night sky and torches burned low as the crowd celebrated and dancers paired off. Trevin tried to cross the courtyard to reach Melaia, but a buxom young woman bobbed up to him. He pressed his palms to hers as the music began. He felt as if he had danced with every woman in the world but the one he wanted. His cheeks ached from smiling.

As he twirled with the grinning maiden, he glanced at Melaia, who danced with King Laetham, both of them obviously delighting in the other's company. At least her partner was not Varic again, Trevin thought as he led his admirer round and round, closer to the princess. When the song ended, he bowed and turned to Melaia as she turned to him.

"Do you have another dance in you?" she asked.

"For you, my lady, I would dance all night." He touched his palms to hers, and the music played. They circled. He felt her pulse in his fingertips, and his hands tingled.

"Do you like the shield?" asked Melaia. "I chose the eagle for you."

"I love it." He laughed. "It resembles a gutted pheasant after a certain prince has dined." He shot an accusing look at Varic.

Melaia's smile faded. "You don't like it."

"Of course I do. I like it because you gave it to me. It doesn't matter if the eagle looks like a half-eaten pheasant or a battered drak. It's a gift from you."

Melaia bit her lip and looked away.

"Truly. I like it."

They formed a ring with the other dancers. As they circled to the right, then to the left, Trevin's heart circled downward. Only a dolt would voice such a slur about a gift from a princess.

They faced each other again, palms together. Melaia said, "I chose the eagle because you wore the eagle mask when we disguised ourselves to get into the palace at Qanreef. The eagle is king of the wind, the only creature who can look into the sun."

Gazing into Melaia's intense eyes, Trevin felt as if he were indeed looking into the sun, but he could feel her tension. "I didn't mean to make light of your gift," he said.

"It's not really my gift. I simply chose the eagle."

"The eagle is perfect. I was too fog headed to catch its meaning."

Melaia did not seem comforted. "I need to speak to you but not here."

"And I need to speak to you."

"Come to my quarters. As soon as we can get away."

Trevin laced his fingers through Melaia's. Step close. Step back. At the last strum of the lyre, a bow.

⚜

The night spun on. Wine and ale flowed, most of it into Varic, though Dwin drank his share as well. Trevin kept a watchful eye on his brother. Like a fly lighting first here then there, Dwin casually laughed his way from Nuri and Iona to Varic and his men.

After Trevin saw Melaia and Serai leave the festivities, he lingered only a short time before heading to the palace and making his way to Melaia's quarters. Serai ushered him inside, then excused herself to the roof garden.

Melaia sat by a window, inspecting a purple flower propped in a gilded finger bowl. "I've not yet seen Peron," she said. "This is her favorite flower." She held the bowl out to Trevin.

He sniffed the blossom. "Smells nice. Like a rose."

"I asked the gardener to plant some in my garden. Somehow Prince Varic heard about it and brought me this one."

"Prince Varic visited your quarters?"

"He heard about my garden and wanted to see it."

Trevin clenched his fists. "He visited your quarters!"

"*You* are visiting my quarters."

"I thought you wanted nothing to do with the cur."

"Trevin!" Melaia set the bowl on the windowsill.

"I'm serious."

"I don't want to marry the prince, but I can't shun him. You heard my father's compromise. I have to keep the weather at Redcliff agreeable until you come back from consulting the Oracle."

Trevin leaned against the window ledge. "Maybe you won't have to wait that long. I requested a meeting with you this morning to tell you something Dwin discovered. Varic's friend Hesel is a gash runner."

"What's that?"

"He transports and sells gash. But that's not the worst of it. For payment he takes not only coin but sheep, goats, and *children* too."

Melaia paled. "Are you certain?"

"Dwin has proof."

"That's sickening," she said. "Have you told my father?"

"I've tried, but I can't get in to see him."

"I'll tell him. First thing tomorrow. I wonder if Prince Varic knows."

"Of course he knows. But he'll deny it."

"If he knows, he's heartless, which is ironic, because the flower he gave me is called true-heart." Melaia stroked the purple petals.

"True-heart," Trevin muttered. "It was certainly not named for the giver."

"The name comes from a folk tale that says if you sleep in a field of these flowers, when you wake, you'll know your true heart on a matter. Do you think if I grow them, Peron might visit?"

"It's worth a try," said Trevin, though he hated to think of Melaia growing a flower that reminded her of Varic.

"At least this blossom is alive, unlike the other one." She led Trevin to a chair adorned with the image of a sunset-red poppy.

"He's a painter?" asked Trevin, disgusted. What else could the jackal do?

"He's an artist, he says, but"—her eyes widened—"this image isn't painted. Varic placed the poppy on a silver net, then pressed it to the wood. When he removed the net, the flower was part of the chair."

Trevin rubbed his hand over the poppy. He felt no brush strokes, no inlays. The bloom seemed to have become wood. He scowled at it.

Melaia ambled back to the window. "Varic says his gift is preserving images in wood and stone."

"Preserving or killing?" Trevin growled.

He moved to stand by Melaia and followed her gaze. Serai and Jarrod strolled arm in arm through the roof garden in the moonlight.

"Two angels, Exousia and Erielyon," said Melaia. "A divine match."

"Jarrod is not pure angel," said Trevin. "He's half-immortal."

"That's beside the point. They're both ageless."

"What about us? If you sense me, I must be Nephili like you. Half-angel, half-human. Are we ageless?"

"I asked Jarrod about Nephili. He says we're not ageless, but he thinks we may live longer than usual." Melaia smiled and stared at the moon.

Trevin studied her perfect profile. "Melaia, about your vow last night, you should know I feel the same about you. I'll gladly be your servant the rest of my life. But if there's a chance I could be more—"

Melaia looked down. "I'm Dreia's daughter, Trevin."

"That's no barrier for me." He bent his head to the top of hers and inhaled her lavender scent.

"It's a barrier for me. I can't marry anyone. I must restore the Tree."

"You lied about the vow?"

"I didn't lie." She looked up at him, her eyes searching his. "I vowed that *if* I married, I would marry you."

"If?"

"I don't know what the future holds. I have to find the kyparis harps and unite them, and what then?"

"The Wisdom Tree will be restored, the angels will have their stairway to heaven, and your task will be finished."

"But a debt must be paid, and somehow I'm part of the price. I don't know what that means. It would be unfair for me to pledge myself to you. I would be playing with your heart."

Trevin paced to the hearth, where a brass lamp burned in place of a winter fire. Her vow to marry only him might be meaningless despite her destined task. If someone didn't discredit the Dregmoorian prince within a season, it wouldn't matter whom she vowed to marry. She would belong to Varic.

Melaia plopped two cushions on the floor near the hearth and sat cross-legged on one of them. As Trevin settled himself on the other, she said, "I have a plan. I've arranged for you to leave tomorrow."

"Tomorrow? I want Lord Beker's counsel before I ride out."

She leaned closer, a mischievous spark in her eyes. "You don't need his counsel. I'm going with you. But tell no one. Not even Serai."

"I thought you meant to tell your father about Hesel's gash business tomorrow."

"True. I must do that." Melaia toyed with her braid. "I'll meet with my father first thing in the morning. Then as soon as I can, I'll sneak out by the Door of the Dead. I've done it before. We'll work out a signal—"

"Melaia!" Trevin huffed. "First you vow to marry no one but me. Then you tell me you can't pledge yourself to me. Now you want to leave with me. I don't follow your reasoning."

"I have to find the harps, Trevin." Her eyes pleaded with him.

He sighed. "I would love to spirit you away, never to return, but I can't. Your father barely trusts me as it is. I'm a new, untested comain. If you disappear the day I leave, he'll know you're with me. He'll accuse me of stealing you."

"You're right. You leave first. Wait for me with the sylvans in the Durenwoods. I'll follow in a few days."

"Think, Melaia. Your father would send a search party, and Varic and his curs would join them. And who would be in trouble? Me first—that's certain—but they would also believe Serai was involved. What about Jarrod? Dwin? The sylvans? Even Hanni and the priestesses would be suspect. Believe me, Melaia, they won't stop looking until they find you, wherever you are. The rest of us will be hanging from the parapets."

Melaia stared at Trevin, her brown eyes wide. He ached to take her in his arms. Instead, he folded his arms over his chest. Why did she have to be the princess?

Tears welled in her eyes. She rose and crossed the room to where her old blue priestess's cloak hung on a peg. "You don't know how awful it feels to be confined this way. Father knows I'm gifted like Mother was, but he thinks the harps, the Tree, and the stairway are only fragments of an ancient tale. Sometimes I question the tale myself." She fingered the cloak. "If only I could look for the harps...but Father won't let me leave the palace. He says my mother abused such freedom and he'll not take that chance with me. He's training me to reign."

"Which proves he's a fair man." Trevin joined her and leaned against the wall. "How many kings would choose a daughter as their heir?"

"Don't you see what that means? He expects me to be here. In Redcliff. Now and forever. But the harps are far more important than a word from the Oracle. Or allies from Eldarra. Or knowing the whereabouts of missing co-mains. You once told me that a slave and a priestess had something in common: neither was free. Nor is a princess."

Trevin wished he knew what to say, but he had no idea.

"You know where I tasted freedom?" she continued. "In the Durenwoods with the Angelaeon. Traveling to Qanreef with you. I knew I was Dreia's daughter. I knew I had her task to complete. But I was free. Was I wrong to acknowledge the king as my father?"

"You saved his life."

"I try to save his life every day. He's either on the mountaintop or in the depths of the gorge. There's no in-between. He wants me to understand and learn, but he won't listen to what I know. He doesn't think I have anything worthwhile to add to the conversation."

"He loves you. He wants to protect you. Doesn't that count for any-thing?"

"Of course it does. And I love him. But I know now why my mother spent so much time away. I'm imprisoned here."

Trevin sat on a trunk and watched lamplight dance with shadows across the walls. Life was a dance. Light with darkness. Known with unknown. The possible with the impossible.

"If your mother had been patient," he said, "if she had stayed with the king, think of the strength of the kingdom. Your father never would have had a reason to doubt her faithfulness. You would have been born and raised here, and who knows—"

"She might be alive today."

He nodded, but his gut twisted.

"I know what you're saying." Melaia sat on the trunk beside him. "I don't want to make the same mistake my mother made, but I need the harps."

"Then I'll look for them. But I won't know where I'm going until I speak to Lord Beker."

She touched his knee. "Go tomorrow. I want you back as soon as possible."

Trevin took her hand and stroked her elegant fingers. "You want me back, or you want the harps back?"

"I should want the harps above all, but"—she blushed and squeezed his hand—"I do want *you* back. The sooner you leave, the sooner you'll return."

"But tomorrow? I'm lost if I have no counsel on where to go. I know only that I'm headed north toward the Oracle."

Melaia brightened. "I made a plan for our journey."

"*My* journey."

"Your journey then." Melaia sighed. "Wait here."

As she left the room, Serai and Jarrod strolled in.

"The night is still warm," Serai said with an enviable lilt of joy. "I'll fetch something cool to drink."

Jarrod settled himself on a bench by the hearth and leaned back against the wall.

"While I'm gone, keep an eye on Melaia," said Trevin. "She's restless."

"I've noticed, but what woman wouldn't be restless with that prince around? I'm on edge too."

"Aren't you always on edge?" Melaia teased Jarrod as she returned. She held out a book to Trevin.

"Isn't this your mother's book?" Trevin took it reverently. "I thought you kept it under lock and key."

"It may help our search," said Melaia.

Trevin ran his fingers over the sign of the Tree carved in the wooden cover.

"Kyparis wood. From the Wisdom Tree." Melaia motioned for Jarrod to look too. "Open it to the page marked by the white feather."

Trevin found the feather and eased open the book. He read aloud.

> *Three from one and one from three.*
> *Music of the living tree.*
> *One sleeps in stone, one touches skies,*
> *One in the hands of mortals lies.*
> *One shall wake, one shall shake.*
> *Three shall light the way.*

Trevin frowned at the page. "How does a riddle help?"

"It's about the harps," said Melaia. Serai entered with a tray of cups and handed one to Melaia. "'One in the hands of mortals' describes the harp I have. Its runes, *Dedroumakei,* mean 'awaken.' It awoke my father from the spell of Lord Rejius."

"Merely a side benefit." Jarrod took a cup. "The Angelaeon believe its true purpose was to rouse us, like a call to battle: time to restore the stairway and its protective Tree."

"What of the one that 'sleeps in stone'?" Trevin asked.

Jarrod studied his drink. "That's the one Dreia took from the caves in Aubendahl."

"It's the one Lord Rejius stole from her," said Melaia.

Trevin steered his thoughts away from the memories of serving the First-born. The sovereign of Camrithia held his allegiance now. He took a cup from Serai as he handed the book to Melaia.

"I suspect the harp Rejius stole is in the Dregmoors now," said Jarrod.

"And the last harp *touches skies*?" Trevin saluted with his cup. "To the search that's done before it's begun."

"How can you say that?" asked Melaia.

"Your father is sending me north, not east. So if the harp Rejius stole is in the Dregmoors, I won't find it up north. As for the third harp, I'm supposed to search the sky. All *while* consulting the Oracle, recruiting allies, and looking for missing comains."

Melaia leafed through the pages of the book, then thrust it into Trevin's empty hand. "This may help."

Trevin scanned the two pages. "Excellent," he said. "These pages are blank."

"Are they?" she asked. "Look again."

Trevin squinted at the pages, then noticed a twitch on one, like a sprinkle of rain. As it broadened and split into misty lines, other strands formed on the opposite page, then sharpened.

"These pages show what the kyparis harps see," said Melaia.

Jarrod and Serai leaned in, and they all watched as if through a window. The lines on the left-hand page undulated like gently flowing waves, but the right-hand page showed a torch flickering in a wall bracket. Tall silhouettes—perhaps columns or robed people—stood in the foreground. Then a man paced into the torchlight.

"Benasin!" whispered Jarrod. "My father."

"You've never seen this before?" Trevin asked him.

"Never." Jarrod frowned at Melaia. "Why didn't you show me?"

"I didn't know it was Benasin," said Melaia. "He's not always present. When he is, his head is down, or his face is in shadow."

"Where is he?" asked Serai.

"From the looks of it, he's in a cave," said Jarrod.

"At Aubendahl?" asked Melaia.

Jarrod shook his head. "I would recognize Aubendahl. Most likely it's the Dregmoors."

"At least we know he's with one of the harps." Melaia looked at Trevin. "Is there any way you could get to the Dregmoors?"

Trevin returned the book to her. "You don't know for sure that's where this cave is. It could be anywhere—the wolf caves, the southern isles, the tribal lands." He raised the fingers of his right hand as he counted. "Allies, comains, an immortal in a cave, a harp in the sky. What else should I look for while I have so much time?"

"Start with the Oracle at Windsweep," said Melaia.

"Oh, yes. The Oracle." Trevin squinted at his right hand. "I'm afraid I'm out of fingers."

Melaia enclosed his hand in hers. "Stop being difficult. That's my job." Her hands were soft.

For a brief instant he sensed their auras together, silver and gold. Trevin knew at that moment he would go anywhere for Melaia. "Where exactly is Windsweep?" he asked.

Serai slipped a yellowed scroll off a shelf and rolled it out on the floor, revealing a map. "You're traveling north." She ran her fingers from a square marked "Redcliff," past the mountains of Aubendahl, across a plain to a dark oval. "This is Tabaitta Canyon. The Oracle dwells on one of its plateaus. People seeking advice from the Oracle usually go to Windsweep to ask their questions."

"Is Windsweep a plateau?" asked Trevin. "A city?"

"It's a pass in the mountains." Serai pointed to a barely legible *W* written on one peak of the jagged line south of the canyon.

A shout echoed from the hallway, then a clamor of voices, Varic's among them.

Trevin drew his dagger, ready to engage Varic. But as Trevin and Jarrod stepped to the door, the voices faded.

Pym burst into the room and slammed the door behind him. "You can thank the Most High for your bodyguards, my lady. The slime prince is drunk and livid. Someone told him you vowed to marry no one but Trevin."

"Who could have told him?" asked Melaia.

"Nash," said Trevin.

"He wouldn't," said Melaia. "He's well trusted—"

"And gone," said Serai. "He's not been seen since he left the king last night."

"No doubt he's on his way out of the country with a pouch of rubies and gold," said Trevin.

"Wherever he is, he's safer than you are, Main Trevin," said Pym. "Varic vowed to kill you the moment he next sees your"—he glanced at Melaia and Serai and made an obvious adjustment to his words—"your sweet face."

"Not if I see his first," said Trevin.

CHAPTER 6

In the dim lamplight of the stable, Trevin strapped his journey packs to Almaron's back. He glanced uneasily at the stable door. He had assured Melaia that Varic couldn't possibly rise this early after being so drunk the night before—he had left Dwin sleeping off *his* merriment—but he wasn't sure that was true.

On the other hand, if Varic didn't show, Trevin had half a mind to climb through the jackal's window, wake him with a dagger, and scare the scorn out of him—just so he would know the new comain hadn't turned coward and run.

As Trevin secured his sword within easy reach, he sensed an approaching presence, silver as moonlight. He smiled. She didn't have to come.

A cloaked figure holding a lantern ducked into the stables.

"Where are your bodyguards?" asked Trevin.

"Sometimes I slip away." Melaia hung the lantern on a peg. "But you were right. They'll find me." From her waist sash she drew a looped black cord. A tiny harp of red-brown wood dangled from it. She slipped it over Trevin's head. "A parting gift." She pulled out a matching pendant and hung it around her neck.

"Are these kyparis wood?" asked Trevin.

"Zilwood, a near match. They're to remind us of what brought us together."

"And now pulls us apart."

"Like it or not, you and I are bound together in the search for the harps."

"I think I like it." Trevin lifted her pendant and held it next to his, forming a heart. He eyed her. Was she blushing?

Melaia smiled and slipped her pendant from his hand. "Here comes Jarrod."

"I've something for your journey," said Jarrod as he entered the stable. Serai stepped out of the shadows to join him as he held out a staff. "I found this at the temple. It once belonged to another traveler."

Trevin felt his face redden. "This was your father's. It should be yours, Jarrod."

Jarrod shrugged. "If you find Benasin, return it to him with my regards."

"All's ready for the journey," Pym called from the stable gate.

Trevin motioned Jarrod close as he checked Almaron's cinches. "Dwin told you about Hesel?"

"He did."

"Melaia knows too. She plans to alert King Laetham this morning."

Jarrod nodded. "I'll support Dwin."

"Watch him, will you? Try to keep him sober and out of trouble."

"I'll keep him busy," Jarrod said with a sly smile. "He'll have to stay sober for the task I have in mind."

Trevin grinned. Did Jarrod think he could make a priest out of Dwin?

A muffled cry came from Serai. She pointed to a shadowed haystack by the side wall, where a foot protruded, half-exposed.

Trevin sprinted to the stack. With Jarrod and Pym he pitched aside clumps of hay. Legs came free. Hand. Arm. Torso. Head.

Trevin jerked back. Nash's eyes stared upward, and his mouth gaped, stuffed full of thick dun mud. Gash.

Melaia covered her mouth with her hands.

"Varic did this." Trevin rubbed his arms, chilled at the notion that Dwin might get involved.

Almaron whickered. Footsteps sounded in the courtyard.

"My guards." Melaia pushed Trevin toward the outer gate. "This place will soon be swarming. Be gone, or you'll not have the chance."

"I can't leave now," said Trevin. "This is our opportunity to prove that Varic's a villain."

"Can you prove Varic did this?" asked Jarrod.

Trevin rubbed his right hand. He couldn't yet, but he might find proof.

Melaia stood tall and looked every bit the princess. "Main Trevin, I want those harps found. Now."

Trevin stiffened and bowed. "As you wish."

When he rose, he saw tears in her fierce eyes. But she was right. If he stayed now, he might never leave. He took Almaron's reins and followed Pym out of the stables into the break of day.

A small, lone drak rode the first breeze of dawn as the new comain and his armsman mounted. They skirted the east wall of the city, then galloped west toward the Durenwoods, where early morning sunlight edged the treetops. Once they reached the woods, they turned north and rode toward Aubendahl. The drak followed them partway, then circled around and headed back toward Redcliff.

❦

Two days of riding took Trevin and Pym to Dahl in the foothills of the Aubendahl range. On the third day, they rode west around the hills, and by noon on the fourth day, they stood gazing across a grassy plain at mountains that spanned the northern horizon.

"Which gap is Windsweep?" asked Trevin.

"I'd say we won't know until we get closer." Pym shaded his eyes. "I'd aim for the middle of the range." He shot a challenging glance at Trevin and nudged his roan into a gallop. "Beat you to the other side," he called.

Trevin whooped and loosened his reins. Almaron fairly flew, swiftly gaining on Pym. Trevin crowed as they took the lead.

Halfway across the plain, Almaron tried to turn east. "Straight on!" urged Trevin. "Straight on!"

Almaron slowed, headed north, then swerved west. It took all of Trevin's coaxing to get him back on course.

Pym caught up. "Twists and turns! Make up your mind. East, west, or north?"

"I'm trying to go north," said Trevin. "This is Almaron's doing."

"I should have made you take the gelding," growled Pym, but he was struggling to control his skittish roan too.

Almaron balked. His ears twitched; his nostrils flared. A few yards ahead, Pym's roan came to a halt as well.

A low rumble swelled in the east, and a dust cloud boiled on the horizon. Trevin squinted. Ahead of the dust surged a wave of galloping horses.

"They're running wild!" cried Pym.

"Hie!" Trevin shouted, pressing his heel into Almaron's flank.

The stallion shot north, quickly outdistancing the roan. Then he veered east and raced toward the oncoming wave.

The din of Trevin's heartbeat in his ears rivaled the rumbling hoofs. There were at least fifty horses in his estimation, a wild-eyed torrent. He shouted at Almaron and tried to rein him aside, but the stallion surged ahead.

Moments before they reached the thundering herd, Almaron turned. The mad gallop engulfed them. Blinding, choking dust made it impossible to see Pym, and the deafening thud of hoofs drowned Trevin's calls. He had no choice but to lean into the sting of Almaron's whipping mane and cling for his life.

The wild throng flooded into a narrowing valley that funneled the horses into a corridor between cliffs. Two abreast, the horses surged into a box canyon the size of the great hall at Redcliff. The herd circled the enclosure and slowed to an agitated walk.

Trevin eased to a sitting position, panting. The horses snorted and milled uneasily, steaming a strong odor of sweat. Pym and his roan were not among them. Trevin wondered if they had made it across the plain or had turned back or… He wiped the back of his wrist across his forehead.

Flexing his right hand, then his left, Trevin looked for a way out of the canyon. A spiked fence had been placed across the entrance, and at least a dozen men swarmed the stone corridor beyond. Trevin nudged Almaron toward the fence, but the stallion held his ground, his head high, his ears alert.

A sharp whinny bounced off the stone walls. Almaron answered with a neigh, then pushed through the churn of the herd toward a horse with a golden coat and white mane that stood by the far wall. As they drew nearer, Trevin gasped. Pure white wings lay folded against the horse's sides.

The winged horse dipped her head as Almaron sidled up and nudged her. She nuzzled him back.

Trevin patted Almaron's sweaty neck. "Did she choose you, or did you choose her?" he asked. "A marvelous choice in either case, but now is not the time to make attachments. We have to find Pym." He looked toward the fence again.

Two men with closely cropped hair stood talking at the gate. Both wore wine-colored tunics and dark brown leggings. One was tall and lanky with a neatly trimmed beard, and the other was shorter and clean shaven. Each carried a bow and quiver of arrows slung across his back.

Trevin waved. "Friends!" he shouted, fully aware that they might be far from friendly.

"Ho!" called the bearded man. "How did you get trapped in the canyon?"

"I was crossing the plain when I got caught in this herd."

The clean-shaven man unchained the gate. "You're lucky to be in one piece," he called. "Where do you come from?"

"Camrithia. I'm Main Trevin. I serve King Laetham."

"We're the horsemen of King Kedemeth of Eldarra," shouted the bearded man. "I'm Haden, and this is Brink." He pointed to the man removing the chain. "We travel with Prince Resarian."

Brink pulled off the chain but didn't open the gate. "I can't raise the fence without risking the release of the herd, so you'll have to come out by this gate. It's not large enough for your horse."

"You're welcome to camp with us," called Haden. "As we cull the horses in the coming days, we'll bring your horse to you."

Trevin's heart sank. How could he know whether or not these men would be true to their word? Besides, he needed Almaron to search for Pym.

"Great barn owls!" Haden stared past Trevin and climbed the fence. "It's the Golden! She's let herself be penned."

Other horsemen came running, shouting, "The Golden! The Golden!"

"The winged one?" asked Trevin.

"Aye, the winged one," said Haden. "Each year she brings in the others, but she always flies before entering the corridor to the canyon. I'll be 'swoggled if she hasn't let herself be caught this time!"

"Can't she fly out if she wants?" asked Trevin.

"Crowded as it is and with those high cliffs? She'd have a hard time getting out. Besides, she looks content with your horse beside her."

"So it seems." Trevin tried again to nudge Almaron toward the gate but to no avail. Instead, Almaron and the Golden edged apart just far enough for him to dismount without being crushed.

Trevin sighed and dismounted, then freed Almaron from the weight of the packs, staff, and saddle. He slipped his sword and scabbard onto his belt, but his shield was lost.

As he removed Almaron's blanket, he eyed the slashes that crossed the stallion's shoulders. He ran his hand over the scars, then studied the Golden, glancing back and forth between the two horses.

His whole body went cold. Almaron once had wings.

"You need help?" called Haden.

Trevin shook his head, swallowing against a choking sensation. Had these men taken Almaron's wings? Did they plan the same for the Golden?

Trevin stroked Almaron with new respect, then shouldered the packs and the saddle. "I'll be back," he said, "and I'll not let them harm your friend."

The calm presence of the Golden and Almaron seemed to gentle the other horses, and Trevin walked slowly so as not to disturb the peace. The herd pressed toward the walls as he crossed the canyon.

As Brink chained the gate behind him, Trevin turned for another look at Almaron. The stallion would not be lonely. Trevin wished he could say the same for himself.

Haden reached for one of Trevin's packs.

"I'll carry it." Trevin clenched his teeth and headed down the walled path.

"Please yourself." Haden tromped behind him. "But if you want help, I've a strong back."

Trevin plodded ahead, his awkward load weighing heavily on him, but if this horseman's hands had taken the wings of horses like Almaron, those hands would not touch his belongings.

Other horsemen joined them as they left the enclosure, and they all trekked the corridor to the plain. At the mouth of the inlet, Trevin had to set down his baggage and rest. The other men strode toward a grove of trees, where their horses stood tethered.

Only Haden stayed. "The prince will be glad to have new company and fresh stories," he said.

Trevin kept his eyes on the plain. "Thanks for your offer of camp, but I need to find my friend. The herd separated us."

"You plan to travel the plain on foot to find him? Carrying your staff, two packs, and a saddle? Unless you have a magic I don't, your friend will be found faster on horseback. I can offer you a mount and men to help in the search."

Trevin faced him. "What are your plans for the winged horse?"

Haden's thick eyebrows arched. "The Golden? We've no plans for her. We didn't expect to corral her in the first place." He narrowed his eyes. "If *you're* thinking of taking her, you'll have to deal with me first."

"You'll not take her wings?"

"Take her wings? You think we're Dregmoorians? That's the last thing we'd do. The Golden's a free creature, and I aim to see she stays that way."

Trevin took a deep breath. "I'm sorry. I misjudged you. My horse bears scars where he should have wings."

Haden frowned. "You know who maimed him?"

Trevin shook his head. "He was found wounded and half-starved, wandering near the Dregmoors. No one thought he would live, and with his scars he wasn't considered a worthy mount."

Haden chuckled. "Worthy, eh? I'd say worthy and then some." He pointed to Trevin's packs. "May I?"

"I'd be grateful." Trevin gathered his staff and saddle as Haden hefted his two packs. Together they strode to the grove. "Tell me about the Golden."

"She's queen of the Windwings," said Haden. "They're perhaps the wisest of the animals. Some say they're gifted to see into the spirit realm and were once able to cross into Avellan and back."

"Avellan?"

"A border city of heaven."

"You mean they reached heaven without the stairway?"

"So the legend goes," said Haden. "I've no notion if it's true, but when I was a boy, Windwings were common here. Then the Dregmoorians began trapping them. Rumor said the immortal Firstborn bred Windwings with common horses to create herds for the Under-Realm, but in order to keep the Windwings from flying away—"

"He severed their wings? Is this still going on?"

"Ended a score or more years ago," said Haden. "Fierce battles were fought over it. In the end Arelin's forces set the Windwings free."

"Who is Arelin?"

"A warrior angel, if you believe in such." Haden eyed Trevin.

"I know one," said Trevin, thinking of Jarrod.

"Oh?" Haden looked at him with interest. "Arelin managed to release the Windwings, but the breeding had already begun, so the horses who rejoined the herd were mixed. Some were Windwings, and some were sired by them but born without wings. Each spring the Golden culls the wingless out of her herd and runs them here to the Edgelands of Eldarra. I think she knows we'll respect and care for them. I confess, I dream that someday the wingless will breed a winged one."

"Almaron obviously didn't escape the Dregmoors with the other Windwings."

"But he did escape," said Haden. "Maybe he's the reason the Golden allowed herself to be penned."

Trevin and Haden stepped into the shade of the grove, and Trevin set down his load. No doubt Almaron had known what he was doing when he ran with the herd—he was running with the Golden. Trevin couldn't blame him. If Melaia were nearby, he knew where he would be.

Several of the horsemen had already ridden back to Prince Resarian's camp, but four who remained at the grove volunteered to help search for Pym. Since Brink had stayed at the canyon as a guard, Haden let Trevin borrow Brink's gelding.

"We haven't a great deal of time," warned Haden. "At nightfall the wolves start prowling. Besides, the prince will likely send a search party for *us* if we don't return to camp by dusk."

"Then let's make quick work of it." Trevin mounted Brink's horse. "My friend Pym will be glad for a meal in good company."

"A man with my own taste," said Haden. "I like him already."

The horsemen headed out in twos, Haden riding beside Trevin. As they scoured the path of the wild herd, clearly defined by flattened grass, Trevin braced himself to find Pym and the roan trampled.

Afternoon crept toward evening. Clouds turned orange red. A distant howl moaned across the plain, echoed by another, making the horses snort and sidestep.

"Wolves are more plentiful when the wild horses run." Haden looked toward the darkening east. "It's time we turn back. Your friend… Is he a seasoned traveler?"

"He is," said Trevin, though he took little comfort in the thought. "As armsman to Main Undrian, Pym has traveled every corner of Camrithia. That's one reason we're here. I've been sent to search for King Laetham's comains. They've all disappeared."

"So we've heard," said Haden. "How did you escape such a fate?"

"I'm newly appointed." Trevin circled back with Haden. The other riders fell in with them, and they cantered toward a sunset that streaked the lavender sky with rose and gold. Trevin kept glancing back over his shoulder, hoping to see Pym galloping toward them.

"One of your comains, Catellus, rode the territory east of here near the wolf caves of Montressi," said Haden. "On the Dregmoorian border."

"I met Catellus once," said a sandy-haired rider. "He helped protect shepherds in the foothills from wolves."

"Won't wolves stalk the horses you've trapped?" asked Trevin.

"Our guards are masters of the bow," said Haden. "As for your friend, he'll most likely make a fire, which should keep the wolves at a distance. If he finds a sheepcote for shelter, he'll have an even better time of it."

They broke into a gallop, passed the grove, and headed toward the prince's camp.

Trevin felt as if his heart had been torn into three parts. One remained at Redcliff. Another lay in the enclosure with Almaron. A third roamed the hills in search of Pym. He yearned to be in each place.

Instead, he was headed away from all of them. He had no heart left for that.

CHAPTER 7

As Trevin and the horsemen rode into the prince's camp, hoots and guffaws rose from a company of men gathered around a bonfire. Savory aromas twisted Trevin's stomach with hunger. He dismounted and looked back at the darkening plain. If Pym hadn't lost his pack, he'd have food, but where would he find shelter?

Following Haden and the other horsemen, Trevin skirted the fire and approached a flaxen-haired young man seated on a stump and bent double with laughter. Trevin couldn't help recalling Dwin at the tavern, but this youth had been cornered by a skinny, bush-haired jester rather than three loathsome Dregmoorians.

Haden pointed to the young man. "Prince Resarian."

The prince wiped his eyes, rubbed his freckled nose, and caught his breath. "A fine story, Dio," he told the jester. His voice held the lightness of youth with an edge of manhood. "Do you have another tale as funny?"

"Maybe Haden has brought a story, a glory, a timely tale, so to say," said Dio.

"Uncle Haden!" The prince jumped to his feet.

Haden strode to the front of the group, and Trevin hung back, watching. *Uncle?* As Haden and the horsemen knelt before the prince, Trevin did the same.

"Rise! Rise!" said the prince. "I heard you trapped the Golden!"

"I'd say she allowed it," said Haden. "Maybe chose it."

"I wish I had been there!" said the prince. "I'll ride out to see her tomorrow."

Wolves howled in the distance, and a momentary apprehension rippled through the group.

Haden clapped his hands. "I've a riddle for you, Resarian."

We trapped a goodly number of wild ones,
Strong and mighty steed,
But one we saw, when we did count,
With two heads and six feet!

Prince Resarian pursed his lips and drummed his fingers on his knees. "One head at the front and one at the rear? Or two side by side?"

"Neither," said Haden. "One at the front and one in the *middle*."

"Grotesque!" said the prince. "Could it be a malformed insect?"

"Not that strange," said Haden.

The prince raised his hands. "I surrender."

"A horse and its rider," said Haden. "Stand, Main Trevin."

"Oho! You trapped a rider!" said the prince.

"Comain of the kingdom of Camrithia," said Trevin, bowing.

"We heard the comains disappeared," said the prince.

"Main Trevin is newly appointed," said Haden.

"Welcome, then, Main Trevin." The prince waved him forward. "Come dine with us."

Haden and the other horsemen wandered off to their duties while Trevin joined the prince and Dio. As they ate, the prince plied him with questions. What was Camrithia like? Where had his travels taken him? What was it like to be a comain?

Trevin answered cautiously, wary of revealing too much information to people he didn't know. Resarian, however, talked freely of his life as prince of Eldarra, growing up in the palace city of Flauren. He was the youngest of four children, but the older three had died in childhood.

"I'm embarrassed to confess I've never been this far from home before," said the prince. "At least not without my father. You see, my mother shields me, therefore my father shields me. I am forced to implore him to trust me with responsibility, to let me prove myself." Resarian swept his arm toward the provision wagons. "This is the extent of the duties allowed me. It peeves me to be assigned the simple task of minding the camp while the horsemen do the 'dangerous' work. I'm quite ready to face the challenges of the wild."

The prince's bravado reminded Trevin of Dwin, but while Dwin hurled himself into action, Prince Resarian hurled himself into words.

Haden returned with a jug of wine and refilled the prince's cup. Then he eased his lanky frame to the ground and refilled Trevin's. "You told me you were searching for the missing comains," he said.

"Perhaps they were captured and spirited away to a magical maze," suggested Dio.

"If only I could journey like Main Trevin and find a magical maze!" said Resarian. "That's a challenge fit for a prince."

Haden filled Dio's cup and his own. "I know of canyons and caves, groves and thickets, but I've never seen a magical maze."

"The dull face of reality." Dio gulped his drink.

Haden leaned back against a tree trunk. "To return to my subject, Main Trevin, you said searching for comains is one reason you're here. What's your other reason?"

Trevin gazed past the bonfire into the black of the woods, wondering if he should mention the harps. "I was advised to consult the Oracle," he said.

"You were headed to Windsweep?" asked Dio.

"I and my friend," said Trevin. "Have you been there?"

"Not I," said the prince.

"Nor I," said Dio. "But legend says Windsweep is where the Oracle gives advice, answers, wise words, so to say."

Howls pierced the night, and the horses shifted uneasily.

"I hope your friend finds shelter, some abode off the road, so to say," said Dio. "After dark, wolves prowl the Edgelands."

"So I've been told," said Trevin.

Dio leaned forward. "I've stories to make your flesh crawl, tales of a hooded figure who wanders the mountains. When men draw near, he throws off his hood to reveal a ravenous jackal with glowing eyes!"

Another howl split the air, and Trevin shivered.

"Or the tale of vulturous draks that lead wolves to prey," said Dio. "The wolves make the kill, and no matter the victim, the wolf pack leaves the prey's head, hands, and feet for the draks to feast on! A sacrifice between beasts, so to say."

Haden cut his eyes toward Dio, and Prince Resarian laughed. "Dio takes pleasure in trying to scare me to the utmost. Sends me to bed with the shakes."

"I'll be the one who retires with the shakes." Trevin laughed in an effort to calm his sense of foreboding. He had seen enough of draks and shape shifters to know that the line between tale and truth did not always fall where he wished. With Pym unaccounted for, he preferred not to spend the night fighting back fears, founded or unfounded.

Trevin eyed Dio. Perhaps the jester knew a story that might be more enlightening than frightening. "Do you know the tale of the Wisdom Tree?" he asked. He had never heard the entire story though it held Melaia in its grip.

"I do!" Dio cradled his lyre, plucked a mournful melody, and sang:

> *Time was, time is, and time will be.*
> *Thus starts the tale of the Wisdom Tree*
> *and two brothers who rivals forever shall be.*

Over the pensive tune Dio told the story. "Rivals they were, Firstborn and Second, in games of skill, games of logic, games of love and life, until rivalry itself became their great game. They rivaled themselves past the grave, beyond death, the knell, the dirge, so to say. You may ask, how so? Listen and learn, my friend:

"In search of the best of all gifts for his father, the Second-born came upon a great Tree bearing a crimson fruit not known in his land. The Wisdom Tree it was, concealing the stairway to heaven, the lightbridge for angels who carry the dead heavenward, skyward, across the veil, so to say. The Second-born plucked its fruit as a gift for his father.

"Enraged, the Tree's guardian angel appeared, demanding he return the fruit, for its flesh held the gift of knowledge and wisdom, and its seeds were forbidden to mortals.

"The Second-born begged the angel to let his father taste such fruit. At last she allowed him a single fruit in return for his vow to bring back its three seeds. Moreover, she required him to bring her the first creature that greeted him upon his arrival home. If he failed to repay this debt, said the angel, she would take payment in breath and blood. Impetuous bargain, reckless pledge, foolhardy promise, so to say. For his niece, the Firstborn's daughter, welcomed the Second-born home.

"Upon hearing his story, the girl offered to return the seeds herself and plead release from his debt. In secret she and her uncle stole away, but the Firstborn discovered their plan, their scheme, their plot, so to say. He followed with warriors, rescued his daughter, and destroyed the Tree so his brother could never repay the debt.

"What of the seeds, you ask? One, the Firstborn ate. The other two, he forced his daughter and brother to swallow, and they became immortal. They have carried their feud, their blame, their game from the time that was, into time that is now, unto time that will be. As far as the mind can see, so to say. As far as the mind can see."

Only the crackle of flames broke the silence as Trevin stared into the bonfire. He had heard Melaia tell fragments of the tale. Dio's version differed in some details, but Trevin saw the entire story now and knew the basic facts were true.

A howl brought him out of his reverie. Small protective fires flared up in a ring around the perimeter of the camp.

Prince Resarian rose, placed one foot on his tree stump, and drummed his fingers on his knee. "Main Trevin, you'll not have to wait for your horse or your friend. I shall take you to Windsweep tomorrow."

"I thought you wanted to see the Golden tomorrow," said Haden.

"On the way to Windsweep."

Haden scratched his ear and eyed Trevin. "Does your friend know Windsweep is your destination?"

Trevin nodded. "We planned to camp in the foothills tonight and reach Windsweep a day or two later."

"In that case I wager he'll meet up with you there." Haden turned to the prince. "You're in charge here, so Main Trevin will have to make his journey alone."

"Horse dung!" said the prince. "Any of these men can keep this camp in order. I'm in *charge,* so I can *charge* someone to take my place while I'm gone, and I can *charge* myself to lead a quest to Windsweep."

Inwardly Trevin groaned. An impulsive prince might slow him down.

"Supervising the encampment is no small task," said Haden. "Prove you're trustworthy here, and some day you'll have your own quest."

"I can prove I'm trustworthy by escorting Main Trevin to Windsweep," said Resarian. "There and back. Simple."

Haden peeled bark off a twig. "Resarian—"

"I'm going. You can come or not. We'll stop to see the Golden."

Haden tossed the twig into the fire. "All right. But if I say we turn back—for any reason—we turn back. Agreed?"

"Agreed." The prince grinned, and so did Haden.

"If we stop to see the Golden, maybe I can get Almaron," said Trevin. "Although now that he's with his own, he may never want my company again."

"If he won't come now, you can ride my horse," said Haden. "We'll have someone bring your mount as soon as they're sorted out."

"An adventure!" The prince crowed. "Dio, come with us and put our journey to song. Oh, the stories we'll tell Father and Mother when we return!"

"We're not out for sightseeing," Trevin warned. "King Laetham wants me back by the end of the season, so I can't afford to lose time. Every day counts." Not to mention that Melaia's future hung in the balance, he thought. Maybe Dwin's as well.

"Does King Laetham think an omen from Windsweep can solve his problems?" Haden looked amused. "Sounds to me as if he sent you on a charmed-owl hunt."

"The king has also asked that I renew ties between Camrithia and Eldarra," said Trevin. "He hopes the two kingdoms, once allies, might be so again."

Haden nodded at Resarian. "Now *that* is a fitting task for a prince, Resarian. Introduce Main Trevin to the court at Flauren. Show him around. You could head there tomorrow."

"I see through that ploy." Prince Resarian laughed. "You're trying to turn me from my quest. I'll take Main Trevin to Flauren after I've shown him to Windsweep."

"And I still need to search for my friend," said Trevin.

"To Windsweep, then," said the prince. "Maybe I'll hear a word for Mother. She believes in oracles and omens and star watching. Sometimes at night she looks north from the tallest tower of the palace to the lights of Avellan in the sky. She says Avellan recedes. Which means the blight expands here in our world."

Dio strummed a dissonant chord on his lyre and winced. "An enchanting tale, a fine fable, a thrilling drama, so to say."

"Some tales are true," said Resarian.

"Camrithia is beginning to experience the blight," said Trevin. "But Avellan—your mother can see it?"

"I've seen it myself," said Haden. "But not everyone believes the tales of Avellan." He looked at Dio, who shrugged.

"I believe it," said Resarian. "Can you see Avellan from the mountains, Uncle Haden?"

"On a clear night you can see it from Ledge Rock." Haden drained his cup. "It's only a bow shot from here."

"It's a clear night." Prince Resarian swept up his cloak. "Let's go see Avellan."

"What about wolves?" asked Dio.

"We'll take torches," said Resarian.

"And daggers," said Haden.

༄

Ledge Rock, a bald protrusion of granite abutting a tree-topped hill, loomed higher than Trevin had imagined, like a giant camel's hump under the broad sky. With Trevin and Haden carrying torches to ward off wolves, their small group climbed a moonlit path to the gently rounded summit of the rock.

"Watch your step." Haden took the lead. "There's a reason it's called Ledge Rock." He raised his torch, and Trevin could see that the rounded slope ended in a sheer drop.

"I'll just sit here." Dio retreated and plopped down four paces back. "Should've brought a cloak," he muttered, rubbing his arms.

"Take mine." Trevin slipped off his cloak and tossed it to the skinny jester.

Prince Resarian sat on the edge of the rock and dangled his legs over.

"Move back," said Haden.

"I'm sitting," said Resarian.

"I'm responsible for your safety." Haden wedged his torch in a crevice. "If you want your parents to let you go on more adventures, don't court danger."

The prince scooted back.

Haden turned to Trevin. "I don't take to courtly life and would have weaned Resarian long ago, filed the edge of nobility off him. But he *is* heir to the throne, so he's under a mite more than normal protection."

Trevin wedged his torch into a nearby crack, eying the prince, wondering what kind of king he would be.

"There!" Resarian pointed. "Barely above the horizon."

"It's easier to see on a moonless night." Haden folded his arms over his chest and gazed across the hilly landscape.

"My mother says most of what we see is the veil, but beyond it lies the glow of Avellan."

Trevin scanned the dark horizon. A wave of light rippled across the heavens like a gentle tide lapping the seashore. Pale colors—pink, yellow, green, blue—slowly swirled through white eddies, creating a sheer, billowing curtain. Trevin could barely make out a gold point beyond the veil.

"You seem to know a lot about Avellan," said Trevin. "I've not met many people south of here who talk about it or study the stars."

"The Erielyon live north of us," said Haden. "And Queen Ambria has long been a friend of the Angelaeon."

Trevin sank to the rock, never taking his eyes from the play of light. "As Avellan grows distant, does the veil recede too?"

"As the tale goes," said Dio, "Avellan was once so near that the light covered the world like a blanket, a cloak, a second skin, so to say, held in place by the stairway to heaven. Climbing the stairway was known as crossing the veil. The queen claims the stairs will rise again when the stars of the beltway align to form a path for the stairs to follow."

"Which happens once every two hundred years," said Resarian. "Mother says when it happens next, heaven will be secured to the world once again. She watches for it."

"Now its light plays in the distance like music, a heaven song, a shimmer of sounds," mused Dio from where he sat behind them. "They say on a windy night you can hear the hum of light even here, but I've—"

His words ended in a scream.

Trevin turned as a wolf landed on Dio.

Haden grabbed the prince, and Trevin leaped onto the wolf, plunging his dagger between its ribs. As the wolf reared back, Haden sliced into its neck.

Trevin shoved the blood-soaked wolf aside and turned to Dio. He couldn't tell if the blood that covered the jester belonged to Dio or the wolf, so he was heartened to hear Dio's voice squeak, "Did he miss my vitals, my members, my innards, so to say?"

"Amazingly." Haden inspected Dio's slashed lyre. "Your shield saved your life. Maybe all of us should wear lyres."

"Can I see?" Resarian sat on his haunches by Haden's torch.

"Let's get Dio back to camp," said Haden. "He has some nasty-looking scratches."

Trevin raised his torch and circled the wolf's body. Tan fur, one black leg, gray eyes.

Varic's dog.

CHAPTER 8

Trevin lay awake in camp that night, wondering if Varic's wolf dog had followed him on its own. Was Varic on his trail as well? What about Hesel and Fornian? For Melaia's sake he hoped Varic had left Redcliff, but he bristled at the idea of Varic tracking him and Pym.

When at last Trevin fell asleep, his terror-dream engulfed him. A hooded figure. A flash of pain. Screams.

He awoke with a jerk, sweating, panting, his heart racing. But he had not cried out, for the camp slumbered on. He clasped the small harp that hung from his neck and tried to keep from tumbling back into the dream.

Trevin roused to a flurry of activity the next morning. While supervising a meal of flatbread, fruit, and dried beef, Prince Resarian divided his company into four groups. He instructed the first to search for Pym, the second to mind the wild horses, and the third to manage the campsite and tend to Dio's wounds. Haden and Prince Resarian formed the fourth group, charged with the task of escorting Trevin to Windsweep to question the Oracle.

Midmorning, Haden, Resarian, and Trevin departed camp, riding three abreast, Trevin on a borrowed gelding, sleek and black. They galloped to the box canyon where the horsemen who ringed its cliffs counted the wild horses.

Trevin stood at the gate and watched the horses mill around the enclosure, flaring their nostrils. Almaron tossed his head as if saluting, but he stayed beside the Golden. The two stood tall, king and queen of the Windwings.

"You'll have him again," said Haden. "Windwings are a brilliant breed and loyal. We'll cull him out and keep him safe for you."

Prince Resarian climbed halfway up the fence. "I dream of someday riding a Windwing. Can you imagine soaring the skies like a bird?"

Trevin could almost imagine it. Riding Almaron full gallop across the plain was as near as he could come to flying.

He headed back down the stone corridor. "Blast!" he muttered. "I hate losing Almaron at a time when I most need his surefooted speed."

Prince Resarian caught up with Trevin. "I've not had the pleasure of riding at a full gallop for any length of time. Such activity falls into the list of dangers from which my mother shields me. If not for Uncle Haden, I would not have been allowed to join the horsemen this year."

Haden strode behind them. "We'll not tell your parents how close the wolf came to you last night. They made me swear by the king's crown I'd bring you back safe."

The prince matched Trevin's pace, his gangly arms swinging. "What were you doing at my age, Main Trevin?"

"How old are you?" Trevin asked.

"Fifteen."

Trevin looked back at Haden. This boy was a man.

"I know," said Haden.

"So what were you doing at fifteen?" asked the prince.

Trevin rubbed his scruffy beard. At fifteen he had been caught climbing down the wall of a caravansary, a bag of food and other loot in his hands, Dwin waiting below. They had seen a hawk but had ignored it until the bird landed and transformed into a man. Lord Rejius. It was his possessions Trevin held. The hawkman offered them a deal: he would spare their lives if they would serve him. So the hawkman gained a young informant at Redcliff.

Not an exemplary life. Better to start the account earlier.

"My parents died when I was nine," said Trevin. "My younger brother and I were taken in by an old schoolmaster for a time."

"I knew you were educated," said Resarian.

"But we weren't inclined to be scholars, so we joined a caravan and worked as donkey drovers. One trip was enough. We were easily hired away by the master of a traveling tent show." He left out the fact that he and Dwin were hired for their sticky fingers and told to pick pouches for the master.

"It kept our bellies full," said Trevin, "but it wasn't the best way to live. As it happened, one day the show master fleeced a nobleman who had connections with a visiting comain. In the ensuing melee, we ran and ended up in Redcliff."

Prince Resarian halted at the corridor entrance, gaping at Trevin. "And now you're a comain entrusted with a magnificent quest! Shall I not have a quest as well, Uncle Haden?"

"Main Trevin is not heir to the throne of Eldarra," said Haden. "But if you're worried I'll make you go back to camp, you can breathe easy. I think you and I can afford to lend Main Trevin our company for a day or two before we turn back."

Prince Resarian ran ahead to their mounts. "Onward to Windsweep!" he cried.

Trevin hung back to walk beside Haden. "You're Resarian's uncle, so you must be—"

"Brother to King Kedemeth." Haden looked sideways at Trevin. "You're wondering why I don't comport myself like royalty?"

"So to say." Trevin grinned.

"Taking Dio's place?" Haden chuckled. "You're not the first to ask such a question. My brother enjoys people, the bustle of the city, the inner workings of kingdoms. I prefer solitude, the peace of mountain and meadow, the interworking of land, sea, and sky. Fortunately, Kedemeth is the firstborn. I wouldn't want the throne."

"I know how different brothers can be."

"You understand, then. I believe my nephew should have a *little* more experience with the hardships of life. I'm protective of him first and foremost because I love the lad, but second because he's Kedemeth's only living heir. Next in line is—"

"You?" asked Trevin.

"I'm afraid so," said Haden. "But I'll be 'swoggled if I spend the rest of my life astride the throne."

Prince Resarian was already in the saddle when Trevin and Haden mounted their horses. They galloped eastward across the plain.

After a time Haden slowed his horse to a walk. He pointed to the ridge along the horizon. "See the cleft in the range to the north?"

Trevin shaded his eyes and studied the backbone of earth until he saw a notch. "West of the tallest peak?"

"That's it," said Haden. "Windsweep."

Prince Resarian scanned the mountains. "Have you been to Windsweep before, Uncle Haden?"

"Some twenty-five years ago. With Arelin." Haden turned to Trevin. "I mentioned him before. He was Angelaeon and as close as a brother to Queen Ambria. Her family ruled in the mountains of Montressi until the Dregmoorians invaded and massacred them."

"All except Mother," said Resarian. "She had already married my father."

"Arelin took to spending the winters at the palace with Kedemeth and Ambria and traveling the mountains in the summer," said Haden. "Until Dreggies nabbed the Windwings. That's when I accompanied him to Windsweep. He sought advice about whether he should try to rescue the horses."

"I wasn't yet born when it happened." Resarian leaned toward Trevin. "My mother told me about it. She didn't want Arelin to go to the Dregmoors."

"Did Arelin hear the Oracle at Windsweep?" asked Trevin.

Haden shrugged. "He said he did. He rode to the Dregmoors, leading a contingent of warriors. They freed the Windwings, but Arelin paid with his life. So did he hear right or not?"

Haden turned north into the foothills, and they headed into steeper mountains, single file.

As dusk descended, wolves began their nightly howl. Haden led the way to the top of a rise where two ancient, crumbling stone walls intersected. Within this half fort Haden tethered their horses and built a fire. Trevin handed a round of bread to the prince.

"I'm following my own path for a change," said the prince. "That's what I admire about you, Main Trevin. You're a young comain, and you follow your own path."

"I follow my king's command," said Trevin.

"But in your own way," said Resarian. "If Uncle Haden and I were not with you, you'd still be traveling these dangerous mountains. Alone."

Haden looked at the prince sternly. "He had a companion."

Trevin felt Pym's absence keenly, but he gave the prince a half smile. "With your admiration I may gain an inch or two in height."

He broke another loaf in half. Maybe he should tell the truth: the admired comain felt woefully inadequate for his quest. On the other hand, what harm would it do to allow the prince this misjudgment? Dwin's tongue would never utter such praise.

The prince was so intent on his side of the conversation that he didn't flinch when twigs snapped on the dark hillside. But Trevin and Haden sprang to their feet, Trevin drawing his sword. Prince Resarian stiffened and hushed. Haden loosened his dagger, slipped silently in front of the prince, and nocked an arrow in his bow.

Trevin peered into the moonlit night toward whatever crept up the slope. An experienced bandit wouldn't make so much noise. Was it a wolf, then? A pack of wolves? The approach was slow and deliberate, circling. Or was the sound meant to distract them from silent attackers uphill? A breeze rustled the bushes. Insects whirred. Wolves howled.

A movement drew Trevin's attention to a thicket. From behind it, barely visible, was…a foxtail?

Haden aimed his arrow.

Trevin squinted and barely made out a sheaf of hair, tousled like an un-weeded garden.

"Hold!" said Trevin. "It's my friend."

"How do you know?" Haden held his bow steady.

"I can see in the dark."

"Bull teats." Haden kept his aim.

"Pym?" called Trevin.

"Main Trevin! It *is* you!" The thicket rustled, and Pym peered out. Then he ducked into the shadows and emerged leading his roan. Haden lowered his bow.

As Pym entered the enclosure, Trevin clapped him on the back. "I thought you'd been trampled. Let me introduce you to the hospitality of Eldarrans."

"Can you introduce me to some victuals as well?" asked Pym.

"Is this is your long-lost companion?" asked the prince.

Trevin made introductions. Haden laid aside his bow.

"I'd keep that bow close at hand, I would," said Pym. "When we encountered the stampede and my roan spooked, she ran south but too far east to make Aubendahl. I had to rest her before I could hope to pick up the trail again. We set out in the evening but didn't get far before we spied travelers who'd not have given us a warm welcome."

"Who?" asked the prince.

"Main Trevin will know them as ruffians," said Pym. "Prince Varic and his two companions."

Trevin scowled as he handed Pym a strip of dried meat and a hunk of cheese.

"I thought you'd be surprised," said Pym.

"You didn't see their dog, did you?" asked Trevin.

Pym bit off a corner of the meat and spoke with his mouth full. "Come to think of it, I didn't see the dog."

"We did," said Trevin. "Haden and I killed it."

The prince's mouth dropped open.

"Dog?" asked Haden. "That was a wolf if ever I saw one."

"Whatever the beast, I'm glad it's gone." Pym bit into the cheese.

Haden paced to the open side of the shelter where the horses were staked. "You said *Prince* Varic."

"Of the Dregmoors," said Trevin.

"Say no more." Haden studied the dark hillside, alert.

Prince Resarian pulled back the string of Haden's bow. "What is the prince doing in the Edgelands of Eldarra?"

"Hunting deer, I guess," said Pym. "They had two dead and laid out nearby. I wager they're hunting other prey as well."

Trevin squatted by the fire. "Meaning me?"

"Meaning you," said Pym.

"Why did Varic follow me north?" asked Trevin. "He was free of me at Redcliff."

"It's a whole season before King Laetham gives a yea or nay to Varic's peace offer," said Pym. "If you were found dead before then, it might shorten the wait."

Prince Resarian let the bowstring go with a *ping*. Haden looked at him. "You'll be traveling with that bow until we return to camp."

The prince whooped, then clapped his hand over his mouth.

Haden narrowed his eyes. "This is not play, Resarian. Remember that."

Trevin turned back to Pym. "Did Prince Varic see you?"

"I think not," said Pym. "I kept my distance. They were loud and having their fill of ale. Speaking of—"

Haden filled Pym's cup. "Why does this prince want you dead, Main Trevin?"

"Why?" echoed Prince Resarian.

"Varic probably wants to prevent Main Trevin from gaining allies for Camrithia," said Pym. "Strong allies will make it easier for King Laetham to refuse the Dregmoorians' peace offer."

Trevin stirred the fire with a stick. "Now that you're found, Pym, perhaps we should visit the Eldarran court at Flauren first. Camrithia needs allies more than a sign from an Oracle."

"But we've almost reached Windsweep." Prince Resarian's shoulders slumped. "Flauren is back east, at least a day's ride past the camp."

"The prince has a point," said Pym.

"Besides, my father may not grant your request right away," said Resarian. "He will say there are strategic matters involved. He always says that, but it's true."

Trevin eyed Resarian with new respect. The young prince was naive but not empty headed. "You're right. Windsweep is closer. Take us there first, then to Flauren. Perhaps you can be a party to our discussions there." He grinned at Resarian's broad smile.

Haden leaned against the stone wall. "If the Dregmoorians offer peace, why the need for allies?"

"The price of peace is marriage between the Camrithian princess and Prince Varic," said Pym.

Trevin stabbed the glowing logs with his stick, sending sparks into the night. "If the princess refuses Varic, we'll have no peace treaty, and Camrithia will need all the allies she can find."

"I hear a tale for the telling," said Haden.

"It would be a tale left unfinished," said Trevin.

The prince drummed his fingers on his knees. "Have you any tales, Arme Pym?"

"I'm no storyteller." Pym took a swig of his ale.

"You're an armsman," said Resarian. "Haven't you seen battles?"

"More than I care to remember." Pym wiped his mouth with the back of his hand. "I can describe the comains of Camrithia for you."

"Good enough." The prince settled back, stroking his borrowed bow. "Tell on."

"I'll start with my master, Main Undrian," said Pym. "Tall, he was, and lance thin. Rode under the sign of the bear. I helped him secure the land along the banks of the Davernon River. Main Gremel was a close friend of his, a well-muscled man. He oversaw the Southern Sea coast and the fortress of Tigerre at the mouth of the Davernon."

Haden strode to the open side of the shelter and stared into the darkness. Trevin tossed the stick into the fire and moved to the opposite wall, sword and dagger close at hand, one ear to Pym's voice, one ear to the night.

"Sharp-eyed Main Vardamis always dressed like a noble," said Pym. "He traveled the highways. No one fared better at keeping bandits at bay." Pym counted on his fingers. "Fourth was Main Brevian, a paunchy fellow, bald as an egg, in charge of all defenses, inspecting fortresses and such like. Fifth, Main Solivius. Jolly, red cheeked, fair haired. He kept the western border secure."

"Don't forget Main Catellus," said Prince Resarian. "I saw him once when I was younger. He has big ears."

"That's him," said Pym. "Husky. Big eared. Expert at the slingshot. He oversaw the northeastern mountain border between Camrithia and the Dregmoors."

"Catellus protected shepherds and their flocks east of here as well," said Haden. "He visited King Kedemeth on occasion."

"My story has a mysterious ending, and true," said Pym. "A little over a year ago, the comains' shields began turning up hither and yon throughout the kingdom, but the comains have never been seen again. Until last night."

Trevin straightened. "What did you say?"

"I saw Main Catellus last night," said Pym. "With Varic and his companions."

"Has Catellus joined the Dregmoorians?" asked Haden.

"Joined them in drink and laughter, at least, from what I saw." Pym ran his hand through his hair. "Now that I think on it, he wasn't laughing that much.

In fact, he looked downright gloomy, but I didn't care to stay and question him."

Trevin paced to the horses and gazed at the dark, hulking mountains. Had Catellus turned traitor? Had the other comains defected as well? Why?

⟵❦⟶

By the time the sun had fully risen the next morning, Trevin and his friends were well on their journey. Windsweep, a wide gap between two peaks, appeared to be near, but the climb proved steep and rugged, and the trail was narrow, forcing them to dismount and lead their horses. To make matters worse, wind funneled through the gap and roared down the mountainside. The closer they came to the notch in the ridge, the stronger the wind blew.

Despite the toad's pace of their trek, by midafternoon they reached Windsweep. Haden led them to a wide-mouthed cave a stone's throw to the west of the gap, its ceiling blackened by the fires of previous travelers. They settled their packs inside.

Pym rubbed down the horses. "I'll stay with the mounts," he said. "I'm more than glad to be out of the bluster."

Prince Resarian bounded out of the cave, Haden on his heels. Trevin followed them to the ridge, where trees grew sideways in a permanent bow to the wind surge. As they neared the gap, they had to yell at one another to be heard.

Once they reached the rift, they discovered they could lean into the wind, supported by its force, as they gazed across Tabaitta Canyon north of the mountains. The prince laughed with delight, though Trevin knew it only by watching his face and hearing occasional snatches of his voice.

Trevin had no idea how he should address the Oracle. He supposed Melaia would pray, but to be heard here, the prayer would have to be loud. He yelled, "I'm Main Trevin of Camrithia. I seek news of the king's comains."

His voice swirled away on the wind. He closed his eyes and strained to hear an answer, but he heard only waves of wind louder than the breakers of the sea.

"I seek a sign, a word from you," he called.

Again he heard only the wild rush of air assaulting his ears. Over and over he called. Nothing.

At length he had his fill of being buffeted on the heights. His throat was dry, his ears roaring. He returned to the cave with Haden and Resarian.

After a long drink of water, Trevin helped Pym lay a fire. The prince practiced pulling Haden's bow with no arrow while Haden spread out the prince's bedroll.

"Haden," said Trevin, "were you in the gap with Arelin when he listened for the Oracle?"

"I was, but he stood there so long I nearly left before he heard anything."

"So he *did* hear a message?"

Haden shrugged. "Said he did. I heard nothing but wind."

"How did Arelin listen? What exactly did he do?"

Haden chuckled. "He did the same as you this afternoon. In fact, watching you took me back twenty-five years. Arelin leaned against the wind with his eyes closed. Finally I saw his lips moving as if he were conversing with someone. I thought he'd gone mad, and maybe he had. When we finally left, he wore a big grin on his face. 'I'm off to the Dregmoors,' he said."

Trevin paced to the mouth of the cave. The mountainside lay shadowed in twilight. "I'm returning to the gap," he said and strode out into the wind.

CHAPTER 9

Trevin shouldered through the whistling gale until he reached the center of the gap. There he faced the wind and stared, squint eyed, across the land that lay north of the mountain range. A river curved like a black snake around the tall, flat-topped towers of earth that rose from the floor of Tabaitta Canyon. The sides of the plateaus looked like sheer cliffs, striated with purple shadow, darkening as he watched.

With arms outspread like an eagle's wings, Trevin leaned into the wind. "I seek the harps made from the great Tree," he yelled, barely able to hear himself. "I seek the comains of Camrithia." He heard nothing. "Can you help me?" He felt crazed talking to the wind.

Seeeeeker.

A shiver shot through Trevin.

Seeeeeker. Seeeeeker.

"I'm a seeker," Trevin called. "Will you advise me?"

Hold fast to the search. Hooooold faaaaast, Seeeeeker.

"Where do I search?" Trevin's words blew back into his throat. He pressed into the wind. "Where are the comains of Camrithia? Where are the harps of the great Tree? Where do I go from here?"

The wind howled. *Seeeeek meeeee. I would seeeee yooooou face to faaaaace.*

Trevin glanced around. The Oracle had a face, not just a voice? "Where do I find you?"

In the caaaaanyon.

Trevin scanned the canyon. Plateaus dotted the landscape all the way to the horizon. "Where in the canyon?" he called.

Only the wild, lonely howl of the wind answered him.

Trevin stayed until darkness swallowed the canyon and the gap where he stood. Only the top of the mountain remained golden in the light of the setting sun, but it, too, quickly faded into night. With the wind thrashing his back, Trevin returned to the cave.

Tomorrow he would venture into the canyon.

❧

A hand shook Trevin's shoulder. He pushed himself to a sitting position and blinked heavily at Haden. "Did I cry out?"

"You were mumbling, but I was going to rouse you anyway."

"My turn at watch." Trevin drew his cloak snug and followed Haden to the mouth of the cave. On the eastern horizon a thread of gray rimmed the mountains.

Trevin turned to Haden, whose profile seemed chiseled from stone. "It's almost daybreak. You stood my watch as well as yours."

"I wasn't tired," said Haden. "I'm in a quandary. Resarian is pressing to stay with you until you get an answer from the Oracle. How long do you mean to be here?"

"I heard my answer," said Trevin.

"And?"

"The Oracle directed me to the canyon. I plan to trek in after daybreak."

Haden glanced over his shoulder at the sleeping prince. "Resarian will want to go with you, but it's against my better judgment."

"And mine," said Trevin, "but I have no authority over the prince."

"He might relent on the matter if he woke up and found you gone."

Trevin nodded. "Tell Resarian he can show me around when I visit Flauren."

Haden smiled. "That I will. By the time we return to camp, your horse should be free. Shall I hold him for you in Flauren or ride him to the canyon in search of you?"

"I can't say where you might find me. I'd best come for him in Flauren."

"Until then, keep the mount you borrowed." Haden grasped Trevin's hand. "I wish you good speed."

To avoid the howling gap of Windsweep, Trevin and Pym backtracked west along the ridge and crossed the mountains at a pass Haden suggested. In the canyon below, dawn's pale rays trickled across the tops of the plateaus while the depths of the gorge slept in heavy gray shadow.

As Trevin headed down the steep, narrow path, he studied the nearer plateaus. Many looked bare, but others bore shadowy brush, and dark patches topped several of the more distant plateaus. Groves, he guessed.

A movement atop one of these caught Trevin's eye. If he looked straight at the dark plateau, the movement stilled. If he looked aside, it returned.

He pointed. "What about that one, Pym? The seat of the Oracle?"

"I'd be hard-pressed to say." Pym squinted at it. "If we could fly like Serai, we could get close enough to see a hut or house atop, but flying's not in my plans."

The wind gusted. *Trusssssst yourself.*

"What did you say?" asked Trevin.

"I said it's not in my plans to fly. The mere thought of Windsweep gave me the wobbles."

The wind whipped Trevin's hair into his eyes. *Trussssst yourself.*

Trevin brushed his hair back and snorted. Himself. Exactly what he did not trust. He had lived as a thief, an informant, and a betrayer, and descending this mountain trail reminded him of another mountainous descent, tailing a caravan...

He fingered the harp pendant around his neck, trying to ward off the past. This was his future.

"We'll try the plateau with the darkest grove," he said. "Something's moving on top." He mapped it in his mind. Three plateaus to the east of the river. Four plateaus north from a light green patch at the canyon rim.

The path down the mountain was rocky, the journey slow. Trevin listened for more windwords but heard only lizards skittering through dry brush, ground mice scrabbling, birds scolding.

By noon they were out of the foothills and stopped to rest their mounts at a spring, where Trevin filled their water skins.

"We're being watched," said Pym. "From above."

Trevin looked up to see two dark spy-birds riding the wind currents. They spiraled slowly and soared out of sight. His skin prickled. Dreia had been followed after she took the harp from Aubendahl, just before her entire caravan was ambushed and murdered. He hadn't considered that he might be courting the same fate.

A scrub-covered plain separated the foothills from the canyon, but the distance across was farther than it looked. By the time Trevin and Pym reached the rim of the gorge, dusk was claiming the canyon floor. They stopped and dismounted.

"We'll soon be in need of more water," said Trevin.

"The only water I see is below," said Pym.

Trevin eyed the ribbon of river winding its way around the flat-topped outcroppings. "We're not likely to make it into the canyon before nightfall."

"We'll quench our thirst yet." Pym led his roan to a stand of thick, rounded plants, drew his sword, and slashed the plant in two. Thin green juice bled out. He handed half of the fruit to Trevin. "Desert pear."

Trevin slurped the sweet juice while Pym gave the last of their water to the horses. As they drank, Trevin realized that the stand of desert pear was the light green patch he had seen from high in the mountains. He scanned the tops of the tablelands and located the one he had marked in his mind that morning. Four north. Three east of the river.

"Drat those draks," said Pym. "They're as pesky as bedbugs."

Trevin watched the birds soar over the canyon and circle back. Then, not wanting to waste daylight, he led Pym along the canyon rim in search of a trail to take into the gorge the next morning.

As the last of the sunlight faded, Pym discovered a trail down. With his sharp eyesight Trevin could have trekked the path at night, but since Pym and the horses had no such gift, they camped beneath the stars, with Trevin and Pym taking turns standing watch.

Early the next morning they set out on the steep, narrow trail, which appeared to be ancient. They walked their horses down, hacking through overgrown brush. When they reached the canyon floor, they headed straight for the river, where they not only drank but bathed as well.

Then they set off to look for the plateau Trevin had seen, counting three east from the river and four north from the stand of desert pear. But while Trevin thought he knew the location of the light green desert pear, he could no longer see it from the floor of the canyon. Nor could he see anything atop the cliff-like formations, which rose like giant columns supporting the sky.

"The Oracle could be on any one of these," he muttered as they rode slowly around the plateaus. "Even if we find it, I see no way up. I've scaled stone walls, but I can't gain footholds here unless I chip out the stone."

He nudged his horse on. In, out, and around they wove as he counted again.

Then, among the vertical striations of one plateau, Trevin spied horizontal lines. He closed his eyes to clear his vision, looked again, and pointed. "A ladder."

Pym frowned. "I don't see it."

"Straight ahead." For the first time in days, Trevin's spirits soared. He was close to the Oracle, close to answers. He felt it. He dismounted, loped to the ladder, and grabbed a rung at shoulder height. "It's carved in the stone."

Pym ambled to his side. "Flustrations! I don't see it." He touched the rock wall, slid his hands up and down, back and forth. "The sun hasn't burned your brain, has it?"

Trevin stepped back and closed his eyes. Was his mind playing tricks on him? When he opened his eyes, he clearly saw the ladder, solid and inviting, rising to the top of the plateau. He climbed two rungs. "I'll show you where to place your hands."

Pym paled. "I can't climb what I don't see."

Trevin jumped to the ground and dusted his hands. "Stay with the horses, then."

"As your armsman, I'm obliged to tell you I'm uneasy about this. We don't know what's atop."

Trevin looked up at where the ladder ended and the sky began. It could be a trap. Or the Oracle. Or the cave where Benasin was held. There was no shortage of sky. The harp could be up there.

Trusssssst yourself.

"You camp here, Pym."

Pym huffed and handed Trevin's sword to him. "In case it's unfriendly up top."

Trevin strapped the blade to his side and grasped the highest rung he could reach. "If I don't return—"

"You'll return."

Trevin turned his gaze upward. "I'll return," he mumbled and began climbing.

By the time Trevin neared the top of the plateau, his arms ached from clutching the rungs. He had looked down only twice to see Pym standing beside the horses. After that, he could no longer look down without growing lightheaded, but he knew Pym would watch until he cleared the top of the plateau.

At the highest rung he paused and wished for his shield. Anyone waiting above would find him an easy target.

He took a deep breath and peeked over the edge.

revin grasped the trunk of a nearby sapling and hoisted himself onto the plateau. The only movement atop came from bees droning among the tiny purple blossoms that speckled the grass. True-heart. A reminder of Melaia. And Varic.

Hurry, Trevin's heart beat. *Find answers and get back to Redcliff.*

A grove of red-flowered trees stood a bow's shot away, but Trevin saw no house, hut, or shelter of any kind. He paced the perimeter of the plateau, his hand on the hilt of his sword. Maybe someone had lived here in ancient times, but it seemed uninhabited now. Where better to hide a harp?

A delicate fragrance drifted from the grove. Trevin wandered into its shade, eying the ground and trunks for a hidden harp or the entrance to a cave. Nothing.

Seeeeeker. The deep, breathy voice spoke behind him.

Trevin turned on his heel but saw no one. "Oracle?"

I'm heeeeere to meeeeet with you, Seeeeeker.

Trevin scanned the trees. "How do I meet face to face with someone I can't see?"

"Here," said the voice, clear, resonant, and warm. "Outside the grove."

Trevin wove his way between the trees. Beyond them an image wavered in the sun, rippling like a reflection on the surface of a breeze-blown pond: an old man with long white hair and a billowing cloak. The man stepped into the grove and vanished.

Trevin stopped, his breath so shallow he feared he wasn't breathing. He tried to step back, but his feet felt rooted to the ground.

The wavering image appeared again only a pace away. The man held up three fingers, the sign of the Tree. "Welcome," he said in a clear, full voice no longer swept thin by the wind.

Trevin raised three fingers and knelt, his head bowed. He found his throat dry and his face warm with shame at the way he had yelled into the wind at Windsweep. It seemed disrespectful now that he faced the ancient Oracle.

"You may rise," said the Oracle. "You have reached me."

Trevin looked up but did not stand. "I was instructed to ask your counsel."

The Oracle gazed at Trevin's chest, and Trevin realized the ancient one was looking at his right hand, held against his heart in the sign of the Tree. "How did you lose your finger?" asked the Oracle.

"I don't remember," said Trevin. "It happened early in my childhood." He shrank under the Oracle's gaze. "Is something wrong?"

"On the contrary, everything is right. Which means you may remove your sword."

Trevin stood, unfastened his sword belt, and placed it on the ground.

The Oracle motioned for Trevin to follow, but as soon as Trevin stepped forward, the man vanished. Trevin paused, and the Oracle came back into view four paces ahead.

"Forgive me," said the Oracle. "I'm accustomed to my own pace. It's not easy to slow down."

As Trevin walked toward him, the Oracle turned and strode across the grass, slowly this time. Trevin followed him to the edge of the plateau, but when the Oracle stepped off into the air, Trevin stumbled back.

The Oracle halted. "You expected the Oracle to spend his days sitting on a stone, spinning wise words into the world?" He chuckled. "To some I'm the Oracle. Others call me Windweaver."

Trevin stared at the ancient. He should have known. Melaia had described each of the Archae who came to her at Aubendahl, but he had thought she was describing a dream. Now he dug his nails into his palms to make certain it wasn't he who was dreaming. "You're Windweaver?" he asked. "The Archon?"

"One of the guardians of the world, yes. At present four of us are active: Flametender, Seaspinner, Earthbearer, and me. And I know you're Main Trevin of Camrithia. Now come, Main Trevin. Walk the circle of the wind with me."

Trevin's pulse shook his entire body, and his knees felt as weak as water.

"You'll never know unless you take the first step. Don't think about it. Just come." Windweaver looked south toward the mountain ridge. "As we walk, we'll discuss your quest."

"As we walk." Trevin crept to the edge of the plateau.

"Don't look down."

Every muscle in Trevin cringed; every ounce of reason cried, *Turn back!* He looked Windweaver in the eye. And stepped off the plateau.

The wind beneath Trevin's feet sprang like a rain-soaked meadow, but it supported him. He felt strangely light as he matched Windweaver's stride, yielding his feet to the buoyant currents. Swiftly they walked, each step covering a half-day's journey for a land traveler.

Windweaver gathered strands of air, thin and sheer. Some he twined together; others he untangled. Then he sent them on their way.

"Winds tend to be unruly," he said. "Sometimes I allow them to dance as they see fit. At other times their wildness is unwise." He drew out a strand and blew it west. "Tell me what you seek."

With effort Trevin drew his mind away from the wonders of the wind and the view of the world from on high. "Harps," he said. "Melaia—Dreia's daughter—believes she must unite three kyparis harps to restore the stairway and the Wisdom Tree."

Their next step took them to the top of the highest tower of Redcliff. As they circled the parapet, a snatch of melody drifted around them. Trevin paused and looked down into Melaia's garden, where she sat on a cushioned bench, playing the kyparis harp, Serai at her feet and—he smiled—Varic nowhere near.

Trevin started to call to Melaia, but Windweaver held up his hand in warning, and Trevin's shoulders slumped. He longed to trade places with Serai. With her wings she would walk the wind with ease, while he, in her place, would be content to bask in Melaia's presence.

"Dreia's daughter is right," said Windweaver. "She must unite the harps. As you see, she already has one. So what do you seek?"

Melaia stopped playing.

"The two remaining harps." Trevin watched Melaia set aside her harp and walk to the side wall. "Also"—he paused, distracted by her intense, searching eyes—"I seek allies for Camrithia and five comains who disappeared more than a year ago. And King Laetham wants a prophecy or a sign from the Oracle."

Windweaver studied Trevin. "You answered questions I didn't ask. You told me what Melaia seeks. You told me what King Laetham seeks. I asked what you seek."

Trevin bit his lip. Didn't Windweaver understand? The king's comain sought what the king told him to seek. He sought what the princess wanted.

Windweaver motioned to him, stepped off the parapet, and strode northwest.

Trevin hesitated only long enough to glance back at Melaia, then caught up with the Oracle. Their pace quickened, but Trevin felt no strain, no weariness in the distance they covered. He recognized Ledge Rock ahead.

Windweaver paused at the mound of granite. "You want to know where the harps are, is that it?"

"Yes." Trevin breathed easier. "Do you know?" He scanned the sky, looking for the veil. The sunlight hid it, but he could hear its hum floating on a strand of breeze that Windweaver snatched and sent spinning south.

"One touches skies." Windweaver stepped off the ledge and headed east. Trevin struggled to keep up. "One sleeps again in stone," said Windweaver. "Hold the edge of my cloak."

Trevin snagged Windweaver's hem and felt as if they flew. Moments later they stood on a peak of gray stone overlooking a clearing surrounded by boulders and leafless trees.

"The Dregmoors," said Windweaver. "Where the dead enter the Under-Realm."

Trevin's right hand began to throb, and he rubbed it as he looked around. Below them a waterfall tumbled from an outcropping. Ahead, the clearing ended abruptly at the edge of a cliff, providing a bird's-eye view of a wooded landscape beyond.

Windweaver shoved the wind on its way. As it whipped past the waterfall, Trevin felt the spray. He heard the wind rush through the bare trees, though not a branch swayed, not a bough tossed.

Suddenly the wind changed direction and whipped back at them with a shower of stone dust and the unmistakable odor of landgash.

As Trevin shut his eyes against the stinging dust, a haze of images flooded his mind. A glint of gold on green. A figure cloaked in black. A smile. A dagger. White light. A bloody tunic.

Trevin fought to open his eyes, but his terror-dream reigned. A jolt of pain pierced his hand. His knees buckled. As he tried to regain his footing, he stumbled and plunged off the peak into the whirling gale.

Windweaver uttered a thunderous command. Trevin didn't understand the words, but the authority was clear. The wind pressed against him on all sides and dropped him into a pile of brush in the center of a broad field of standing stones.

Trevin crouched there, hugging his aching hand. The cliff edge lay a dozen paces behind him; water cascaded in the falls a dozen paces ahead.

"Perhaps I should have warned you." Windweaver appeared, striding across the stone field. "Rogue winds frequent these mountains."

Trevin flexed his right hand and grimaced as he rose.

"We stand where the Wisdom Tree once grew," said Windweaver, "a kyparis so tall its top was not visible from the ground, so wide it extended across this field from side to side and from here back to the waterfall. You could feel the energy of the stairway within it, a flow of light bridging the near and the far, the now and the always."

Trevin tried to envision the Tree engulfing the spot where he stood. "The place seems desolate now."

"Even the trees have turned to stone." Windweaver gazed at the clouds as if he were trying to remember the Tree. Then he strode to the edge of the cliff.

Trevin ran after Windweaver and grabbed his cloak. Within moments they were again walking the wind, and the pain in Trevin's hand vanished.

For a while Trevin simply watched as Windweaver swept some air currents out to sea and reeled some in. He heard no sound but the roar of wind and the rush of waves.

Then Windweaver paused. "What were we discussing?" He caught a wisp of breeze and sent it north. "Ah, yes. You wished to ask about the comains."

"Five of them," said Trevin.

At once they paced the air above the battlements of Alta-Qan, the castle at Qanreef on the Southern Sea. Another few steps and they strolled above the

Durenwoods, where the Archon's winds set the treetops dancing. "Do you seek anything else?" he asked.

"A word or sign for King Laetham," said Trevin.

A few more strides returned them to Eldarra, Prince Resarian's realm. Then they strode across the Dregmoors again. They moved so quickly that within another step they reached Qanreef. Again and again they paced a giant circle with Redcliff at the hub.

Windweaver motioned to the lands they circled. "Do you desire all this?"

"All this?" Trevin laughed. "That's nonsense."

"I'm not in the habit of talking nonsense." Windweaver calmly paced the wind. "Do you desire all this?"

Trevin let his gaze roam the countryside, cities, towns. One circuit, two. Night was falling, leaving the land below in shadow. He shook his head. "I've no desire for these lands."

Windweaver nodded.

"If I may ask—," said Trevin.

"You may."

"Is all this yours to give?"

"It is not," said Windweaver. "But a man's desires show his true nature, don't you think? Many seek outwardly what they can find only within themselves."

With one more step they returned to the plateau. Windweaver disappeared into the grove. Weary, Trevin lay back in the grass among the purple true-hearts and inhaled their rosy scent. He wished Melaia were here to watch the stars appear. But she wasn't, and as the stars brightened, his hopes faded. He had expected Windweaver, the great Oracle, to give him some direction, some answers.

Windweaver returned carrying a bundle and a flask. "The heavens are best viewed from your angle," he said. "Unless you walk into them. But we've done enough walking for now. We've completed many cycles of the wind. Three days' worth."

Trevin sat up, tense. "We've been gone three days?"

"Time passes differently when you travel the edge of it as we did," said Windweaver. "You're in a hurry?"

"I have to be back at Redcliff with news of allies and comains and harps and some word or sign for the king before harvest moon."

"As for the king's sign, you are that sign."

Trevin frowned. "I could get myself hanged telling him that."

"You won't have to tell him."

Trevin could feel the Archon studying him. He shifted uneasily.

"You served Rejius, the immortal Firstborn, for some time," said Windweaver.

Trevin rubbed his hand. Would his past never let him go? "I and my brother."

Windweaver handed him the flask and untied the bundle. "Rejius drew you into his vengeful game of hawk and hare. He allows Benasin to escape, then hunts him down."

Trevin took a gulp of chilled springwater, relieved the Archon understood that he and Dwin had been pawns. "Doesn't Rejius ever tire of his game?"

"On the contrary, he delights in it. The challenge is different each time Benasin escapes. Besides, the time required to find his brother is of no consequence to Rejius."

"Because he and Benasin are immortal," said Trevin.

"Just so. However, we of the Angelaeon are determined that this game will be Rejius's last." Windweaver handed Trevin a fist-sized round of bread.

Trevin took a hefty bite and was surprised to find a tangy golden jam inside. Apricot. He eyed Windweaver, wondering if the Archon had seen him give Melaia a dried apricot at Treolli as a guilt offering.

But Windweaver lay on his back, gazing up at the stars. His face was inscrutable.

Trevin licked at the jam. The dried apricot at Treolli had cost him dearly in coin—and this trip was costing him dearly in time. He needed answers. "I've been told the stars will soon align," he said, hoping to turn the conversation back to the harps.

"The time is right," said Windweaver. "The game will be lost or won not only for the Angelaeon but for this world, for if the stairway is not restored, if the Wisdom Tree is not rerooted, the opportunity will not return for two hundred more years."

"So we'll get another chance." Trevin picked a pit out of the jam and sucked the fruit off it.

"In two hundred years, yes. But by that time the blight will have decimated the world, and the immortals' game will have destroyed thousands upon thousands of its inhabitants."

"In that case my most pressing task is to find the harps. Do you know where they are?"

Windweaver leaned on one elbow. "You think I've given you no answers, but it's you who have not answered me, Seeker."

Trevin turned the pit around in his palm.

"Main Trevin?"

Trevin looked into Windweaver's searching eyes.

"What do you seek?" asked the Archon.

Trevin closed his fist around the pit as the question sank in. "Myself," he murmured. "I seek myself."

CHAPTER 11

Trevin awoke on the plateau the next morning in a blanket of fog heavy with the smell of rain. He couldn't see Windweaver, but as he looked toward the indistinct shape of the mist-shrouded grove, he could feel the Archon's presence. He saluted with the sign of the Tree.

In answer a stiff breeze riffled his hair. Then Windweaver was there, handing Trevin's sword belt to him. "I walk the wind again today," he said. "You will move on. But we've not seen the last of each other."

Trevin fastened the scabbard to his belt. "Then you'll hear if I call to you?"

"I am not omniscient. If I'm nearby, I'll hear. If I'm not"—he shrugged—"I may catch a snatch of your voice on the wind. Or not."

"But I can return to Windsweep, and you'll hear."

"Only if I'm nearby. Not everyone hears from the Oracle at Windsweep."

"I heard you in the aerie," said Trevin, "and in the woods near Drywell."

"I often greet you when I pass." Windweaver held three fingers to his heart. "You'll feel me in the wind." He turned and vanished.

Wind gusted, fog swirled, and the voice whispered. *Hold faaaaast to the search, Seeeeeker.*

Trevin stood listening until the gray world around him grew still. Since the edge of the plateau hid beneath fog, he crept toward it, feeling his way to the sapling that had supported his climb up. Belly to the ground, he clutched the thin trunk with both hands, edged his legs over the rim, and lowered himself until his toes felt the top rung of the ladder, slick in the wet air.

After the first few rungs, the fog thinned, and Trevin chanced a look straight down at the canyon floor. It was a shadowless maze. Near the foot of the ladder lay a banked campfire and Trevin's staff, but Pym was nowhere in sight, nor were the horses. Three days was no doubt longer than Pym had ex-pected to wait, but surely the armsman would not have given up yet. He had probably led the horses to water.

Thunder rumbled in the distance, and Trevin jumped the last few rungs to the ground. He took up his staff and poked the ashes of the campfire. Re-cently used. Pym would return, and he would have questions: Did the Oracle speak a message for the king? What about the harps and comains?

Trevin sighed. He was returning as empty headed as he had gone.

Voices echoed off the cliffs.

"Pym?" called Trevin. The talking stopped. He circled the base of the plateau. "Pym?"

As he rounded the west side of the cliff, he saw a horse tethered to a scrub tree, but it wasn't Pym's roan or the sleek black he had ridden. A few more paces brought a large stone into view.

On the stone sat Prince Resarian, his chin raised proudly but fear in his eyes. Beside him stood Varic, inspecting the edge of his sword.

"See?" Resarian said. "I told you Main Trevin was somewhere around here."

"Of all your fool ramblings, it's the only intelligent thing you've uttered," said Varic.

Trevin leaned casually on his staff, but his mind raced. Where was Pym? Haden? Varic's companions? "What are you two doing here?" he asked.

"I am having my adventure," said Resarian.

"Indeed," said Varic.

Resarian folded his arms. To keep them from trembling, Trevin suspected. "I slipped away from camp in the early morning just as you did, Main Trevin. A clever strategy. I wanted to return your horse to you. I rode him to the edge of the canyon, where I was accosted by Prince Varic and his surly friends. They're most ill humored."

Trevin winced. No doubt Resarian felt free to salt his talk with barbs now that his favorite comain had shown up to rescue him.

"We were more than happy to accompany this jabber-jaw to find you," said Varic.

We? Trevin looked around. A crackling streak of thunderlight jagged across the clouds.

"Hesel and Fornian have gone after the fellow who chased your horse," said Varic. "When they return, Hesel will escort the prince to the Dregmoors while Fornian and I return your dead body to Camrithia so the king will know justice has been meted out to the murderer of his personal servant."

Resarian's eyes widened with alarm.

"How did I get accused of murder?" Trevin slid his right hand down his staff and nearer his sword.

Varic tested the heft of his blade. "Hesel was accused of gash running and forced to divulge the name of his contact in Redcliff."

"And he named me," said Trevin. *Turn the tide,* he thought. *Move swiftly. One good cut to Varic's leg, and hold the jackal hostage. When Hesel and Fornian return, trade Varic for horses and leave the Dregmoorians to find their way out of the canyon on foot.*

"Murder is just one in a long list of your crimes," said Varic. "Thief, informant, turncoat. Not even animals are safe from you. Prince Rattle-Tongue told me what happened to my dog." He pierced a stand of desert pears with his sword. The juice oozed out and puddled on the ground.

"How did Hesel get off free?" asked Resarian.

"He didn't," said Varic. "Fornian and I led him out of Redcliff in chains, destined for the Dregmoors, where he will be justly repaid. We decided to take the northern route to find his murderous accomplice."

"You've found me," said Trevin, "so let the prince go."

"And forfeit the bounty paid for his blood? Hesel would be none too happy about that."

"Why the prince's blood? Take mine. Now, if you want."

"Yours won't do. You see, gash can't maintain youth unless it's mingled with blood. The younger the blood, the better the results."

"*Tohdlit.*" Trevin's stomach churned. "Children."

Varic's eyebrows rose. "I'm impressed."

"I am not a child," rasped Resarian.

"You're on the old side, I'll admit," said Varic, keeping his eyes on Trevin. "But with royal blood, who knows?"

Trevin steadied his breathing. This was not the best place for swords. Boulders, scrub trees, stands of desert pear, and the sides of the plateaus jagged at dangerous angles. But Hesel and Fornian could return at any time. Not the odds Trevin wanted, but his fingers itched to draw his sword. If Varic would turn his attention to the prince...

"Where's my horse, Resarian?" asked Trevin.

"He bolted to escape a net thrown by Prince Goon here."

Varic punched Resarian in the stomach. It wasn't the kind of attention Trevin intended, but he took the opening. As the prince slumped to the ground, Trevin dropped the staff and swept out his sword.

Varic grabbed Resarian, who gasped for breath, and thrust the tip of his blade at the prince's throat.

Trevin froze, sword poised, muscles tensed. "If you want me, take me in a fair fight."

"A fair fight?" Varic shoved Resarian aside and slipped his sword into its scabbard.

At the unexpected move Trevin eased up. In a flash Varic swept off his silver mesh sash, whirled it in the air above his head, and let it fly.

Trevin knocked the net away with his sword, but the mesh jerked the blade out of his hands, and both weapons fell to the ground, the pommel of the sword under the net.

Varic drew his sword and lunged.

Trevin dodged, grabbed his staff, and blocked Varic's next strike. The staff wasn't sharp, but it was longer than Varic's sword, and between parries, Trevin struck Varic, connecting once with a shoulder, once with a thigh.

"You four-fingered misbegot..." Varic seethed. "I know you're after the throne. You thought you could hide. No longer!" He struck back.

Trevin parried with the staff. Its length was a hindrance around the boulders. He had to make sure he didn't get boxed in, unable to maneuver. In addition, he didn't know how long the staff could take the sharp edge of Varic's sword. With every hit he expected it to splinter.

All the while, Trevin was aware of Resarian trying to rise. Then the prince seemed to give up and simply crouched there, holding his belly.

Trevin ducked a wild swing from Varic. He could see why Hesel and Fornian did Varic's fighting for him. Varic was not a skilled fighter. His right defense was weak, though he made up for it with an overabundance of ferocity. His swipes were vicious. Trevin stepped sideways, alert. If he stumbled or dropped his guard, he knew Varic would lunge in for the kill.

Resarian began crawling slowly across the ground. Hoping the prince would run or at least take refuge behind a rock, Trevin twisted left, leading Varic's attention away from the prince.

Then he saw where Resarian was headed. As the prince slipped Trevin's sword away from the net, Trevin took heart. Two against one. Even though he had been punched, Resarian would be the fresh man in the fight.

But Resarian did not take up the sword. Instead, he tried to slide the blade to Trevin. Resarian clambered back to his boulder and motioned to Trevin, pointing at the sword.

Trevin would have to move to a weaker position to retrieve the sword, his back to the cliff face. But he saw no other choice.

He dodged Varic's cut, wove around a scrub tree, tossed the staff aside, and grabbed the hilt of his sword. The pommel was as flat as a piece of parchment and as cold as frost. The balance felt strange. But Trevin met Varic's next swipe with a strong stroke.

With new courage Trevin went on the attack, concentrating on Varic's weak right. He felt hemmed in, with boulders on each side and the cliff face behind him, but he pressed Varic, looking for an opportunity to wound his legs or lunge and skewer him through the chest. Either way, the fight would be over. And Varic was tiring. So was Trevin, but if he could stay alert, he would find his advantage.

Then Varic made a desperate swipe to his right. His weak right. Trevin met Varic's blade and sent it flying.

The sky rumbled. Trevin cut toward Varic's legs, but Varic dodged, reversed direction, and grabbed Resarian, holding him as a shield.

"Let Resarian go." Trevin panted. "Your quarrel is with me, not him." Trevin kept his sword pointed at Varic, ready to run him through as soon as he released the prince.

Varic's beetle-black eyes glittered hatred. In one swift move he rammed his living shield toward Trevin's sword.

As Trevin jerked back, his elbow hit the stone face of the cliff.

Resarian's eyes were wide, his mouth open as Trevin's blade slammed through his chest, but the cry came from Trevin.

Resarian coughed and shuddered.

Varic staggered back.

Trevin slumped to the ground with the prince. His head buzzed; his whole body shook. The sound of galloping hoofs seemed like a distant dream.

Then Varic yelled, "This devil attacked Resarian! I tried to fight him off, but he knocked my sword from my hand and turned on the prince."

Trevin looked up, gaping as Haden and Dio rode in with three horsemen. Haden leaped from his horse, tearing off his cloak. He reached the prince in two strides, pulled the sword from his chest, and pressed his cloak to the wound.

But Resarian was dead.

Haden backhanded Trevin.

Trevin tumbled sideways, tasting blood, his head and neck glittering with pain. Two horsemen jerked him to his feet, and Haden swept the sword to Trevin's throat. "I believe this is yours," he hissed.

Varic calmly retied the silver mesh around his waist. "Main Trevin is wanted for murder in Camrithia. I was sent to bring him back to the gallows. If only I had found him sooner—"

Fury shot through Trevin like a pike. "Liar!" He wrestled against the grip of the horsemen. "Dregmoorian filth! You're the murderer!" He would strangle Varic. Pummel him to death. Feed his carcass to draks.

"You see? He's a raging madman," said Varic. "I can help you hang him here and now. Or I can take him off your hands and haul him back to Camrithia."

"We have our own justice," growled Haden, backing away from Trevin. "Our gallows work as well as those in Camrithia. You may follow us and add the Camrithian charges to ours. Our court will want to hear what happened."

"Of course," said Varic. "You'll want to hear from the guide who helped me track Main Trevin. We heard angry voices and rushed in just as the prince was attacked. The prince's horse spooked and ran, and my guide rode after it."

"Scum!" yelled Trevin. "You had no guide."

"Too blinded by rage to see him?" Varic mounted his horse. "I'll go find him. He'll meet you at the Eldarran court. As for me, I'm expected to report back to King Laetham. I'll assure him that the murderer was hanged."

He rode away as the horsemen bound Trevin to the gnarled trunk of a scrub tree.

The wind gusted. Haden turned back to the prince, moaning, "It's my fault." He hugged the prince and rocked back and forth. "My fault. My fault."

My fault, thought Trevin. Large drops of rain plopped onto the dry ground. As Dio and Haden cloaked the prince's body, Trevin sank until only the ropes held him upright. His terror-dream rose to meet him. The cloaked figure. The searing flash. The blood.

Trevin felt numb, mind and body. His thoughts would not connect to make any sense. Not even when Pym rode up on his roan, leading Almaron. Not when Pym spoke to him. Not when the horsemen led him to Almaron with his hands bound. Guilt lay as heavy as a cloak of stone around his shoulders as Prince Resarian's wide-eyed death happened again and again in his mind. A true comain would have struck the final blow at Varic. A true comain would have saved the prince's life.

As the group headed out of the canyon, rain pelted down.

꒰ঌ

For two days and two nights, Trevin rode bound in the midst of the horsemen as they carried their fallen prince west into Eldarra. He was aware of Pym at his side, caring for the horses and trying to coax his comain to take food and water, but Trevin had no will to eat or drink. His entire quest was for naught. He had destroyed the chance of a secure alliance with Eldarra and hampered the search for the comains and harps. But the deepest wound to his soul was the thought that he would never see Melaia again.

Like a tide, waves of hopelessness rushed in and out of Trevin's mind, crashing against a constant, immovable cliff of grief and shock. His failure to handle Varic's confrontation had caused the prince's death. He had held the blade. His hands were stained with the prince's blood.

From the border of Eldarra to the capital city of Flauren, news of Resarian's death outpaced the horsemen. By the time the riders entered the palace city, black flags flew from towers, and black cloth draped market stalls. Mourners lined the road, and people spoke in hushed tones.

Guards hauled Trevin straight to the dungeon. They took his pouch, belt, and harp pendant and insisted Pym remain outside the small, damp cell while they locked the barred door. Trevin curled up in a corner and closed his eyes.

"Don't worry about Almaron," called Pym. "I'll take good care of him. And I'll make sure you get food and fresh water. As you've seen, the whole land is in mourning, but as soon as they can turn their thoughts to you, I'll speak on your behalf." He paused. "I have to go now. When I return, I'll ask you to tell me what happened." He paused again. "Flustrations, Trevin. Do you hear me?"

Trevin made no answer. He despised himself. He was better off being hanged right here, right now. He heard Pym sigh and trudge away. He remembered the dungeon at Redcliff when Melaia had balked at rescuing him. She was right. He should have died there. He drew his cloak tight and fell into a fitful doze.

Some time later Pym returned with food and water. "The prince's body will be buried tomorrow." He scooted bread and soup toward Trevin.

Trevin turned away. He wanted only to sleep.

"You could at least tell me what happened," said Pym. "How can I speak for you if I know nothing?"

Trevin hid his face in his hands. What could he say? His bloodguilt went back to the foothills of Aubendahl, and now he would pay for it.

He heard Pym pacing the cell. Then the door scraped open, and Pym left.

That night Trevin's terror-dream returned in full force. The cloaked, hooded figure lunged at him with a dagger, and he could not fight back. He awoke in a sweat, his right hand throbbing. He clutched his hand to his chest and shivered uncontrollably.

CHAPTER 12

For a week Trevin's lone daily visitor was Pym, who brought food and water. At first Trevin refused it, but he finally grew too weak to resist when Pym dripped broth onto his tongue or squeezed water into his mouth from a cloth. He felt ashamed of being suckled like a baby for the sole purpose of staying alive long enough to go to the gallows.

Each day Pym scratched a mark on the cell wall with charcoal so Trevin could keep track of time. But Trevin didn't care about time. Even if he were acquitted, which was unlikely, his time for seeking comains and harps would be gone.

On the eighth day Pym brought news that the king's council had taken up Trevin's case. "They allow me to attend their gatherings," he said. "I've put in a good word for your character, but I can't answer their questions about what happened the day their prince died. Only you can do that." Pym stared at him with eyebrows raised.

"They'd not believe me," Trevin croaked.

"Mysteries and miracles!" said Pym. "You've found your tongue, you have." He tugged Trevin to a sitting position and squatted in front of him. "You said they'd not believe you. You're half-right. Some will find no satisfaction for their grief until the prince's murderer is punished, and they're so set on comforting themselves with revenge, they willingly believe you're guilty."

Trevin closed his eyes. Varic had won. The Eldarrans would do his dirty work for him.

"Wait!" said Pym. "I said you're half-right. Which means you're half-wrong. Some on the council support you. They believe you're innocent."

Trevin opened his eyes and snorted. "Who?"

"Dio was the first to stand for you."

"Dio is a bard," said Trevin. "He can't be on the council."

"Eldarran law requires all kinds of folk to be on the council."

Trevin's hands trembled as he brought the cup of broth to his lips.

Pym pulled a piece of bread from his pouch. "Eat this. I'll return as soon as I can."

Trevin nibbled on the edge of the sharp-tasting bread, set it aside, and shut his eyes. He was grateful for Pym's support, but it was of no use.

⚜

When Trevin heard the clank of the cell door, he roused. Pym strode in, followed by Dio and Haden.

Trevin tried to read Haden's face. Dark circles rimmed his eyes, and his jaw was clenched. Trevin ran a hand through his hair and attempted to rise.

"Stay seated," said Pym. "We want you to regain your strength."

"For that purpose we bring you a gustatory gift, so to say." Dio opened a pack and pulled out four cups and a jug of ale. "Except for drink, I see you have all the comforts of the palace. The palace pigsty, that is." He handed out the cups and filled them.

Haden sat on the floor across from Trevin and looked him firmly in the eye. "It was your sword."

Trevin looked down at his cup. "It was."

"The only tale being told is Prince Varic's," said Haden. "I want to hear you tell it."

"Is Varic here?" asked Trevin.

"No, but Main Catellus is," said Pym. "He claims he was Varic's guide, and his story matches Varic's. He says you flew into a rage because Prince Resarian rode your horse."

"That's a lie," said Trevin. "Catellus wasn't there." He leaned his head back against the cold wall. "Even if I'm acquitted here, I'll never be allowed to return to Redcliff after Varic spreads his story."

"Flustrations!" said Pym. "Did you think I'd let that happen unopposed? I sent the swiftest Eldarran rider to Redcliff with a warning about Varic's lies. I didn't know the true story, but I knew the lie he would carry back."

"You've left us with little to tell the council," said Dio. "Only a modicum of a message, a snippet of support, so to say. How can I write a true and proper ballad of the last adventures of the prince"—his voice broke—"unless I know what really happened?"

Pym paced the cell. "If you don't give another view of it, the lie will win."

Haden leaned forward. "You say Varic lied, you say Catellus lied, but you held the sword. I saw it with my own eyes." His gaze bored into Trevin. "What's the truth?"

"The truth is, I failed Resarian." Trevin stared into the grimy shadows of the cell, but in his mind he saw Resarian sitting on the boulder.

He cleared his throat and gave his account. By the time he finished, all heads were bowed.

Haden stared at his folded hands. "Catellus says otherwise."

"I've never even seen Catellus," said Trevin.

"Did *you* see Catellus in the canyon, Haden?" asked Dio. "I didn't."

Haden shook his head. When he looked up, his eyes were moist. "What you say makes sense, Trevin, but Catellus's report makes sense too. I'll have to weigh it. However, I assure you that the council will hear your story when it meets this evening."

Trevin rubbed his right hand. "I doubt anyone on the council will believe me."

"I believe you," said Dio.

"And I." Pym held his head high. "I'm a visiting member of the council."

Trevin half smiled in spite of himself. "Then only two on the council will believe me."

"You judge Eldarrans harshly," said Haden. "The council has no desire to hang an innocent man. We want to weigh our choices and make a just decision. We'll consider both sides overnight, and your case will be put to a vote tomorrow."

They drained their cups, and then Haden and Dio took their leave.

Pym sat on the floor beside Trevin and drew a small pouch out of a fold of his waist sash. "This came for you from Redcliff in answer to my message."

Trevin took the soft leather pouch, drew it open, and removed an object wrapped in cloth. He laid it in his palm and carefully unwrapped it. "A dried apricot," he said, his throat tightening.

"One apricot?" asked Pym. "That will hardly fill your belly."

"It's not meant to fill my belly but my heart," said Trevin.

Pym rolled his eyes. "That makes all the sense in the world."

"Was there no message with it?"

"There was a sealed scroll for the king of Eldarra," said Pym. "Sealed with King Laetham's signet."

"It probably confirms that I'm accused of Nash's murder." Trevin turned the apricot over in his hand. At least Melaia didn't hold him responsible for Nash's murder or believe the tales about Resarian's death. She didn't know the full extent of his guilty past, but what she knew, she had forgiven.

"I questioned Catellus about the other comains," said Pym.

"Does he know what happened to them?"

"He says he was up north when they disappeared. Says he knows nothing about it. He's been in Montressi doing his job, guarding the northern border. It's a short, desolate fringe of the country, wolves posing the greatest danger. Of all the comains, he was the loner. Had one armsman and no men-at-arms on call."

"Wasn't his shield found abandoned like all the others?"

"It was. He claims his armsman stole it and fled. End of tale. Push him further, and his face goes hard as stone. I thought he'd be friendlier to me as a fellow Camrithian and Main Undrian's armsman."

"No doubt his word, along with King Laetham's scroll, will outweigh my story in the council."

"We'll find out tomorrow. I'll let you know as soon as the votes are cast."

"And if the votes go against me?"

Pym glanced at the door. "In that case I'll work for your escape," he said softly.

"What if you're not successful?"

Pym scowled and trudged to the door, then turned. "If we're not successful, then what happens next is up to you. You can be dragged to the gallows like a simpering fool if you want, but I prefer to tell Melaia you strode to your death tall and confident like the innocent man you are." He tapped on the bars, and the guard let him out.

Trevin's chest tightened as he remembered his last morning at Redcliff. He wished he had roused Dwin to bid him farewell. He wished too that he had pledged his love to Melaia in no uncertain terms.

Still, he would be her eagle. On the way to the gallows, he would look straight into the sun. And he would see her face.

He rose and slowly paced the length of his cell, then breathed a laugh. He didn't fear death, but hanging as a criminal would be a useless death. Why couldn't he have died fighting, taking an enemy down with him, or at least saving Prince Resarian? The prince's death—*that* was useless.

Except—Trevin wiped his eyes with the back of his hand—the prince's death had probably saved his life. Which was wrong. All wrong. He should have died, and the prince should have lived.

Trevin sank to the floor, his head bowed.

꧁ꙮ꧂

The next morning a guard brought Trevin's meal, which he devoured. Then he paced his cell and tried to keep his mind from straying to the discussion taking place in the council room. He ran his hand through his hair. Maybe he would be allowed to get it trimmed or tie it back. He scratched his beard and decided he wouldn't shave it but have it neatly clipped. If he planned to die like a man, it wouldn't hurt to look like one.

Pym's voice echoed down the corridor, joined by Haden's and Dio's. They sounded agitated.

Pym appeared first. "You're standing!" he said. "That's an improvement."

The guard unlocked the door, and the three men stepped into the cell. Trevin studied their faces, but they were unreadable. "What's the news?" he asked.

"It was a draw," said Haden. "Out of eight council members, four called you innocent, four guilty."

"It's a rarity," said Dio. "An uncommon happenstance, so to say. Four believed your story and the scroll from your princess that vouched for your character."

"The scroll was in my favor?" asked Trevin. He wondered if King Laetham knew Melaia had sent it.

"But four on the council believed Catellus," said Pym.

"I can't lie about what I saw, Trevin," said Haden. "You held the sword."

Trevin looked from Dio to Haden to Pym. "What now?"

"You're to come to the council chamber yourself," said Haden. "You'll be tried tomorrow by the eye of the sword."

CHAPTER 13

Trevin squinted as he stepped out of the keep into the blinding sunlight. He had been released into Haden's custody until evening, when he was scheduled to appear before the council. Pym had gone to purchase suitable clothing for the occasion.

The city of Flauren still lay cloaked in the black of mourning. Black flags flew from every tower of the palace, which crowned a hill of fir trees in the center of the city. Its rosy granite towers stood in tiers, the shortest in front, tallest in back, each encircled with balconies. Wind rippled the black drapes and vines that cascaded from the balconies, giving the impression that the palace shuddered.

Shops were open, foot traffic brisk, but the mood of the city was subdued. Trevin felt the stares of the townspeople and heard their murmurs as Haden led him through the streets toward the horsemen's quarters by the stables.

"Where will my trial by sword take place?" Trevin struggled to keep up with Haden, relying on his staff to steady him. "Will I be allowed a weapon?" Even with a weapon, he knew his weakness would be a fatal disadvantage.

"You misunderstand," said Haden. "But I suppose no one informed you. Do you remember what I told you about Arelin?"

"A great sage and warrior. Angelaeon. Died in the Dregmoors freeing the Windwings."

"Before Arelin left for the Dregmoors, he gave Queen Ambria an extraordinary sword. The blade is wider than most, highly polished like a mirror."

Trevin eyed Haden's careworn face. "Do they spear me with it and see if I survive?"

Haden snorted. "You face the blade, and it reflects your true character. The eye of the sword, they call it. It shows your worth."

Trevin grimaced. "If the sword reveals truth, it will show that my hands killed the prince."

"But you were not at fault?" Haden paused at the entrance to a narrow, shadowed street and faced Trevin, his face set. "I don't know what to believe. Every time I close my eyes, I see you over Resarian's body, your bloody sword in his chest."

"I see it too," said Trevin. "I'm at fault for not protecting Resarian. I backed off when I should have pressed Varic. But I would never have harmed Resarian. Never. I would rather have died in his place."

Haden's accusing glare softened. "If your heart is steadfast and honest, the sword will reflect it."

"I'm doomed, then," said Trevin. "My past isn't clean. I did a devil's bidding when I knew it was wrong. Deceit, betrayal, thievery, spying. How's that for my worth?"

Haden smiled sadly. "I'd say you've shoveled more than your share of dung. My past isn't snow pure either, but it's behind me. What's past is what's gone."

"What's past is what haunts me. I might as well walk to the gallows now."

"Give the sword a chance, Main Trevin. The greatest courage a man can have is to look himself in the eye."

Haden headed down the narrow street, motioning for Trevin to follow.

Trevin realized that Haden had trusted him to come all this way without a guard. Which meant that, for all Haden's doubts, the horseman believed in him. Trevin stood taller, breathed deeper, and followed him to a dirt courtyard.

The sweetly pungent smell of hay and horses drifted from a long, low stable. Beyond the stable, fenced fields extended to the north wall of the city. Trevin studied the grazing horses and picked out Almaron.

"Pym's taken good care of your horse," said Haden.

"What about the Golden?"

"She flew as soon as we herded the horses out of the canyon, but we've seen her in flight over Flauren. The herd stirs every time she appears. Especially your stallion."

"Almaron's not mine anymore." Trevin felt empty, voicing his decision. "He should stay with his kind."

Haden's eyebrows rose, but his smile deepened. "You'll set him free?" He placed a firm hand on Trevin's shoulder. "I hope the same for you."

⁓ঞ⁓

Trevin could eat only a few bites of the stew Haden provided for his supper. His beard was newly trimmed, his hair pulled back in a short tail, his new dark gray tunic plain but spotlessly clean. Yet his heart felt anything but clean. The dirt of his past clung to him, accusing him, announcing the condemnation to come.

The overcast sky lent Flauren's granite towers a strange pall as Trevin and Haden headed to the palace. Dio and Pym met them at the entrance and escorted them to the king's council room, where the evening breeze wafted through tall latticed windows, bearing the scent of fir trees and the sound of black drapes flapping from the balconies. Two long tables extended into the room from a dais, which held its own table.

Trevin counted six people garbed in various shades of gray standing in the center of the room, deep in conversation. The orange shimmer he sensed told him at least one was Angelaeon. They looked up as he walked in.

A lean man with silver hair left the group and strode to Haden. "Is this the comain?" he asked.

"It is," said Haden. "Main Trevin, this is Lord Shuldamar, head councilman."

Lord Shuldamar gave a nod. "You should know my opinion carries no greater weight than any of the others here. Come meet the rest of the council and your accuser."

Pym nudged Trevin. "Main Catellus," he whispered. "The burly one. Big ears. Flighty eyes."

Shoulders tight, stomach knotted, Trevin approached the people who had discussed whether he should live or die. He knew they assessed him as they met him, but no one's eyes expressed scorn. Even Catellus nodded, though his jaw was clenched and his lips tight. Trevin was greeted cordially by the silversmith Zalmon, the farmer Gwibbin, the carpenter Mithel, and the one Angelaeon, a woman arrowsmith named Toryth.

The door at the left end of the dais swung open, and a page stepped into the room. Everyone hurried to find chairs at the side tables, but no one sat. Haden motioned for Trevin to stand behind the seat between him and Pym.

Main Catellus stood directly across the room. Trevin's eyes met his for a moment, and Catellus quickly looked away. Trevin did too, glad the table hid his shaky legs.

A buxom, dark-haired woman entered the room, followed by a slender lady, gowned in black and veiled. She wore a simple gold crown. They moved to the last two chairs on the dais and stood facing the council. Trevin couldn't help staring at the somber veiled figure, Queen Ambria, Prince Resarian's mother. He could not see her face, but he had no doubt that she studied her son's accused murderer. He gripped the back of his chair.

Next came a sturdy young woman with loose-flowing brown hair who bore a bow and quiver on her back. She was uncloaked, and the short, wide sleeves of her black gown revealed muscular arms as well as a dagger at her waist. A sunset-red light emanated strongly from her as she stationed herself in a corner behind the queen.

Then a sharp-nosed, clean-shaven man entered, followed by black-robed, stalwart King Kedemeth, a shorter version of Haden, ruddy and pleasant looking. He took his seat beside the queen. Chairs scraped across the floor as everyone else sat.

King Kedemeth folded his hands on the table. "Lord Shuldamar." His rich voice resonated like Haden's.

Shuldamar stood and bowed. "Majesty."

"I understand the council came to no agreement regarding the case of the accused."

"That is correct, Majesty."

"So he will be put to the eye of the sword," said the king.

"A rare occurrence," said Shuldamar, "but reasonable in this case."

"So shall it be." King Kedemeth spoke to his advisor, who then left the room. "Before we invoke the sword," said the king, "I should like to question the young man."

Trevin's heart drummed in his ears. He rubbed his moist palms on his leggings. Lord Shuldamar motioned for him to stand, and he rose, trying to ignore the weakness in his knees.

"Main Trevin of Camrithia," said Lord Shuldamar.

The king held his head high. "Step forward."

Trevin walked to the dais as calmly as he could and bowed. "Majesty."

King Kedemeth stared at his clasped hands, then eyed Trevin. "Why did my son ride alone through the desert to find you?"

Trevin tried to speak, but his mouth felt as dry as dust. He hung his head.

The king's voice softened. "Look me in the eye, Main Trevin. If you wish to confess, you may do so now and avoid the sword."

Trevin looked into the king's eyes and saw only a longing for honesty. He took a deep breath. "Resarian died by my sword, sire, but Prince Varic was the murderer."

"Outrage!" Main Catellus rose. "Prince Varic is highly respected, but this deceiver—who calls himself a comain—is a smooth-talking rebel, a leader in the coup against King Laetham in Camrithia, where he is wanted for the murder of the king's personal servant. What's more, he's a suspect in the disappearance of the Camrithian comains. He was trying to escape his capture when he struck down the prince. I witnessed the murder myself."

King Kedemeth, calm as a tower in the wind, said, "I believe the council heard Main Catellus's testimony, did it not?"

"Aye, Majesty," said Shuldamar. "We turned the matter inside out."

The king nodded and studied Trevin. "The sword will show the truth about you. What I want now..." His voice wavered, and he cleared his throat. "What I want now is the truth about my son. Why was he alone in the desert?"

Trevin rubbed his right hand. "The prince said he was looking for adventures of his own. He spoke of his yearning to prove himself a man. And he did. He faced Varic's threats with courage. Varic wanted *me* on the point of his sword. If only..." Trevin's voice grew hoarse as he said, "I'm sorry. Resarian died a brave and honorable man, sire."

A quiet sob came from behind the queen's veil. The king bowed his head. All was silent except for the drapes flapping on the balcony.

King Kedemeth looked at Trevin and smiled sadly. "Thank you. That is what I wanted to know."

The king's advisor returned, carrying a black cloth draped across both arms. He transferred it to the king, who descended from the dais, the queen following. She folded back the cloth, revealing a sword.

Together they faced the council, and the queen swept her veil back over her crown. Trevin's heart quickened. She had Prince Resarian's flaxen hair, his brown eyes, his upturned nose, his thin mouth, but her eyes were red rimmed, her cheeks streaked with tears.

"Main Trevin," said the king, "Queen Ambria will hold the Seer's Sword before you and place it in the best position to reflect your likeness. The council members will view it. You may look, if you wish. If necessary, the queen will interpret what we see."

Trevin clasped his hands behind his back and tried to steady his breathing as the council members gathered. Haden nodded at him. Dio stood by his side. Pym's hand rested on his shoulder.

Queen Ambria took the hilt of the sword with both hands, faced Trevin, and angled the tip toward the floor.

Trevin felt cold and sweaty. Starving boy, cutpurse, thief, the immortal Firstborn's spy, drak-keeper, betrayer, Angelaeon pledge, comain, killer. Which would it reveal? Worse, it might show nothing but the terrible empty chasm of his soul.

Holding the flat of the blade toward Trevin, the queen stepped slowly forward. She kept her gaze on the sword, as did the king and the entire council. She paused and adjusted the slant of the blade.

Trevin had intended to look, but he couldn't. He closed his eyes, every heartbeat shaking him from head to toe.

He heard gasps. Then the queen cried out, and the sword clanged to the floor.

CHAPTER 14

Trevin opened his eyes and looked around the council room. The queen had fainted, and the king pillowed her head on his lap as her handmaid fanned her. Dio stood wordless. Haden scratched his ear. Pym ran his hand through his hair. The other council members mumbled among themselves.

Except for Main Catellus. Guards wrestled him back into the council room. To admit to false charges?

Queen Ambria roused and murmured to the king.

"Are you certain?" King Kedemeth frowned.

Trevin went cold. The sword had shown the truth. Lackey of the First-born, traitor to humanity, the prince's blood on his hands.

The king helped the queen into a chair. She squinted at Trevin. "Come here, young man."

Heart pounding, Trevin knelt before her.

"Hold out your hands," she said.

He raised his trembling hands.

The queen took his right hand in hers, drew it to her cheek, and closed her eyes.

Trevin gaped at Pym, who shrugged.

The king motioned to a servant. "We'll have wine."

"Bring cheeses and groundnuts as well," said the queen.

Murmurs rippled around the room as both servants and council members drew closer, craning their necks—to see him, Trevin realized, feeling as bewildered as they looked.

King Kedemeth pointed to Catellus. "Lock him away until I can question him."

A short scuffle ensued as Catellus protested, but the guards wrestled him out of the room.

Queen Ambria released Trevin's hand and directed the council members to push the tables together.

Trevin stepped back and drew Pym aside. "What did the sword show?"

Pym stared at him. "You didn't see it?"

"Like a coward, I closed my eyes."

"It showed you as a broad-shouldered man, clean shaven, hair gathered back at your neck. Your eyes burned with resolve, and your right hand was raised in the sign of the Tree." He held up three fingers. "And your hands! They glowed like molten metal, they did."

"That's not me," said Trevin.

"Why not?"

"I'm bearded. And I had my hands behind my back."

"Flustrations! The king didn't say it would show your *image*. He said it would show your character. If you want proof, the man's small finger was missing."

Trevin stared at his hands. Was that why the queen had asked to see his hands? To confirm that the reflection in the sword was his?

"Come!" Queen Ambria motioned for everyone to sit as she and the king took seats along one side of the lower table. The sword lay before the queen. Servants poured wine and offered cheeses and groundnuts.

When everyone had settled into drinking and eating, the king spoke. "Queen Ambria and I continue to mourn. However, we understand that the sword's revelation is good news. Feel free to enjoy it. Main Trevin is innocent, and his story of Resarian's death is true." He turned to the queen. "You know how to say this better than I, my dear."

Queen Ambria scanned the faces of her guests. "Most of you know of Arelin, a dear family friend who died in the Dregmoors, where twenty-five years ago he took on the task of rescuing captured Windwings. We received occasional messages from him, his last arriving over twenty years past with troubling news.

"Arelin's life was in grave danger, as was the life of his one-year-old son, whom he was sending to me. He asked me to care for the child until his return. Unfortunately, the child never arrived, and we never heard from Arelin again. We assumed both had been murdered."

Queen Ambria stood, uncovered the sword, and offered it to Trevin. "By the grace of heaven, Arelin's sword can now be presented to his son."

Trevin blinked at the queen.

"Come, son of Arelin," she said. "Receive the Seer's Sword."

Trevin slowly rose. "How do you know I'm the one?"

"Dear me, didn't I say? In the first place, your reflection in the sword looked exactly like Arelin. Second, his message said I would recognize the little one by his right hand, missing the small finger."

Trevin stared at his right hand. His body went cold, and his eyesight dimmed. He tried to keep from slipping into his terror-dream, but he could not overpower it. The cloaked, hooded figure loomed full in his mind, along with the stench of landgash. His hand was spread out on a ball. A hard ball. Smooth. Shiny. Green. A dagger swept toward him. He saw the spray of blood, felt searing pain, heard screams.

As his mind drifted in and out of the dream mist, Trevin felt the queen take his right hand and place it on the hilt of the sword. He breathed easier. The images faded. The coldness subsided. Like a lifeline, the queen's touch tugged him back to the present.

"Raise the sword, Trevin," she said. "Look into it."

With both hands he lifted the sword and stared at the reflection. Broad shoulders. Long hair gathered at the neck. His hands glowed like coals, the right one raised in the sign of the Tree. The face was his but more confident. Older. Wiser.

He was certain the image did not show who he was now, but he could not deny that it showed the man he wanted to be.

❧

Trevin and Pym stayed as guests in the palace that night. The queen herself ushered them to their beds, which were soft and fragrant. Pym began snoring as soon as he lay down.

Trevin sat at the window of the tower room, gripping the harp pendant Pym had returned to him and gazing into the star-filled sky, trying to piece together his life. Had Lord Rejius, the Firstborn, known his spy was Arelin's son? Had Lord Rejius had anything to do with Arelin's death?

And what about Dwin? Trevin remembered being four years old, almost five, when his brother was born. Until then he had been the only child of Caedo the stonecutter and his wife, Besalai. Dwin had quickly become their father's favorite. Now Trevin knew why.

Strange. The man who had held him and taught him to chip stone and climb rock was not related to him. They had sweated together and washed up together, and Trevin had grieved Caedo's death as keenly as if the man had been his true father.

Then shortly after their father—Dwin's father—had died of an illness, Trevin and Dwin had found themselves grieving over their mother, who died in childbirth along with the baby, leaving her young sons on their own.

But was Besalai his mother? Had Arelin sent her with their son out of the Dregmoors? If so, why hadn't she gone to Flauren?

"You still awake?" Pym rose on one elbow and blinked heavily at Trevin. "You're missing precious time. We're unlikely to find accommodations this soft for the rest of our journey."

"My real father was an angel." Trevin moved to his bed and sank into the thick mat. "That changes things."

Pym ran a hand through his hair. "It explains a lot, like seeing invisible cliff ladders, but it doesn't change much. You're still a comain. You still have your duties. You've not forsaken them, have you? Did you find the Oracle? Ask for advice?"

"I asked." Trevin yawned. "But the Oracle told me only what I already know."

"That's a disappointment, it is." Pym eased himself back under his covers.

Trevin closed his eyes and saw Windweaver untangling threads of air. *You think I've given you no answers, but it's you who have not answered me, Seeker.* Had Windweaver answered? Maybe his answers were like air currents, real but unseen.

Drapes flapped in the breeze outside on the balcony. Trevin thought of another palace, another tower. Redcliff. He and Windweaver had been discussing

Melaia, and there she was. Second stop, Ledge Rock. They spoke of the harps, and Windweaver quoted part of the riddle, *one touches skies,* as the hum of the invisible veil floated on a strand of breeze.

Trevin sat up with a jolt. "I've been senseless!" he whispered.

Long before Dio, Haden, and Resarian had taken him to Ledge Rock, he had seen the veil of Avellan. In Melaia's book. On the page with lines that rippled like a stream. Melaia had said the page showed what the harp saw.

"Pym!" he said. "The Oracle *did* answer my question. One of the harps is at Ledge Rock!"

Pym answered with a snore.

Trevin plopped back into his thick mat. Where exactly was the harp? Atop the hill? In a cave?

He lay awake for a long time, tossing around possibilities. When at last he fell asleep, his terror-dream returned. This time when the figure lunged at him, Trevin struck it with a gleaming sword, and his attacker shattered into thousands of tiny shards that blew away on the wind. Even so, Trevin awoke panting, sweating, and trying to identify the figure who haunted his dreams. Was it Rejius?

Or could it possibly be Arelin?

❧

Court attendants arrived the next morning to escort Trevin to the baths. Pym was already there, soaking and grinning as a servant scrubbed his back.

"I thought you didn't like soap," said Trevin.

"They said they'll rub me in oil after so I don't get the itches." Pym spluttered as water cascaded over his head.

Trevin immersed himself in the warm pool beside Pym. "I think I know where to look for something we're seeking."

"Harps or comains?"

Trevin glanced at the servants. "You'll see. It's a short ride."

"I doubt we can go today," said Pym. "You're to meet with the king and queen."

Trevin's shoulders slumped and were promptly sudsed. Then he was rinsed, rubbed down, oiled, and given another new tunic. Thinking of the beardless image in the sword, Trevin asked for a shave.

While Pym went to the stables to watch the horsemen work with the wild ones, a servant escorted Trevin to King Kedemeth and Queen Ambria, who strolled arm in arm along the balcony that encircled the tower housing the royal quarters. A guard was stationed at each door, and the warrior woman Trevin had seen in the council chamber trailed them. He sensed her sunset-red aura.

King Kedemeth motioned for Trevin to join them, so he paced silently behind the king and queen, his back prickling at the sound of the warrior woman's footsteps and the thought of the dagger in her belt.

Trevin turned his attention to the city spread around the palace. But the black-draped awnings and window dressings, the gray- and black-robed towns-folk, and the overcast day itself brought memories of Resarian's death. He bowed his head. Perhaps he should never have left Redcliff.

King Kedemeth cleared his throat. "You told me why Resarian followed you to the canyon," he said over his shoulder, "but you've not told me why *you* were there."

Trevin gazed south toward Redcliff. "It's a long story."

"We have time," said Queen Ambria.

"Officially we are in mourning for a fortnight more," said the king. "We're not expected to deal with any but the most urgent matters of state."

"In that case," said Trevin, "I'll begin with a princess."

King Kedemeth grinned. "The perfect place to begin."

Trevin gave him a half smile, conscious of the harp pendant under his tunic. He told them that Melaia had been discovered as the king's lost daughter. Briefly he described Lord Rejius's attempted coup and the missing comains.

But the king and queen had heard it all before. For them the news was the Dregmoorian peace offer, King Laetham's desire for allies, and his wish for a word from the Oracle.

Queen Ambria halted and turned to Trevin, staring at him with a puzzled look. "The Oracle?" she murmured. "Arelin, the Oracle led you astray."

King Kedemeth touched her arm. "Ambria, this is Arelin's *son*."

Trevin rubbed his clean-shaven chin. Did he look that much like his father? Maybe he should have kept his beard.

The queen's face paled, and her hand fluttered to her forehead. "Of course. That's what I meant. Quite."

The king patted her arm. "I've never been to Windsweep, Main Trevin, but I'm told the Oracle can be frustratingly cryptic, if he speaks at all. Did you hear anything?"

"I did, sire. I ventured into the canyon at the bidding of the Oracle. I believe I'm also to visit Ledge Rock."

"A half-day's travel from here," said King Kedemeth.

"Is it safe?" asked the queen.

"Ambria," the king chided. He linked his arm in hers and led her around the balcony.

As Trevin followed their slow stroll, he gazed at the horizon, itching to be on his way. Could he truly be this close to finding another harp? "I'd like to explore Ledge Rock this afternoon," he said.

"If you left for Ledge Rock now, you wouldn't arrive before nightfall," said the king. "Besides, I hoped you would join me when I question Main Catellus this afternoon."

Trevin rubbed his brow, frustrated. He was so close to completing one of his tasks. Cell bars no longer held him back, yet he was still being detained. "But I must—"

"You understand, don't you?" Queen Ambria's hand fluttered to her head. "It's simply not safe, Arelin. We cannot allow you to leave."

revin matched King Kedemeth's stride as they headed toward the keep, two guards flanking them.

The king looked sideways at Trevin. "I apologize for Ambria. She isn't herself. I'm afraid she's overwhelmed by the death of Resarian and the shock of discovering Arelin's son."

"I heard Arelin was like a brother to her," said Trevin. "His loss must have been a great blow. No doubt she's wrestling with painful memories."

The king motioned his bodyguards to fall back, then spoke quietly. "Arelin was the closest friend of Ambria's older brother. I feel certain Ambria would have married Arelin if her family hadn't pledged her to me. She has never told me such, mind you, but I'm sure of it. I tell you this only to explain why her mind wavers."

Trevin's mind snagged on a prickly thought: for all he knew, *she* might be his mother. "Is she—" Trevin checked himself. He wanted assurance, but the question was far too personal.

The king nodded his understanding. "She has always been faithful to me. No doubt about that. With a little rest she'll think clearly once more. She's a brilliant woman, you know."

"She sets the standard too high for me," said Trevin. "I'll never attain Arelin's stature."

"Don't limit yourself. It's not beyond reason to think you'll one day be Arelin's equal."

Trevin didn't want to argue the point, but he was only Nephili. He would never be an angel like Arelin.

The king paused at the door of the keep and placed a hand on Trevin's shoulder. "I grant you the freedom to come and go as you please, but I hope you will honor us by completing the time of mourning here in Eldarra."

"Of course." Trevin felt ashamed that he hadn't thought of it himself. It was the least he could do to honor Resarian, even though he longed to be on his way.

"But you may certainly visit Ledge Rock whenever you wish," the king said. "I'll see to it that Ambria doesn't stop you."

"In that case I'd like to go first thing in the morning."

"A good time. I've asked the doctor to give Ambria a potion to help her rest at night. She'll be sleeping soundly when you leave."

❧

Main Catellus bowed to the floor when Trevin and King Kedemeth entered his cell with two guards.

"Rise," said the king. "We want some answers, and you're best advised to make them truthful."

Catellus stood, his eyes flitting from the king to Trevin. "Telling the truth will be one burden lifted." He hung his head. "But I've another weight that will only grow heavier with the truth, sire."

"Which is?" the king snapped.

"I fear for my son."

"What does your son have to do with this?" asked the king.

"He was my armsman. Marco. He's little more than a boy."

"Where is he?" asked Trevin.

"I don't know." Catellus's eyes moistened. "I joined Varic only to save Marco. If Varic finds out I crossed him, he'll bury the boy alive."

Trevin clenched his jaw, hoping Varic hadn't sent the boy into the Dregmoors with Hesel.

"How long have you cowed to the Dregmoorian's threats?" asked the king.

"Almost two years. Varic rode into the mountains to hunt wolves and 'capture images' as he put it. He brought rolls of papyrus, inks, charcoal. He's good with sketches, and he does amazing work with silver nets. Marco was fascinated watching him."

"I've seen some of his work," said Trevin, remembering with disgust the flower pressed to Melaia's chair and the flattened pommel of his sword.

Catellus wrung his hands. "I never felt at ease with Varic, but mountain men can be strange, so I shrugged it off. Now that I look back on it, I see we never got to know him well, while he learned plenty from us. When Marco bragged about me being a comain of Camrithia, Varic asked for tales about the comains. I told him, naturally, spinning stories before the fire at night."

"What did you tell?" asked Trevin.

"Names. The regions where the comains worked. The weapons they were skilled in. That sort of thing. All as a tale, but a tale told true. Marco loved hearing valiant stories."

"As did Resarian." King Kedemeth pressed the bridge of his nose.

Catellus shot a pleading look at Trevin. "After a season two other men showed up. Friends of Varic."

"Hesel and Fornian?" asked Trevin.

Catellus looked surprised. "You know them?"

"Unfortunately." Trevin nodded for Catellus to continue.

"All three pressed me to join them in a villainous scheme. They tried to bribe me with a drink they call gash, saying it would make me live forever. I laughed in their faces. Then they offered me jewels, the likes of which I'd never seen."

"I've seen those too," said Trevin. King Laetham no doubt still wore his ruby ring. He wondered if Melaia wore her medallion.

"I refused the jewels," said Catellus. "Being a mountain man, what would I do with gems? Their friendly mood changed then. They threatened to force gash down Marco's throat until he choked. They would have done it too. Had the boy pinned down. What could I do?" Catellus's hand shook as he rubbed his forehead.

"What did they want from you?" asked King Kedemeth.

"Treason, that's what. I see now I unwittingly opened myself to the offer. Varic was always bragging about his skills and his wit. One day I'd had enough of it, so I did some bragging myself. I showed him the scroll King Laetham signed, appointing me comain. I boasted that Marco learned to write by studying the scroll and had the boy show Varic how he could copy the king's signature so close it looked like the king's own hand." Catellus wiped his eyes. "My bragging cost me my boy."

Trevin stepped closer, wishing Pym could hear Catellus's story. "Go on," he said.

"Varic and his friends wrote a summons to each comain," said Catellus, "and they forced Marco to sign the messages in King Laetham's handwriting. Then they took Marco to deliver the scrolls."

"What did the messages say?" asked King Kedemeth.

"It was the same on each scroll," said Catellus. "A call for the comains to come straight to Qanreef. Varic and Fornian rode with Marco to make sure he delivered the scrolls; Hesel stayed behind to make sure I stayed quiet. Before they left, I gave Marco my shield and dagger, hoping he'd bide his time and make a sure escape." His voice broke, and he cleared his throat. "Varic and Fornian returned without my son."

"Perhaps Marco escaped," said Trevin.

Catellus shook his head. "When I asked about Marco, Varic told me the boy is fine—and will be as long as I serve him. Otherwise, I'll not see Marco again. Not alive."

The king clenched his fists and stood nose to nose with Catellus. "So you stood by while my son was murdered? You forfeited the life of my son for yours?"

Catellus held up his hands and backed into the wall. "I lied. I swear. I was nowhere near. Varic ordered me to stay at the campsite. When he came galloping back, he sent me to the court at Flauren and told me what to say. I didn't know the truth of the matter. I swear by the Most High."

King Kedemeth shook his fist in Catellus's face, hissing, "Spineless." Red-faced and obviously working to restrain his fist from pounding Catellus, the king turned to Trevin. "This comain has dishonored his office, his king, and his country, and he has direly offended me. But since he is Camrithian, I shall allow you to decide his fate."

Trevin stepped back, stunned. Death? Flogging? Banishment? Surely the decision was too weighty for a comain to make, even if he was Arelin's son. "Can his case go before the council?"

"If that's your decision." King Kedemeth glared down his nose at Catellus.

Trevin studied the burly comain and saw the only honest path he could take. "I served the enemies of Camrithia for a time," he said, "because Lord

Rejius threatened to harm my brother if I didn't comply with his orders. But I've been given a chance to make up for it, and I can give you the same, Catellus. I'd like to see you make reparations."

The king's eyebrows rose. "How exactly would he do that?"

"He would help me find the rest of the comains, free them if they're alive, pursue their murderers if they're dead."

"Fair," said the king, "if Catellus can be trusted."

"He might say the same of me," said Trevin.

Catellus knelt. "I'll make amends as best I can. I'd like nothing better than to see Varic and his friends get their due."

King Kedemeth glared at Catellus. "See that it happens." He strode to the cell door. "I hope you find your son," he growled as he stomped out.

Trevin feared his decision had offended the king. He started to follow him out, then turned to Catellus. "Did you know your shield was found abandoned?"

Catellus bowed his head. "Aye," he said. "I fear the worst."

❧

Astride a gelding gifted him by Haden, Trevin raced Pym and his roan across the plain toward the foothills and Ledge Rock, reveling in the freedom of the ride. At the base of the granite hill, they dismounted and staked their horses.

Trevin led the climb to the ledge that looked toward the hilly horizon, where a golden shimmer brightened the sky momentarily, then faded.

"That's the veil," said Trevin.

"What is?" asked Pym.

Trevin tried to explain it.

"Might be like the ladder," said Pym. "Clear as air to you, clear as mud to me."

"Do you hear the hum?" asked Trevin.

"That I hear." Pym angled his head. "I'd say the sound is behind us."

Trevin looked uphill. A dark smudge streaked the ledge where he and Haden had killed the wolf dog. Beyond, atop the hill, stood a grove of trees. "Touching the sky," he murmured.

He concentrated on the hum. When the breeze gusted, it grew louder. When the wind calmed and the tree branches stilled, so did the hum. He sprinted uphill.

The hum was now a clear melodic strain accompanied by a burbling sound. As the breeze nudged the treetops, Trevin followed the lonesome melody to a sweet-sap. Each branch cradled a bevy of doves, their coos rippling like water in a brook.

Then the ground trembled, and the doves rose from the tree, quibbling.

"The horses are spooked," shouted Pym, scrambling downhill to secure them.

One shall shake, thought Trevin. He unsheathed the Seer's Sword and thrust it out at an angle to reflect the tree. It took him a moment to see the mirror image of what he was looking for, but when he found it, he whooped. Nestled in the treetop was a harp. Only the wind strummed its strings.

But as the melody grew, so did the undercurrent in the ground. Trevin looked back at Pym, who held the horses' reins with all his might, trying to soothe them. Trevin set his sword and scabbard aside and climbed into the quivering tree. Branches lashed at him. Twigs snagged his hair. Leaves whipped his face.

"Hold back, you unruly winds!" Trevin yelled.

Hold faaaaast, came Windweaver's reply. *I plaaaaay for yooooou.*

"I see the harp," Trevin called. "You can stop playing."

The mournful melody continued.

Clinging to the trembling limbs, Trevin gradually gained height, but the higher he climbed, the more wildly the branches tossed. At last he reached the base of the harp. But as he locked his legs around the shuddering trunk and tried to dislodge the harp, the tree lurched with a loud crack and tipped sideways. Trevin wrapped his arms around the harp, clamping the strings to silence them.

"Peace!" he yelled as the tree tilted. "Peace!"

The wind calmed to a breeze, and the ground stopped shaking, leaving the tree bent at a steep angle.

You seeeee the harp's miiiiight. Uuuuuse it wiiiiisely.

"I will," Trevin muttered at the sky, although he suspected Windweaver had moved on and was already striding the cliffs of the Dregmoors. He flexed his fingers and carefully pried the harp from its resting place.

The climb down proved easier than the ascent. Branches seemed to pull themselves out of the way to allow the harp to pass. When Trevin's feet touched the ground again, he snatched up his sword and scabbard and made his way back to Pym.

Pym's eyes were wide. "You stilled the earth!"

"I stilled the harp, but it nearly shook me out of the tree." Trevin held the harp at arm's length, admiring the red-brown wood and the dark runes along its back. "I can't play it for fear of causing a quake."

"You can play?"

"Somewhat." Trevin covered the harp with his cloak and secured it to his saddle. "Dwin and I worked with a traveling tent show for a time. The master taught me to play harp and cut pouches. I was more skilled with pouches."

Trevin mounted his gelding and took one more look at the trees atop Ledge Rock. Now that Windweaver's lead had taken him to the harp, Trevin suspected the Archon had answered all his questions. He watched doves flock back to the leaning sweet-sap as he pondered walking the wind.

The answers hit him like thunderlight. He crowed, "Pym! I see!" and took off at full gallop toward Flauren.

revin dismounted and waited at the city gate until Pym caught up with him. An official-looking group of men inspected the outer walls. Merchants and laborers paced in and out through the arched gateway, buzzing with talk about the earthquake.

Pym rode up and dropped from the back of his roan. "You rode like a madman," he huffed. "What did you see? Were ghouls after us, or were you intent on leaving me behind again?"

"I figured out Windweaver's answers," said Trevin as they walked their horses through the bustle of foot traffic.

"Windweaver?" asked Pym.

"Windweaver is the Oracle."

"I should have known. All that blustering at Windsweep."

"I walked the wind with him," Trevin began to explain.

Pym held up a hand. "It's beyond my ken. Just tell me what he said."

"As he left Ledge Rock, he said that one harp 'touches skies.' Ledge Rock is where we found the harp. Then he said, 'One sleeps again in stone' as we were headed to the Dregmoors, a land of stone mountains and caves. Which is exactly where Jarrod suspects Lord Rejius took the stolen harp."

"What about the missing comains?"

"We spoke of them as we stood on the parapets of Alta-Qan. It makes sense. Catellus said the messages to the comains summoned them to Qanreef."

"I searched Qanreef high and low," said Pym. "Could the comains have been shipped as slaves to the southern isles?"

"We'll go to Qanreef and find out."

Pym grinned. "When do we leave?"

Trevin wanted to say tomorrow, but as they walked past the black-draped shops, he knew it wasn't possible. "As soon as the days of mourning are over," he said.

"Thirteen more days," Pym groaned.

"Thirteen more long days," said Trevin.

༺๑๛

Trevin expected King Kedemeth to call for him that evening to ask about the journey to Ledge Rock. But the maid who served supper said the king and queen would be sequestered for a day or two with a visitor who had come to pay respects in the wake of Prince Resarian's death. That night Trevin made sure the harp was securely covered and locked in a chest at the foot of his bed.

The next morning, with little to occupy himself, Trevin took his new sword to the training yard. His muscles needed the workout, and Arelin's sword had a different heft. The blade was wider, the feel of the handle still unfamiliar to his hand.

Trevin went through the motions of simple passes, but he had to keep stopping to wipe away tears. He had not swung a blade since Resarian's death, and he couldn't help reliving the incident. He realized that while weak muscles and a new sword were good reasons for working out, the driving force behind it was guilt. His mistakes in the canyon had cost Resarian his life. He couldn't undo his errors, but he could practice until the right moves came by instinct.

Advance. Retreat. Cut to the shoulder. Cut to the legs.

Trevin sensed a presence, sunset red. The warrior woman. He gritted his teeth and put more power into his swings.

Diagonal to the right. Diagonal to the left.

"Breathe," said a husky female voice.

"I am," he muttered through his teeth. Advance. Thrust.

"Let the sword lead," she said.

Trevin growled and whirled to face her. If he hadn't already been catching his breath, he would have done so at the sight of her winsome smile, her flowing brown hair, and her garb. She wore a tunic and leggings.

"I thought you might like a sparring partner, hmm?" She tied back her hair.

Normally Trevin would have welcomed a partner. But the warrior woman? He huffed. "Don't you have guard duties?"

"The king and queen are together and going nowhere. The king has guards enough. I'm available." She drew her sword and nodded at his. "You were born to it."

Trevin shook his head. "No doubt you were. But I wasn't. I was taught by second-rate masters in a traveling tent show."

Her laugh was warm and throaty. "It has nothing to do with your birth or who trained you. It's what you tell yourself as you fight. *I was born to this.*" She took a fighting stance.

Trevin positioned himself. A woman. He would never have believed it. Swordplay with a woman.

"Focus," she said. "You are a blade with an alert mind and agile legs."

And with that, they began the most strenuous workout Trevin had ever experienced.

"Balance!" she snapped. "Control!" she cried. "Evade—body first!" she shouted. "You were born to it!"

By the time they finished, Trevin's sword arm ached, and his legs were sore, but he knew his sword better. He knew his own weaknesses better. And he knew his strengths.

The warrior woman threw him a towel and mopped her own face. "Meet you here again tomorrow, hmm?" She shouldered out of the gate, then leaned back in. "My name is Ollena," she said, "in case you need to get me a message."

"Mine," Trevin gasped, his hands on his knees, "is—"

"Trevin," she said. "I know."

❧

For the next two days, Trevin allowed Ollena to work the stiffness out of his sword muscles and the smugness out of his protective pride. With clearer focus and cleaner moves came greater confidence. Each day he chanced a look at his reflection in the sword, wondering if he would see anything different. Each day the same wise, assured face looked back at him.

As they left the grounds together on the third day, a servant trotted up with a message from the king, requesting Trevin to join him in the library that evening. Trevin visited the baths, trimmed his scruffy new beard, and donned his dark gray tunic.

At the appointed time an attendant arrived and led him to the library, a columned room with scroll niches covering the north and south walls. On the west wall, shelves lined each side of a wide latticed window. In the center of the room, two lampstands threw warm light on a gaming table, where King Kedemeth sat.

Trevin bowed.

The king waved him over. "Join me for a toss of the dice?" He narrowed his eyes. "I presume you are honest at gaming."

Trevin took a seat opposite the king. "I am, sire. But if I were dishonest, I would say the same."

The king chuckled. "I must take my chances, then."

Trevin studied the cross-shaped game board. Four squares were carved within each arm of the cross and in the center. "Thief and Guard?" he asked.

"Or Fox and Geese," said the king, pouring white and gray pebbles out of a pouch. "We call it Attacker Defender."

"I've few coins to wager," said Trevin.

The king waved the comment away. "We'll play for the challenge of it." He scooped the pebbles into the center of the board. "Do you wish to attack or defend first?"

"Defend, sire, if it's all the same to you."

"Defending and attacking are *not* the same," said the king, "though there are strategic matters involved in both."

Trevin remembered Prince Resarian quoting his father's words. *Strategic matters.* He smiled sadly.

King Kedemeth scooted two gray pebbles to Trevin. "You may defend. I rather feel like attacking tonight. I've spent the last three days with Ambria and her friend. Two women can leave a man tired of defending and ready to attack something. In this case, your fortress." He counted out twenty-four white pebbles for his attackers.

"In Camrithia we call this game Dregs and Cams." Trevin positioned his two gray defenders on intersecting corners within his fortress, the arm of the cross nearest him.

"Dregmoorian attackers, Camrithian defenders?" The king stationed his white attackers on points across the rest of the board. "Thus King Laetham's quest for allies."

"Exactly. We of Camrithia are the two gray pebbles. If we had allies we could rely on, we would feel more secure."

Trevin assessed his options. Numbers were to the king's advantage, but the king's white pebbles could move only toward the fortress and were not allowed to jump the gray. Trevin's two gray pebbles had more flexibility. They could move anywhere in any direction and jump attackers to capture them. But he had to protect his fortress. If attackers filled the open points in his fort or trapped his two defenders, the king would win.

King Kedemeth scooted an attacker forward. "I wish I could send troops back with you, but we've not had a standing army since the Erielyon overcame the Vilnyri and pushed them into the fire mountains in the far north."

"I've never heard of the Vilnyri." Trevin moved a gray pebble.

"Leatherwings." The king moved.

"Like bats?" Trevin moved. "I thought Erielyon were the only winged angels."

"Leatherwings are not angels." The king moved a white pebble. "I'm into your fort!" he crowed. "The Erielyon lands are a buffer between us and the Vilnyri now. I hear that the leatherwings have contented themselves with forming their own reclusive society. We are at peace."

"Camrithia is a buffer between Eldarra and the Dregmoors." Trevin captured the white pebble in his fort.

"And Montressi is a buffer to our east." The king scratched his beard, pondering his next move. "So besides the occasional pirate attack on our western coast, we've had few interruptions to our peace. Our 'army' consists of small local militias that guard their own villages and towns." He made his move.

Trevin captured the pebble.

"Ah! I didn't see that one," said the king. "I'm not thinking." He made another move. "My own horsemen are trained in defense, of course. In the autumn each year, they go out in twos to train the militias and make certain of their readiness. What I'm saying is, I'm not sure how many would actually come to Camrithia's aid."

Trevin moved his pebble to a better defensive position. "You realize that if Camrithia falls to the Dregmoorians, Eldarra will be next."

"I know. It's in our best interest to help stabilize Camrithia. But it's unlikely I can get my people to leave the peace of their homes to fight on Camrithian soil." He moved a man to the entrance of Trevin's fortress. "However, I believe you'll find that help may arrive from a different quarter, and a stronger one."

"Oh?" Trevin looked up with interest.

"Angelaeon. They will gather here within the week." The king studied the board, then shook his head. "You have me blocked again."

❦

Pym spent his days in the stables and fields with the horsemen. Trevin trained at swords each day with Ollena and played Attacker Defender in the evenings with King Kedemeth.

The king parceled out information about his kingdom as they moved their pebbles. Trevin found the inner workings of Eldarra fascinating and asked questions that King Kedemeth seemed glad to answer. But occasionally when Trevin glanced up from the game board, he found the king intently watching not his moves but him, which Trevin found disconcerting.

Two days of mourning remained when King Kedemeth announced— over Trevin's rare win as Attacker—that a good number of Angelaeon had arrived and would meet on the morrow.

Trevin had felt their presence gathering in strength. "Prince Resarian told me the queen is a friend of the Angelaeon and believes the stairway to heaven will rise again when the stars of the beltway align," he said, scooping the pebbles into a pile.

"That she does." The king paced to the open window and gazed into the night sky. "She's mystical about it. I'm more practical. I believe what I see. I've seen Windwings, and I've seen Erielyon. They're an odd bunch but trustworthy friends. As for the stairway and the tree that supposedly protected it... What's it called?"

"The Wisdom Tree," said Trevin.

King Kedemeth chuckled. "I'm not denying it's real. It may well be. But I don't rule my kingdom based on it." He shrugged. "I'll believe it if and when I see it."

"What about your people? Do they feel the same?"

"Some follow my leaning; some follow Ambria's. We tend to be an easygoing people, welcoming all types to our kingdom as long as they keep the peace."

Trevin dropped the pebbles into their leather pouch.

"What about you?" asked the king. "Now that you know you're Arelin's son, are you inclined to join the Angelaeon?"

"I joined them months ago. At Ledge Rock I found one of the harps meant to restore the stairway." Trevin pulled the drawstring of the pouch tight. "I'm in it up to my neck."

⊱⋆⊰

The windows of the council chamber stood unshuttered to the warm day. As Trevin strode in, he marveled at the difference a change of perspective could make. The last time he entered this room, he was a prisoner facing the gallows. Now he was an honored guest walking into a room shimmering with the light of angels, their colors a welcome contrast to the gray they all wore. If he had not sensed them, he would have assumed they were the normal variety of townsfolk—dark, light, stout, lean, rustic, stately, all dressed in mourning. Ollena, the queen's bodyguard, armed and alert, stood in the corner behind the dais. She gave him a brief nod.

As Trevin rose from his bow before King Kedemeth and Queen Ambria, a woman stepped up to the queen, leaned close, and spoke to her. A thin black cloak hid the woman's broad shoulders, and her dusky hair was pinned back at the nape of her neck. Trevin sensed her familiar blue, calm presence.

"Livia?" he said.

She turned with a broad smile. "I'm glad to see you're well. Last time I saw you grow a beard, it was not by your choice."

Trevin scratched his chin. "Dungeons have that effect on me."

Livia drew him to a bench by the window. "I should have made time to meet with you last week, but Ambria needed my full attention. I felt I could be of some comfort, since I lost my own son, Sergai, last year."

"You were the visitor sequestered with the king and queen?"

Livia nodded. "They told me about discovering you, Arelin's son. I didn't know Arelin well, but I was delighted by the news."

King Kedemeth cleared his throat. The room quieted, and the angels found seats. Trevin placed his hand over the harp pendant that lay under his tunic. Seeing Livia made him ache to be with Melaia.

"Welcome," said the king. "I hold the Angelaeon in high esteem. As you know, my wife, Queen Ambria, watches the skies and assesses the progress of the stars, eager for the time when the stairway to heaven can be restored along with the Wisdom Tree." He glanced at Trevin with a twinge of a smile. "It appears the time is near."

Queen Ambria, regal and controlled, gave a nod as King Kedemeth continued.

"Perhaps you've heard that Arelin's son, Trevin, has been our guest for a couple of weeks. He has discovered… That, I shall let him tell." He motioned for Trevin to rise.

Trevin felt insignificant in such great company, a feeling heightened by a group in the back corner who sat with arms folded, scowling at him. But Livia, her chin high, looked at him expectantly, so he rose, trying to exhibit the confidence of the man in the eye of the sword.

One glance at the king reminded Trevin who was in charge, at least in this chamber. He took a deep breath.

"Each of you is well respected," he said, "and I value your presence. I know Dreia spent time here in the north. I serve her daughter, Melaia, who pledged to continue Dreia's task of uniting the harps. She has secured one of them, and we believe the harp stolen from Dreia is in the Dregmoors. With the guidance of Windweaver, I found the third harp here in Eldarra."

Whispers floated through the room. The scowlers talked among themselves.

King Kedemeth raised a hand, and the voices quieted. "Trevin is a comain of Camrithia. He will soon return to Redcliff. I ask that some of you travel with him to assure King Laetham that the northern lands are Camrithia's allies and to offer aid as needed."

One of the scowlers—a stout, surly angel with a bulbous nose—stood.

The king nodded. "Nevius?"

"We can talk about restoring the stairway all we want," said Nevius, "but Dreia was murdered trying to unite the harps. If an Archon failed, why should we believe a Nephili will succeed? This Melaia may be Dreia's daughter, but I'm not of a mind to follow her to my death."

Livia leaned forward. "That's exactly why she needs our help. She was born 'breath of angel, blood of man' for the express purpose of restoring the Tree. Those of us who know her are confident she'll do everything in her power to fulfill her task, with or without our help. Wouldn't it be better to lend our aid and take part in the Tree's restoration?"

"I agree," said Toryth, the arrowsmith from the trial council, her concerned face creased in wrinkles. "We can affect the balance of power so Dreia's daughter can succeed."

"Will we go to war?" asked a white-haired man. "I lost more than half my friends in the Angel Wars after the fall of the Tree. I've no desire to repeat the experience."

Ollena stepped forward. "If I may—"

King Kedemeth nodded.

"War is a valid concern." Her husky voice filled the room. "But I heard from a reliable source that when Arelin invaded the Dregmoors, Rejius lost a devastating number of his malevolents. I should think the immortal Firstborn would be reluctant to commit to a full-scale war, hmm?"

"A reliable source?" asked the white-haired man. "How many malevolents did the Firstborn lose?"

"I can't give you a definite count." Ollena stepped back to her place.

"Nor can I," said Livia, "but we know they usually work in squads of six. Rejius sent two squads to attack Dreia."

Trevin wiped sweat from his forehead. Two squads to attack an unsuspecting caravan. It was a slaughter. He wished he had never heard of the Firstborn.

"By the Asp's estimates," said Livia, "there are twelve squads in all. That's fewer than one hundred malevolents. If enough of us organize—"

"The Asp!" Nevius snorted. "Is that your *reliable* source? You trust information from an informant no one knows? His reports are likely disseminated by the Firstborn to entice us into a war we can't win. Besides, if we're to believe reports from Camrithia, the Firstborn has plenty of Dregmoorian raiders. We'd be badly outnumbered if he sent them into battle."

"The raiders are gash warriors," said Livia, "kept alive by drinking gash, a poor experiment gone awry. They're not angels, and they're not indestructible."

"They're not completely human either," said Nevius. "I'd not like to come upon a contingent of them. Perhaps they couldn't kill you, but they'd take you to someone who could."

Trevin sank into his seat, disappointed. He knew that angels did not always agree with one another, but he had expected more unity at this meeting.

Ollena stepped forward again. "My mother, Toryth, and I are Exousia."

Trevin glanced at Toryth. Mother and daughter, warrior angels both.

Ollena glared at Nevius. "We are ready to fight and die so *you* can ascend the stairway back to Avellan. For *your* freedom, sir."

"And if you lose?" grumbled the white-haired man. "You'll be forever entombed in stone in the Under-Realm."

Livia stood, her eyes smoldering. "Where is your courage, man? We're servants of the Most High, father-mother of the universe. The breath of the heavens has been breathed into us."

"Tell me," said Nevius, "where was the Most High when the Tree was destroyed? During the Angel Wars, where was our creator? Our father-mother left us abandoned. Orphaned."

Flames appeared above an unlit brazier and swirled into the form of a dark-skinned woman with wild copper hair. Trevin straightened, hardly breathing. He knew she was an Archon, for Melaia had described her along with Windweaver and Seaspinner.

King Kedemeth rose, as did several angels. Queen Ambria gripped the table, and others leaned forward. Nevius glared down his nose, his face set.

"Flametender," said Livia. "Welcome."

"Do I hear voices of rebellion?" Flametender scanned the room.

"Not rebellion. Reason," said Nevius. "Returning to Avellan is a worthy goal, but we are few and unsupported by a higher power. Why don't we admit that it's unlikely we'll ever return?"

"You cease to strive for yourself and the rest of society?" hissed Flametender. "Suit yourself, but you should know I've spoken with Earthbearer."

The angels exchanged glances as they murmured the name.

"Earthbearer is on our side?" asked the white-haired man.

"Earthbearer is on his own side and supports others as it pleases him," said Flametender.

"It pleases him to play god," said Livia.

"That could be to our advantage." Flametender paced around the room.

"I will start with some elementary facts for the benefit of those here who are not Angelaeon."

Trevin felt a hot draft as she passed by.

"The Under-Realm is divided into the Shallows and the Deeps," she said. "When Rejius, the immortal Firstborn, destroyed the Wisdom Tree and its stairway to heaven, he became responsible for the spirits of the dead who could no longer ascend to Avellan. He led them into the Shallows through caves in the Dregmoors, where he created an entire kingdom."

"With Earthbearer's permission?" asked King Kedemeth.

"Earthbearer welcomed Rejius as he welcomes all who enjoy exploring the beauties of the underground," said Flametender. "But over time Rejius stripped the Shallows of its precious gems and minerals and used them to experiment with alchemy. He uncovered the dark arts and applied his discoveries to the spirits of the dead."

Trevin rubbed his right hand. He had seen the results of Rejius's dark arts: shape shifting, draks, gash warriors.

"While Rejius has been toying with spirits," said Flametender, "Earthbearer has been toying with Rejius, unaware that the Firstborn has grown tired of experimenting on spirits. I informed Earthbearer that Rejius no longer waits for people to die but uses the living—even children. Gash is most effective when it's mixed with human blood."

Queen Ambria shrank back.

"Children?" A red-cheeked woman gaped.

"Until they stop growing," said Flametender.

Trevin squeezed his eyes closed. At least Resarian never had to face that fate.

King Kedemeth's fist hit the table. "What the blazes keeps you from going after him, then?" He glared at Nevius, who paled.

"Surely Earthbearer will destroy the Firstborn," Nevius said tentatively.

"I suggested it," said Flametender, "but Rejius is immortal, made so by the seeds of the Tree. He cannot be destroyed unless the Tree is restored."

"By breath of angel, blood of man," said Trevin, staring at her.

"Precisely," said Flametender. "Still, Earthbearer will no longer countenance the Firstborn's cruelties. He wants Rejius out."

"To where?" asked Livia.

"Upground," said Flametender. "Earthbearer is pressing Rejius to take himself and his charges into the world."

"How?" asked King Kedemeth.

"By forcing fires and molten rock upward," said Flametender.

"Landgash?" asked Trevin.

"For a start," said Flametender.

Nevius rubbed his bulbous nose. "This changes things."

"Your mind, I hope." Flametender's fiery gaze swept the group. "It may be easy to ignore the Firstborn when he is underground two kingdoms away. It's another matter when he is upground on your own doorstep. The time to stop him is now."

She paused and narrowed her eyes at Trevin. "You're the one who walked the circuit with Windweaver."

Trevin straightened.

"He's Arelin's son," said Ambria.

Flametender extended her hands to Trevin. "Place your palms on mine."

Intense heat radiated around Trevin, and he hesitated. But the request was no more strange than Windweaver telling him to step off the plateau, so he pressed his palms to hers.

He felt as if he were touching a flaming brazier. He expected to feel searing pain but instead felt only an intense heat that swam up his arms. His fingers, hands, and wrists glowed like molten metal, like the image in the sword. Sweat poured down his face and chest.

Flametender murmured softly as if in prayer.

Sciai eolin,
Ciarai pyrin,
Nai librein.

It was the old tongue, Trevin was sure, the same language as the runes on the harps, which he couldn't read.

Flametender backed away, and Trevin stared at his hands, expecting to see them charred beyond healing. But they looked the same as always, even the space where his small finger should have been. He looked up, wordless.

Flametender swept to the brazier, faded like a dying fire, and was gone.

CHAPTER 17

On the last day of mourning, Trevin crouched alone in the library, rummaging through a trunk of ancient-looking scrolls, searching for one that might contain a key to translating the old tongue. Even Livia, the only other one close enough to hear Flametender's words, did not know the old tongue. She said it had been handed down orally and only a few knew it these days.

"A lost cause," Trevin muttered, tossing the final scroll back into the trunk. "I can't even remember all the words anymore. *Cia eo toccia* something."

He closed the lid. The other angels who had witnessed Flametender's touch agreed she had given him some sort of gift, though no one knew what. At swords with Ollena, he showed no sudden remarkable improvement. He borrowed Haden's bow, but Ollena still hit more bull's-eyes than he did. He even tried a slingshot but completely missed the target. He was baffled. Ollena suggested there were other kinds of gifts just as valuable. Trevin thought he detected a trace of relief in her voice at knowing her prowess would remain unchallenged.

Pym had consoled him with the thought that the gift might be a greater measure of courage or wisdom. Trevin hoped for both as he moved to the window and peered through the intricate lattice. He could see King Kedemeth and Queen Ambria standing below in a grove of marble headstones, two black-gowned figures arm in arm by Prince Resarian's tomb. As they made their way back toward the palace, Trevin knew he too had to visit the grave.

He took a last look at the library, the gaming table, the pouch of pebbles that would go unused tonight because of the court dinner signifying the end of the days of mourning. He would ride out on the morrow, and who knew if he would ever return? He would miss Flauren.

The heady fragrance of roses filled the air around the tombs in the burial gar-den, and the colors of the blooms rivaled a room full of Angelaeon. A beautiful place to rest in peace. Though if the Angelaeon were right, Resarian's spirit, which should have crossed the veil by the stairway to heaven, had instead en-tered the Under-Realm. All the more reason to help Melaia unite the harps and restore the Tree.

"Resarian," Trevin whispered, kneeling by the rosy granite obelisk in-scribed with the prince's name. "Forgive me." Trevin bowed his head as the full weight of his guilt bore down on him.

The dinner that night was an occasion of restrained joy, a celebration of Prince Resarian's life but respectful of the sadness that would remain for some time to come. As the homage to the prince came to a close, an attendant brought Trevin a summons to the royal apartments.

After Trevin made his farewells to council members, courtiers, and serv-ants he had come to know at Flauren, the attendant led him to the king's spacious private sitting room. On the west wall, a wide window stood open to the night sky. Along the north, brass lamps hung over a table that held traver-tine goblets and a bowl piled with fruits. Lamps on stands shed light on the south wall, where fresh flowers filled the summer hearth, gracing the room with the fragrance of a garden.

King Kedemeth rose from a chair by the hearth, and Trevin bowed.

"I thought of bringing Attacker Defender," said the king, "but Ambria forbade it."

"That's a shame," said Trevin. "I feel lucky tonight."

"Trevin." Queen Ambria entered with a handmaid, and he bowed. "I hear you plan to leave on the morrow," she said. "You must return to us soon." She smiled, but her eyes held a deep sadness. She had officially mourned for almost thirty days, but Trevin knew her private pain came with no end date.

Nor did his. He dared not make a promise that would give her false hopes. "I've enjoyed my time here," he said. "After the dungeon part."

The king chuckled and motioned for Trevin to join them beside the flowering hearth. "I know you want to retire and get some rest before your journey, so we won't keep you long," he said. "I wanted you to know that after considering our discussion with the Angelaeon, I have decided to commit Eldarra as a full ally to Camrithia."

Trevin breathed deeply. Another task complete. "King Laetham will be greatly encouraged."

The handmaid gave each of them a travertine goblet of fruited wine. King Kedemeth took a sip, then cleared his throat. "The queen and I have a wish," he said.

"A desire." Queen Ambria patted her chest.

"A hope," said the king. "We lost Resarian."

"But we found you," said the queen.

King Kedemeth set his goblet aside and took Queen Ambria's hand. "We want you to be our son."

Trevin coughed on his wine. "You what?"

"We want you to be our son," said the queen.

Trevin could find no words. They both looked expectant, but he couldn't have been more disconcerted if they had hit him over the head with the lampstand.

"It's sudden, I know," said the king.

"If events had gone as your father intended, we would have raised you as our son, a prince of Eldarra," said the queen.

"But if I took your offer," said Trevin, "I'd be—"

"Crown prince," said the king. "You would inherit the throne."

Trevin exhaled slowly. He felt foolish gawking at the king and queen, but he could hardly grasp their offer, much less find words with which to reply. He, the future king of Eldarra?

"Don't refuse simply on the grounds that you have no royal heritage," said the king. "I shall become your royal heritage."

"What about Haden?" asked Trevin. "Isn't he the natural heir?"

"We've spoken to Haden," said the king. "He insists he doesn't want to rule. He says he can think of no better heir than you."

"Me," Trevin croaked, trying to fit his mind around the breadth, the height, the depth of the offer.

"You told me you've spent a good deal of time making your way around the underpinnings of Laetham's court," said the king.

"Underbelly is more accurate," said Trevin. "A vile underbelly at that."

"Not bad schooling if one is to mount the beast and hold the reins," said the king. "You've proved honest and faithful. You remained here to mourn when you could have bolted from Eldarra the moment you were acquitted. You've reasoned intelligently with me and made wise judgments—"

"We've seen your character in the eye of the sword," said the queen.

Trevin ran his hand through his hair. "Even so…"

"Livia vouched for you." Queen Ambria's eyes searched Trevin's. "She encouraged us to ask you."

"And the Oracle recommended it." The king studied his wine.

"You consulted the Oracle?" asked Trevin.

King Kedemeth looked up sheepishly. "He came to me. It seems you are destined to reign, and I readily recognize it."

"But how can you be certain I'm right for the throne?"

The king drained his goblet. "One can never be certain. One can only be courageous or cowardly. I have the courage to make the offer. Do you have the courage to accept?"

Trevin felt his face grow warm. He had never known a land more agreeable than Eldarra. Even in prison he hadn't been treated cruelly. The laws were fair, the people friendly. He stared at the blooms on the hearth. "I'm humbled, sire," he said. "I'm honored. I'm grateful. But I can't answer you yet. I don't wish to offend, but I've not fulfilled my duties to King Laetham or Princess Melaia."

"Look at me, Trevin," said the king.

Trevin looked up to see the king leaning toward him with the most sincere, guileless, respectful, undaunted gaze he had ever seen.

"Your answer reveals the courage of integrity," said the king. "I expected such. Fulfill your duties to Camrithia. After that, if you accept our offer, I shall be honored to call you 'son.'"

"*We* shall be honored." Queen Ambria's eyes sparkled.

Trevin felt a warm, solid sense of belonging, a grand purpose expanding in his chest like a deep breath. As he left the king's quarters that night, he knew that becoming heir of Eldarra would be his goal.

As heir of Eldarra, he would be worthy of a Camrithian princess.

Overnight the black drapes disappeared from the towers of the palace and the streets of Flauren. By the time Trevin led his gelding out of the stables, packed for the journey, dawn washed over the rosy palace walls. The entire city seemed to be waking not only to a new day but also to renewed life. Trevin knew that in Flauren he could become the man whose image he had seen in the sword.

King Kedemeth and Queen Ambria, cloaked against the early morning chill, appeared and greeted Trevin. The queen studied him with concern. "Did you get the parcel of bread and fruit I told Cook to send?"

Trevin patted the overstuffed pack tied atop the bundle containing the kyparis harp. "Enough to share."

"I expect you to." The queen slipped his cloak from where it lay across his mount's back and handed it to him. He had intended to leave it off, for being midsummer, the early chill would soon dissipate. But he pulled the cloak over his shoulders.

Queen Ambria made sure it was snug. "Keep yourself safe," she said, "and come back soon. Very soon."

King Kedemeth clasped Trevin's hand. "I wish you good speed in completing your goals for Camrithia. A selfish wish, I confess, but I, too, hope you'll return soon. I have much to teach you about Eldarran affairs of state."

Neither the king nor the queen admitted any possibility that he might turn down their offer of adoption. Trevin wished he could assure them that he would accept. He couldn't. But he didn't want to dash their hopes either.

"I'll return as soon as I can," he said. "If I accept your offer, I'll have a great deal to learn. It may take a long time."

"Long enough to play round after round of Attacker Defender," said the king. "Keep up your skills while you're gone." He tucked a drawstring purse heavy with coins into Trevin's hand. "Don't wager it all away."

"Thank you, sire. I'll tell Pym to keep me honest." Trevin tied the purse to his belt.

"Main Trevin," Haden called as he strode out of the stables. "I believe I have something of yours." He held out a shield that had obviously been pounded back into shape. A lopsided eagle decorated the front. "I found this trampled on the plain. Pym said it belongs to you, so I took the liberty of having it repaired."

Trevin examined the shield and smiled. The eagle had been repainted to somewhat better effect. As he tied it to his packs, he thought of the beauty with the rich brown eyes who had given him the shield. Soon she would greet him at Redcliff, and he would clear his name. He glanced around for Pym, eager to be on the way.

"Don't forget," said the king. "Varic stands accused of murder in Eldarra. I want him brought to justice."

"Yes, sire." Trevin mounted his horse. Justice would require him to refrain from killing the scum himself. He would need a caravan load of self-restraint to keep Varic alive long enough to return him to Eldarra.

Pym and Catellus led their horses from the stable. Trevin checked that Arelin's sword was close at hand and his shield and staff tied to the packs behind him.

Livia, Toryth, and Ollena approached—Livia with a smoky gelding, Toryth carrying a bow and a quiver of arrows, Ollena leading a bay mare and wearing a tunic and leggings like a man, though a comely one with long brown locks. The women nodded to the king and queen.

"I'm joining your company, Main Trevin," Ollena announced in a husky voice. "For your protection, hmm?"

Livia stifled a smile.

Trevin raised his eyebrows. "For my protection?"

Astride their horses, Pym and Catellus exchanged bemused expressions.

"Queen's orders," said Ollena.

Trevin started to protest, but King Kedemeth held up his hand. "Queen's orders are nonnegotiable. At least if you want to keep the peace."

Queen Ambria smiled smugly.

"I assure you, my daughter is a skillful warrior." Toryth handed Ollena the bow and quiver. "I would have joined you myself, but I have duties here."

"Yes…well…" Trevin did value Ollena's swordsmanship and skill at the bow. And Livia was coming with him. No doubt she would welcome the company of another woman. He nodded. "Welcome, then," he said. "We'll all protect each other."

"Agreed." Ollena slipped her bow onto her back.

Trevin looked around but saw no other angels approaching, nor did he sense any others. "Five in our company," he said, disappointed that more angels didn't consider him worthy of their support.

Livia mounted her gelding, and Ollena gracefully swung herself onto her bay. Trevin nodded his final good-byes to the king and queen and Haden. Then he nudged his gelding and headed down the waking streets of Flauren, listening to the clop of horses behind him, carrying Livia, Ollena, Pym, and Catellus.

As they neared the main gate, Trevin sensed three auras, one forest-green, one violet, and one midnight-blue. When he saw three Angelaeon mounted and packed for travel, he grinned. With Livia and Ollena they would make almost a full squad of angels.

An almond-eyed, soft-spoken man named Sorabus introduced himself first. In the ranking of angels, he was of the Thronos, reputed to be gifted negotiators. He introduced Xenio, who wore his black hair in long braids and was ranked as one of the Kuriotes, expert leaders.

Trevin nodded at the third angel—stout, bulb-nosed Nevius, who explained that he was an Archangel, guardian of people, skilled in politics, and determined to fight anyone who would abuse children.

In the interest of time, Trevin agreed with the group's suggestion to take the most direct route south through a high mountain pass. As they headed out, he was acutely conscious of being Nephili and suspected that his wise, experienced companions assessed his every move.

Then he realized he was the one assessing himself, trying to live up to the title "son of Arelin," which had gained him respect in Eldarra. He fingered the hilt of his sword. He might look like Arelin, but how could he live up to the character of someone he had never known?

The pleasant rolling hills that graced the first part of their journey soon became more rugged. As they approached the mountain border of Eldarra, two draks appeared over the peaks ahead. Trevin wondered who spied through their eyes. Varic? Rejius? A third drak joined them, a smaller one.

Ollena whipped her bow toward the skies.

"Hold!" shouted Trevin.

The arrow flew at the circling draks. One plummeted to the ground.

"What are you doing?" he cried.

"They're spy-birds," said Nevius.

"I know they're spy-birds," snapped Trevin.

"They rarely come in range," said Xenio.

"Of course Ollena's range is greater than most," Sorabus conceded.

Trevin galloped to the fallen bird. Its gray eyes stared blankly. He dismounted, knelt by the body, and examined its hands.

Livia squatted beside him. "Is it—"

"Disgusting, hmm?" Ollena dismounted beside Trevin as the others rode up.

"Ask me before shooting draks," said Trevin.

"For pity's sake, why?" asked Ollena.

"Because one of them may be a six-year-old girl, as close as a sister to Melaia."

"This one?" asked Catellus.

Trevin shook his head. "The hands are too large for a child." He scanned the sky.

One drak hugged the tops of the mountains. The other had disappeared.

"Ghast! A six-year-old? I'll kill the Firstborn myself," Ollena muttered as she pulled the arrow out of the drak.

❧

Dusk found Trevin and his company camping in the foothills of the mountains. Trevin joined Ollena to hunt for fresh meat and was gratified to find that while she could shoot a cony at a remarkable distance, only he could locate it afterward in the gathering darkness.

Later, as they all sat around the campfire after supper, talk turned to their destination. Redcliff.

Pym leaned back against a tree trunk. "What I'm wondering, Trevin, is what happens at the gate. If there's still a warrant out, which is likely, you'll be arrested."

"Disguise yourself," Ollena suggested from where she stood watch on one side of the staked horses, Livia on the other side.

"Could work," said Pym.

"Maybe Sorabus can negotiate our way in," said Trevin.

Sorabus looked up from stirring the coals, his almond eyes reflecting the flames. "Then Nevius can maneuver through the politics of getting you out of prison."

"If you're willing to rot while politics drags its feet." Nevius rubbed his bulbous nose.

"I suggest we take Main Trevin in as a prisoner." Xenio retied the end of one of his black braids. "We tell the guards we come from the north, bringing a wanted man. Once inside, we keep to the back streets and go where we please."

"The temple," said Trevin. "The priest there is Angelaeon. He'll know whether it's dangerous to show my face." Jarrod could also send for Melaia, who among other things could advise him of King Laetham's mood. They would just have to avoid Varic. If the prince was there.

Everyone grew silent, listening to wolves bay in the distance. Ollena climbed to a boulder on the uphill side of the camp.

As the other men bedded down, Trevin ambled over to Livia. "You're eager to see Serai," he said.

"A mother is always eager to see her daughter," said Livia. "Perhaps as eager as a young man is to see the girl he loves."

"Is that why you suggested me as heir to King Kedemeth—so I would be of rank to marry Melaia? I thought angels didn't interfere with human will."

"We don't. We influence circumstances. We counsel. But we allow you to make your own choices." Livia paced beyond the horses and sat on a stump.

Trevin followed and took a seat on the ground beside her.

"Windweaver suggested you as the logical heir," she said, "and I saw the sense of it, due to your heritage and the life Arelin intended for you. If it eases your relationship with Melaia, all the better."

Trevin gazed north toward Flauren, wondering if he should tell King Laetham about Kedemeth's offer to make a comain his heir. Would that please the king or anger him? "What do you know about King Laetham's melancholy?" he asked.

"Laetham is what we Angelaeon call a Breaker. Like waves that swing in tides, high then low. Though King Laetham tends toward the low."

A lone wolf howled, and Livia pulled her cloak tighter.

"What causes a person to become a Breaker?"

"I suppose it depends," said Livia. "I happen to believe King Laetham is beset by the guilt of falsely accusing Dreia of being unfaithful and banishing her. He lost a wife he loved and almost lost a daughter."

Trevin's stomach knotted. He hadn't realized he and the king shared a gut-gnawing core of guilt.

Livia eyed him. "We all bear guilt for something we've done or not done," she said. "The difference with King Laetham is that he can't forgive himself. He drowns in his guilt. The harshest judgments are often the ones we place on ourselves."

Wolves wailed to each other. Trevin offered to take Livia's watch, but she insisted on fulfilling her turn, so he slipped back to the campfire and chucked another log on the fading flames.

As Trevin lay down and drew his cloak around him, he realized he hadn't warned anyone that he might wake in the night with a terror-dream. The fear of screaming out made it hard to fall asleep in a group like this. But he had not suffered a terror-dream in over a fortnight. Perhaps the phantoms of his sleep were gone.

Still he found it hard to close his eyes. *The harshest judgments are often the ones we place on ourselves.* He stared at the flames licking the fresh log. Guilt was a searing fire, he thought. A burn deep in the soul. Would he, like King Laetham, let that burn define him and control the rest of his life?

CHAPTER 18

Draks shadowed Trevin and his companions every step of their journey south, but as they neared Redcliff, it was the ground that claimed their attention. Rivulets of gash had turned the path ahead into a maze. Trevin was appalled at the change that had occurred in the six weeks he had been absent. The earth seemed leprous, and the air swirled with the stinking steam that rose from the bubbling, dun-colored mud.

"I'm not easily sickened," said Pym, "but these earth gashes make my stomach clench like a fist."

"And mine," said Trevin, though he knew a greater part of his unease was due to a sense of foreboding. He couldn't count the number of times he had instinctively placed his palm on the hilt of his sword and flexed his fingers.

At last the walls of Redcliff came within sight, but instead of feeling relief, Trevin grew only more wary. He sensed no malevolents, for which he was grateful. The trouble was that he sensed *nothing*. The only angel presence he discerned rode with him.

By the time they reached the west wall, daylight was waning. Sorabus took the lead, and the others formed a ring around Trevin, who pulled up his hood. They cantered toward the bridge that rose from the valley to the main gate but slowed when they reached it. The bridge was as bare as a bone picked clean, the iron doors of the main gate shut tight as a casket.

"Flustrations!" said Pym. "You'd think they'd leave the gates open a mite longer."

Sorabus led them across the bridge, positioned around Trevin as they had planned, but before they could pound on the gate, a voice called, "Who wants entrance?"

They looked up to see a guard atop the wall. His companion held an arrow nocked and ready.

Trevin glanced at Ollena. He suspected she could impale the archer before the man could twitch his finger. Her hand lay near her bow, but she and the others held their peace.

Sorabus called, "We're a company of allies from Eldarra. Armsman Pymbric is with us."

"Wait there." The guard bobbed out of sight.

As their mounts impatiently snuffed and snorted, ready to be done with the journey, Trevin looked south over the bridge toward the valley where he was appointed comain. No animals grazed the fields, no hut lights glimmered, and no one traveled the roads. Stinking wraiths of steam spewed from cracks in the ground and dissolved in the chill evening air. A shiver ran up his arms.

Livia sidled up to him. "The Angelaeon presence at Redcliff is small," she said, "but it's here."

Trevin tried to discern the colored light, hoping to sense Melaia, but the scraping of the gate bolt dragged his mind instead to the sound of his jail door in Flauren. The Eldarran cells were better than those at Redcliff. He shuddered to think King Laetham might clap him in irons before hearing the truth.

The gate door opened a crack, and the guard appeared with a torch. After studying the group, he frowned. "Main Trevin? We thought—"

"He was found not guilty," snapped Ollena.

"But we've brought him here to answer to Camrithian charges," said Sorabus.

The guard snorted as he tugged the door open. "You've a long wait, then. Unless you want to ride to Qanreef."

"Why?" Pym stirred his disheveled hair.

"The king's in Qanreef."

"Qanreef!" said Trevin. "The court doesn't go to Qanreef until after the harvest festival."

"You think there'll be a harvest this year?" The guard closed the gate behind them. "Half the city has left for hither and yon."

"The princess is gone as well?" asked Trevin.

"The lot of 'em," said the guard. "They feared they'd be trapped here by these gashes opening all around. Farmers can't produce; no foodstuff's coming in. Some of us have stayed, but how long we can hold without a bulk of supplies arriving is anyone's guess." He nodded at the rest of the company. "The inn's boarded up. Not expecting guests, as you might imagine."

"Is the temple open?" asked Livia.

"You might try there. Jarrod's stayed." The guard waved them on and headed back to his lookout.

Trevin led the group through the dim city streets, his eyes on the towers of the palace, every window dark. But as they neared the inner wall, he sensed Jarrod waiting at the gate. A twinge of anger pinched him. Why hadn't Jarrod gone with Melaia? As an Exousia and Melaia's half brother, Jarrod should be a permanent part of her protection.

As they approached the inner gate, Jarrod opened it and held a torch high. "Weary travelers?" He waved them into the inner courtyard. "I sensed you coming and sent the steward to prepare some rooms on the ground floor of the palace."

Trevin dismounted.

"Horses to the stables across the way," Pym told the group. "I'm familiar with its workings."

"You might not find much fodder," said Jarrod.

"We'll scrape up something," said Pym. "Could use your hair. It's the right color."

Jarrod protectively flipped his tail of hair over his shoulder as Trevin retrieved his sword, his staff, and the pack holding the harp. Pym took the gelding's reins and led the rest of the group to the stables.

Livia hung back. "I suppose Serai isn't here?"

"Unfortunately not," said Jarrod. "She accompanied the princess to Qanreef. Now that Main Trevin is back, I'll go to the coast too."

"I expect we'll all journey to the coast." Livia headed for the stables.

"You're welcome to stay at the temple tonight," Jarrod called to her.

"If the steward has prepared rooms in the palace, I'll stay with the other woman in our group," Livia called back.

"Another woman? I didn't notice," said Jarrod.

"The orange-red angel dresses like a man," Trevin said.

"Obviously passes for one."

"Just don't challenge her to a fight."

Trevin plodded behind Jarrod past the temple's porch columns and through the arched doorway. The altar room lay in shadows. Except for Jarrod's torch, the only light came from the priest's quarters off the curving corridor that echoed with their footsteps.

"Is Dwin here or in Qanreef?" asked Trevin.

"Neither. Dwin has other responsibilities."

"You've already made him a priest?"

"A priest?" Jarrod looked amused. "You believe it's in Dwin's nature to be a priest?"

"No, but—"

Jarrod slipped his torch into a hall bracket and entered his quarters. "Dwin's a spy."

Trevin halted in the doorway. "How long has he been spying?"

Jarrod set out pottery cups. "He started—on his own—the day you found him at Drywell. He recognized Fornian as someone who had visited Redcliff before, and he thought he might find out who the Dregmoorians were. He made a few mistakes—"

"A few mistakes!" Trevin barked.

"And then he tried to redeem himself by getting information on them at Redcliff, which is how he learned about Hesel's gash running."

"Why didn't he tell me?"

"He did. He said you didn't believe him. Said you were none too happy about the idea."

"Brilliant. He must have figured that out when I said *no spying.*" Trevin hung his sword and scabbard on a peg. His own spying had been costly, and not just to him. He had hoped to spare Dwin the same grief. As he leaned his staff in a corner and set his pack on a bench, he told himself to calm down. "So King Laetham needed spies?"

"Dwin works for the Angelaeon."

Trevin plunked down on a stool beside the table. "Can't you angels do your own spying?"

"We have our limitations." Jarrod poured cider. "Malevolents sense our presence too easily. Humans can go places we could never hope to enter."

"Such as?"

"The Dregmoors." Jarrod handed a cup to Trevin. "The Asp needed eyes."

Trevin clapped his cup down on the table, and cider sloshed out. "Dwin is in the Dregmoors? Blast it, Jarrod! You might as well have sent him into a live lava flow."

Jarrod tossed him a cloth to wipe the spill. "Dwin volunteered."

Trevin hissed and scrubbed at the table.

"Was *your* mission successful?" asked Jarrod.

"In part. I met with the Oracle."

"And?"

"The Oracle is Windweaver."

Jarrod burst into laughter. "Windweaver? The mysterious Oracle! I should have guessed. Did he give you a word for the king, a sign, an omen?"

Trevin shook his head. He wasn't about to say he was the sign, a ridiculous notion. He retrieved his pack and untied it. "I also found a harp. The one that *touches skies*. But don't play it unless you want the earth to quake." He gently lifted the harp from its wrappings.

Jarrod stroked the wooden frame. "Now here's a good omen. Melaia will be delighted."

"Can you interpret the runes?"

"*Tremulakei.* Tremble."

"Well named," said Trevin. "So you know the old tongue?"

"I learned it for keeping the histories at Aubendahl," said Jarrod.

Trevin started to ask about the words Flametender had spoken, but he couldn't recall them, and as he returned the harp to his pack, the weariness of the journey fell over him. He felt as empty as the palace. Melaia in Qanreef. Dwin in the Dregmoors.

He went back to his cider. "Why didn't you go to Qanreef?"

Jarrod selected a loaf of bread from a shelf. "Melaia insisted I stay here and wait for your return. She feared you would hear the news from someone else."

"What news?"

"Her betrothal to Varic was made public within a fortnight of your leaving."

Trevin stared into his cider, his throat tight. "Isn't there a customary waiting period?"

"Two months," said Jarrod.

"Then it's not consummated."

"Melaia legally belongs to Varic. The decree is binding."

Trevin rubbed his forehead. "The king led her to believe he wouldn't pledge her to Varic—at least until I returned. He betrayed her."

"He doesn't see it that way, I'm sure." Jarrod chucked a wooden plate of bread onto the table and sat. "Varic accused you of Nash's murder and asked for permission to bring you to justice. The king agreed, but Varic returned—"

"With the news that I killed the prince of Eldarra."

Jarrod studied Trevin. "Did you?"

"It was Varic's doing."

Jarrod tore off a piece of bread. "Nash died at Varic's hand as well. Dwin snooped around and discovered that a little over a year ago Varic forged messages to the comains and secured the scrolls with the king's seal, which he got from—"

"Nash?"

"Nash. Who was presumably paid quite well for sealing the scrolls."

Trevin tore off a hunk of bread. "So Varic had been in Redcliff before?"

"Fornian. That's what made Dwin suspicious. When Varic and his friends arrived at Redcliff with Dwin, Nash became greedy and asked a higher price to stay silent. Varic ensured his silence, but it was Nash who paid the price."

"Dwin discovered all that?"

"Hesel let it slip over their cups one night."

"Does King Laetham know all this?"

"Dwin brought the accusation in private to Lord Beker, along with the list of accounts he showed you. Beker took it to the king. Since the only proof was the list of accounts, Hesel was banished as a gash runner. Varic took him away in chains to his justice in the Dregmoors."

Trevin snorted. "Varic gave Hesel his freedom."

"And King Laetham got the matter off his shoulders. Hesel didn't return."

"Did Dwin find out what happened to the comains?"

"No." Jarrod brushed crumbs from his robe. "Nor did he discover what the messages said."

"That *I* know," said Trevin. "I found Main Catellus."

"Where?"

"In Eldarra. It's a long story, but he says the messages summoned the co-mains to Qanreef."

"Qanreef," Jarrod mused. "I'm sure Pym is eager to follow that trail."

Trevin leaned back against the wall, exhausted. "Does the king truly be-lieve I killed Nash and Prince Resarian?"

"Melaia never believed it, and she asked me to tell you so. As for the king, I think he hoped you wouldn't return so he wouldn't be forced to conduct an inquiry. He's hungry for peace with the Dregmoors."

"Even if it includes selling his daughter to a Dregmoorian snake? Do you know why they take children as payment for gash? Children's blood mixed with gash gives the drink its youth-renewing properties."

Jarrod paled. "All the more reason for the harps to be united as soon as possible." He stared at the pack on the bench. "You might try to see the advan-tage of Melaia's marriage to Varic."

"Advantage? If Melaia is wed to Varic, she'll be taken to the Dregmoors."

"Exactly. It's almost certain the third harp is there. Melaia's marriage could give her the opportunity to find it. Besides, some of us believe the harps must be united in the Dregmoors."

Trevin scowled at Jarrod. "You didn't tell Melaia that, did you?"

"I did."

"You *want* her to go into the Dregmoors?"

"I want her to have hope. If she's forced to marry the boor, at least she might see some purpose in it."

"Why unite the harps in the Dregmoors? The Durenwoods would make more sense. Or Tabaitta Canyon. Or Eldarra."

"Because the Wisdom Tree stood in the Dregmoors before Rejius de-stroyed it."

"Blast it all, Jarrod!" Trevin rose, his fists clenched. "How can you be so calm about this? You've no qualms about seeing your half sister married to a conniving murderer?"

"Of course I do, but—"

"But nothing!" Trevin leaped up and kicked his stool at the stone hearth, where it split with a crack. He stomped to the corner and grabbed his staff. "Melaia charged me with the task of finding the harps. *You* stop the marriage. *I'll* go to the Dregmoors."

CHAPTER 19

Trevin stormed out of the temple into the moonlight, stabbing the flagstones with his staff at every step. If events had gone as planned, he would have presented the harp to Melaia tonight and escorted the company of Angelaeon to King Laetham first thing the next morning as proof of the alliance with Eldarra. He would have summoned Catellus to shed light on the problem of the comains. He would have spoken the truth about Varic. As Trevin had imagined it, King Laetham would thank his comain and refuse to wager his daughter to Varic in trade for a peace that would be superficial at best.

"Fool plans!" He whacked a tethering post.

"Betrayed by the king, hmm?" asked a husky voice.

Trevin turned as Ollena emerged from the shadows beside the temple wall. He was not surprised he hadn't sensed her, because his mind was raging.

"You were eavesdropping," he said.

She shook her head. "Just guarding. I couldn't help but overhear as I walked by the temple window. Care to stroll the perimeter with me?"

Trevin exhaled slowly. A walk would help him cool down. In silence he followed Ollena up the stone stairs to the top of the inner wall surrounding the palace and its grounds. She smelled like sandalwood. A comforting scent.

They strode halfway around the palace before Ollena spoke. "I hope you're not offended that I heard your conversation. Keen hearing is one of my gifts."

Trevin wondered what else she had heard. "Keen eyesight is one of mine." He nodded toward the opposite wall where Catellus's burly form paced in the darkness. "Maybe we all keep an eye on each other."

Ollena's husky chuckle warmed him. "I wanted to tell you I know how it feels," she said. "I was betrayed once."

Trevin shot her a questioning look but said nothing, not wishing to pry into her private affairs.

For a moment they strolled in silence. Then Ollena said, "I was not always as humble as I am now."

Trevin looked away, twisting his mouth in an effort to keep from laughing aloud.

"About seven years ago I journeyed into the foothills of Montressi to take part in an archery contest. I made friends there with a man named Orin, who was a worthy opponent. The contest came down to the two of us."

"And you won," said Trevin.

"I did. Proudly. Orin invited me to join him and his friend Rikin in a hunt before they returned to their homeland. I was smitten by Rikin's dark-eyed charm. He spoke like a lover, said his heart was mine." Ollena trailed her hand along the top of the parapet. "Eldarrans have a saying: 'Like cats, flatterers lick and then scratch.' I should have known better. But I was in love with love, hmm?"

Trevin eyed Ollena. Her sunset-red energy intrigued him now that they were not sparring but simply talking as friends. "You obviously found him out. And I wager you slew more game than the men did."

Ollena chuckled. "I flaunted myself to gain their admiration. One evening over the campfire, Rikin and Orin asked my secret for spotting game. I told them I didn't see game but knew its exact location and size by its sound, because keen hearing is my gift. That night I heard them whispering while they thought I was asleep. They planned to lure me into their service as a spy. The wretches!"

"You confronted them?"

"Actually, I ran," she said. "They tracked me, but with my hearing I knew when they were nearby. They gave up long before I reached the box canyon."

"Betrayal by the king is one thing," said Trevin. "Betrayal by someone who plays the lover is another matter." Even as he spoke, he realized he had done the same thing to Melaia the previous fall when he'd led her and her harp to Lord Rejius. He pressed his hand to the harp pendant. She had forgiven him. It was more than he deserved.

Ollena gazed at the palace, where flickering lights shone from three windows on the first floor. "I brought some Eldarran sweetmeats with me for the journey. They're in my room. Would you like some?"

Trevin eyed the dome of the temple. "I should head back to Jarrod. He has a stool he needs me to mend."

❧

Early the next morning Jarrod met with Trevin and the group from Eldarra. Jarrod reported skirmishes between malevolents and Angelaeon along the Davernon River, the border between Camrithia and the Dregmoors. The malevolents seemed intent on keeping routes open for raiders. In addition, encampments of gash warriors had been spied on the northeastern bank of the Davernon.

After debating the situation, the group decided to divide into two. Sorabus, Xenio, and Nevius would stay in Redcliff to arrange for deliveries of supplies from the north and to coordinate the efforts of the Angelaeon. Meanwhile, Trevin and the others would ride south to Qanreef.

Once the meeting adjourned, Trevin wasted no time getting his group on the road. He headed out of Redcliff with Pym, Catellus, Livia, Ollena, and Jarrod. They wove around the steaming landgashes in the valley south of Redcliff but did not follow the highway over the hills. Instead, they took a trail that led to Stillwater. Trevin had walked the same path by moonlight the previous fall with Pym, Livia, and Melaia, who had been angry with him at the time. Even then he had already lost his heart to her.

Late in the afternoon on the second day, the group crested a hill and saw the city of Navia across the field ahead. Trevin swallowed a knot of guilt. Last autumn he had sent Dregmoorian raiders south from Treolli. Not specifically to Navia, but that was where they ended up.

Trevin eyed the city for signs of damage as they approached. The overlord's tower still dominated the buildings, topped by four cornerstones that looked like hands beseeching the sky. The white dome of the temple was intact but streaked with soot, and the city walls still stood, though they were flame scarred.

He led his companions through the rebuilt main gates and found the city a strange mix of new whitewashed houses and charred skeletal frames. Fortunately, they found an inn in good condition, though the innkeep, a puff-jowled man, warned that he had only meager provisions.

"I'm running low on account of the number of travelers passing through on their way west," he said, "but my wife will do her best to fill your bellies." He led them past two long tables of sour-faced customers and upstairs to rooms that overlooked the common area.

"Why so many travelers of late?" asked Trevin.

"The east bears the brunt of the blight right now," said the innkeep. "Their farms are scored by landgashes. Many are giving up, hoping for better living elsewhere."

"They're leaving the east part of the kingdom open for the Dregmoorians to stroll right in," murmured Jarrod.

"Aye, and the raiders still ply their trade, sure enough." The innkeep opened the doors to three rooms.

Trevin wasn't surprised that raids continued in spite of the betrothal, but he wanted to hear this man's view of it. "I thought we had a peace treaty," he said, stacking his packs with Jarrod's in a room not much bigger than an alcove at the Redcliff palace.

"The royal betrothment brings the hope of peace," said the innkeep, "but I wager we'll not have true peace 'til the marriage is official, signed and sealed. 'Til then, Navians are afeared these raiders will take it into their heads to venture here again. Even if they don't, with Lord Silas abed and not long for this world, I'll not be surprised if our locals skirmish over who'll be the next overlord."

"Lord Silas is dying?" asked Trevin. He had first met Melaia at the overlord's villa when he was a kingsman working for Lord Rejius and she was a Navian priestess. He admired the old man for being faithful to King Laetham in spite of thinly veiled threats from an impertinent kingsman.

"I hear Lord Silas has sent for his son." The innkeep headed back downstairs.

Jarrod nodded to Trevin. "I'll guard."

Trevin followed the innkeep. "The overlord's son, Yareth—wasn't he banished to the western tribes for supporting the coup? Would he try to return?"

The innkeep simply shrugged, pointed Trevin to the empty end of a table, and helped his wife hand out drinks.

Ollena and Livia joined Trevin. Then Pym and Catellus came in from seeing to the horses. Jarrod looked on from the railing above.

The drink was an overwatered wine, the meal an overwatered stew, and the other customers an over surly crew, who were quick to leave the table once Trevin and his friends sat down. Only two drinkers lingered over their mugs. But they, too, retired early, as did Pym and Catellus.

After Ollena finished her meal, she took Jarrod's place at the rail upstairs, and he made his way to the bowl and mug saved for him. Livia stayed at the table, staring into the flame of a bowl lamp sitting on the hearth, which sent a flickering glow into the common room.

Trevin paced the floor, trying to balance a knife, tip down, on the wooden plate he held flat on his palm. As the knife fell, he snatched its hilt from the air. "Two days to Qanreef," he muttered, positioning the knife on the plate again.

"One thing you might want to know before we get to Qanreef," said Jarrod, sopping up his stew with thin flatbread, "is that King Laetham met a lady he wishes to marry."

"Who?" Trevin eased his finger off the hilt of the knife, leaving it standing on its tip.

"She claims she's a noblewoman from an island in the Southern Sea," said Jarrod. "Presumably she sailed to Qanreef to recover after the death of her husband. By the looks of her, she's quite wealthy."

Trevin's knife clattered to the plate. "How did King Laetham meet her?"

"She came to Redcliff to visit, having heard tales of its unusual towers of red clay—and its handsome king."

"'Claims'? 'Presumably'?" asked Livia in a low voice. "Do you have reason to be suspicious?"

"No real reason. Just instinct," Jarrod murmured. "She seems overly solicitous toward the king."

"What does Melaia think of her?" asked Trevin.

"Melaia agrees with me," said Jarrod.

Livia refilled Jarrod's cup from a pitcher on the table. "Melaia has had the sole attention of the king since she has known him. Now she's sharing his affections. That's not an easy adjustment."

Trevin stood the knife on its tip again. "What does the lady call herself?"

"Beautiful, probably," said Ollena from the railing upstairs.

Trevin grinned up at her and murmured, "Never try to keep a secret from an angel with the gift of keen hearing."

Ollena saluted with the dagger she was polishing.

"Her name is Lady Jayde," said Jarrod.

"Maybe the king's interest in Lady Jayde will take his mind off giving Melaia to Prince Varic," said Trevin.

"You might wish it," said Jarrod, "but before Lady Jayde followed the king to Qanreef, she tried to convince him that a double wedding would be a 'most wonderful occasion.' You can imagine Melaia's response."

Trevin scowled at Jarrod. "Your sympathy overwhelms me."

"Angels are not to interfere with human will," said Jarrod.

"Hang this not-interfering-with-human-will." Trevin caught the knife as it fell. "Whose human will? Varic's? Lady Jayde's? Melaia's?"

"Or yours?" Jarrod scooted his bench to the wall and stretched his legs on it full length.

Livia headed for the stairs. "If we intervened, in whose behalf would we work, Trevin?"

"We're to allow you humans to work out matters among yourselves," said Jarrod.

"Nephili too?" asked Trevin.

"Nephili too." Jarrod closed his eyes.

Trevin huffed. "Even if we all end up miserable in the process?"

"I'm told you learn by your mistakes."

"Do you learn by yours?"

Jarrod's eyes snapped open, and Trevin glared at him, fully aware that he had dealt a low blow. Jarrod had made a deadly mistake when he failed to protect his mother, Dreia—which made his failure to guard Dreia's daughter all the more disturbing.

"You should be protecting Melaia right now," said Trevin, "but you're nowhere near her."

Jarrod stared into the shadows, his jaw clenched.

Trevin tossed the wooden plate onto the table, rebuking himself for pointing out Jarrod's guilt while hiding his own. An impulse to confess bit his conscience, but he shook it off. His was not an insignificant confession, and Jarrod was no ordinary priest. Jarrod was more likely to kill him than absolve him.

Trevin sighed. "Is there no way to nullify the betrothal?"

"I'll do what I can," said Jarrod. "But the most important task is uniting the harps. As I said before, Melaia's marriage may place her in a position to accomplish that task."

Trevin passed the hilt of the knife from his right hand to his left and back again. What if Melaia reasoned like Jarrod did? What if she agreed to marry Varic in order to gain access to the Dregmoors and the third harp?

Trevin stabbed the plate. Melaia wanted the third harp; he would bring it to her. He would go into the Dregmoors and bring it back. Then she would have no reason to go into the Dregmoors, no reason to marry Varic.

"*Phadai cordin nes duta periccin,*" said Ollena, studying the hilt of her dagger.

Trevin eyed her. "What did you say?"

Jarrod smiled, his eyes closed again. "The old tongue. It means 'the path of the heart is not without risk.'"

Trevin murmured, "So the one whose gift is keen hearing knows the old tongue."

"Spoken truly, Main Trevin," said Ollena. "What's your point, hmm?"

"You heard Flametender's words in Flauren, didn't you?"

Jarrod opened one eye. "Flametender?"

"Do you remember her words, Ollena?" asked Trevin.

She sheathed her dagger and thought for a moment. "*Sciai eolin, ciarai pyrin, nai librein.*"

"Which means?" asked Trevin.

"Seed of wind, heir of fire, born to free," said Ollena. "Flametender named you."

"Named me?" Trevin yanked the knife out of the wooden plate and slipped it into its sheath. "Couldn't she have been less cryptic? A simple name like Gadrian or Phineas or—"

"Arelin's son?" asked Ollena.

"That's clearer than Flametender's riddle," said Trevin.

Jarrod straightened. "Arelin's son?"

"You're looking at him," said Ollena.

"Heaven's orbs!" said Jarrod.

Trevin scowled at Ollena. "Why didn't you tell me Flametender's words before?"

"For one thing, you didn't ask," said Ollena. "For another, naming is usually done when a baby is born. It affirms the child's heritage and proclaims her destiny."

"Or his." Jarrod studied Trevin.

"Or his." Ollena grinned. "I thought if I said it was a baby's naming, a certain comain would be insulted."

Trevin bit his lip. Insulting. Demeaning. Exactly what he was on the verge of saying. He swallowed his words.

Ollena peeked into the room at the end of the hall, then leaned over the rail. "Livia's still awake. Why don't you ask her about naming? She's done it with her own children."

Trevin headed upstairs. Ollena opened Livia's door and waved him in.

Perched on a low stool, Livia was combing her dusky hair by the light of an oil lamp. The upper curve of her wings was visible beneath her loosely wrapped cloak.

Trevin hesitated, feeling like an intruder.

Livia gave him a motherly smile. "I'm afraid the only seat left is on the floor."

"I'll not keep you long," said Trevin, taking the offered seat. "When your children were born, did you have a naming for them?"

"Two at once." Livia stopped combing and stared into the shadows of the room as if she were looking into another time.

"Sergai and Serai," said Trevin.

Livia began combing again. "All Angelaeon have namings for their children. Why do you ask?"

"Ollena knows the old tongue. She said Flametender's words for me were a naming: Seed of wind, heir of fire, born to free. I hoped you might know its meaning."

Livia worked at a tangle. "When the Wisdom Tree was destroyed, and the stairway to heaven with it, angels trapped in this world were separated from friends and family in Avellan."

"So angels have children even outside our world?"

"The process is a bit different, because in our pure form, we are light. We call it melding. It's—"

"I'm sure Jarrod could tell me." Trevin shifted, uneasy.

Livia smiled slyly. "I'm more familiar with melding than he is. As I was saying, in the heavens melding is a complete intermingling of one angel's essence with another, a combining of light, of colors, of our deepest selves. Light begets light."

Trevin nodded, his face warm. "You then have a naming for your children."

"That ritual began with those of us trapped here. We wanted our children to know their ancestry and have a vision for their destiny as Angelaeon. So we speak a naming over them at birth and repeat it on their naming day each year, though we don't usually speak it in the old tongue. Your naming is quite short. Some are much longer."

"Seed of wind, heir of fire, born to free," mused Trevin.

"Windweaver and Flametender graced you with their own heritage," said Livia. "And they foretold your destiny—born to free."

"Free what? Who? How?"

Livia shrugged. "Destiny is a matter of the future."

"Then what good is it to know your destiny?"

Livia's eyebrows rose. "It's a great good. You measure decisions by your destiny. When you know your destiny is to free, you ask, in every situation, which decision will lead to freedom."

"What will lead to freedom?" Trevin asked as he rose. "That's a simple way to make decisions."

"Simple is not the same as easy," said Livia. "And you should know that a naming is not carved in granite. The named are free to accept or reject it."

"So angels have choice too. Even in Avellan?"

"Even in Avellan."

"How do I accept the naming?"

"You live it. Or not." Livia began tying her hair back.

Trevin bade her good night and stepped into the hallway, where Ollena was still stationed. "I know," he said. "You heard."

She smiled sheepishly. "I can't help it."

Trevin leaned on the rail, staring at the glow of the lamp on the hearth below. If the named were free to accept or reject it, what about those who spoke the naming? Windweaver and Flametender didn't really know him. What if they discovered they had made a mistake? Could they later renounce the named?

CHAPTER 20

Before dawn touched the sky the next morning, Trevin strode to the stables, his mind on another stable and another dawn. It seemed a lifetime ago that he had last seen Melaia. He drew the harp pendant from his tunic. With its mate it formed a heart, and for him that heart represented a promise. If his destiny was to free, he would free Melaia to keep her vow.

Trevin sensed Ollena and slipped the pendant back under his tunic.

"Early, hmm?" She scooped feed into a leather bucket.

Pym walked in bleary eyed, and before long the rest of the group gathered. They were among the first to leave Navia when the gates opened.

The farther south they traveled, the fewer landgashes they found until at last they left the rifts behind them. On their second day of travel, they encountered the sultry sea air, and by late afternoon they reached the tall grass and marsh meadows that signaled the approach to Qanreef.

Trevin craned his neck, watching for the citadel of Alta-Qan to come into view. At last he saw it rise from the horizon. He knew Melaia would soon be taking her evening meal. Alone? With the king and his court? He hoped she was not alone with Varic.

As they neared the white stone walls of the city, Trevin's company once again encircled him. Jarrod took Sorabus's place as spokesman, ready to escort the accused murderer into the city if necessary.

Trevin pulled up his hood, his heart in his throat. She was near. So near.

The gate guards turned out to be Angelaeon and had sensed their approach. One hailed Jarrod as a friend.

"Tarzius!" Jarrod clasped the guard's hand. "I sense others of us here."

"Six hither and yon on the walls," said Tarzius.

"I'll be at the temple," said Jarrod. "Should I expect Angelaeon at the palace?"

"Only two or three." Tarzius waved them in. "We've had no trouble."

No trouble, Trevin thought as Jarrod led them through the gates. Trouble was no doubt coiled in the palace, waiting to strike.

They guided their mounts down roads lined with whitewashed clay houses shadowed in the lowering sun. Ahead, the sea lapped at the wharves, its waves glimmering in the last golden rays of daylight. Trevin eyed it all, but his gaze kept returning to the palace.

He rode up beside Jarrod. "Do we stay at the temple tonight?"

"The Full Sail will be safer," said Jarrod, "until we determine the mood at court."

"Lead on," said Trevin.

Jarrod headed toward the wharves. Trevin wanted to ride straight to Alta-Qan, but the Full Sail would be more hidden and would afford the protection of the angel Paullus. And Cilla, Paullus's new wife, would know the latest news from the palace, which Trevin was eager to hear.

The heights of the mountainous sea clouds caught the last rays of the sun as the travelers dismounted in front of the Full Sail. Pym and Catellus led the horses to the stable while Trevin, shouldering the pack that held the harp, trudged behind Ollena, Jarrod, and Livia into the tavern. They seated themselves at an empty table, and Trevin set the pack at his feet.

Cilla bustled in from the back room, a buxom woman with a head of brown curls and the aura of angelic yellow. She was laden with mugs, which she served to sailors across the room. Trevin could tell Cilla sensed her angel guests, for she glanced their way as the rowdy sailors teased her.

When she had plopped down the last mug, she turned to Trevin's table, asking, "Drinks, dinner, or both?"

"Both, Cilla." Trevin grinned. "And rooms for the night if you have any."

Cilla's hands flew to her cheeks. "Trevin! Jarrod! And Livia! I took you for vagabond angels!"

"Most likely we look the part," said Jarrod.

"Tired and hungry." Cilla wiped her hands on her apron. "Just you rest. I'll fetch out a feast." She hurried through the back door, calling, "Paullus! Paullus!"

Trevin sensed the angel's presence stirring. A moment later burly Paullus burst from the back room and strode across the tavern. "Welcome!" he boomed. His shirt lay open halfway to his waist, making it hard to tell where his beard left off and his dark, curly chest hair began. Trevin and Jarrod stood to meet him and were engulfed in his arms, a greeting Trevin ranked alongside being hugged by a bear.

Paullus bowed to Livia, then drew back and eyed Ollena. "You're Angel-aeon too."

By the time Trevin introduced Ollena, Cilla was back with full mugs of ale. As soon as Pym and Catellus joined them, the first serving of a peppered fish stew and brown bread appeared.

"The bard Caepio is at the palace tonight," said Cilla, setting out honey for the bread. "He's there most nights now, furnishing music for the king's parties."

"An excellent performer," said Paullus. "Deserving of a royal audience."

"Parties," Trevin grumbled, picturing Melaia dancing with Varic. He squeezed his bread so tight a chunk crumbled into his stew.

"The king's dancing now, is he?" asked Pym.

"I hear his music is either to celebrate his joys or soothe his woes, depending on his mood," said Cilla.

Trevin dipped the rest of his bread into the thick, dark honey, the color of Melaia's hair. "And what is his mood today?"

"A bit woeful now that Lady Jayde is off visiting her homeland," said Cilla. "I imagine when she returns, he'll feel like celebrating again."

"The king can choose any woman he wants," said Trevin. "Why Lady Jayde?"

Cilla tapped her chin thoughtfully. "She's youthful. A raven-haired beauty. Full of energy. Flirtsome. I suspect she knows how to keep the king's mind off his worries."

"Do you hear talk of a wedding?" asked Trevin.

"Oh, there's talk aplenty," said Cilla. "Qanreef's rolling in rumors."

"Some say there'll be a double wedding," said Paullus, scratching his hairy chest.

"So Melaia's wedding hasn't happened yet?" asked Trevin.

"Not unless they've done it on the sly, which I doubt," said Cilla. "If I know the king, he'll make a grand time of it. The whole town will be decked

out. But I doubt the princess will wed until Lady Jayde returns from her trip."
She turned to Pym. "Are you still looking for comains?"

"Have you heard news of them?" asked Pym.

"Could be a dead-end tale," said Cilla, "but I overheard a bunch of wharf
hands trying to outbrag each other about the most famous person they'd
ever seen. One claimed he'd seen all the comains and their armsmen traveling toward Alta-Qan, one at a time over the span of a fortnight." She headed
to the back room.

Trevin turned to Catellus. "That would match your story."

"Maybe we've found the shaft of the mine," said Catellus.

"We should examine shipping records," said Pym. "Comains and armsmen would fetch a fair price as slaves in the south islands."

Catellus's brow furrowed as he turned back to his stew.

Cilla set out a dish of dried fruit—dates, plums, and apricots. Trevin mopped the last of his peppered fish with another piece of bread, popped it into his
mouth, and washed it down with ale. Then he snatched up an apricot.

"I'm going for some fresh air," he said. "Would you watch my pack,
Ollena?"

She drew the pack next to her. "Stay close, hmm?"

Trevin palmed the apricot and wove his way out of the tavern. He crossed
the torchlit street to a tethering post where he could get a better view of Alta-
Qan. Atop the chalk bluff to the east, the palace rose like a dark hulk out of a
sea speckled with moonlight.

Trevin had heard what he wanted to hear. Melaia hadn't married Varic.
There was still time. But how much? Turning the apricot over and over in his
hand, he paced one street nearer the palace, his eyes on the towers. Her room
would be in the rear, impossible to see from this vantage point. Up another
street he strolled, then another and another until he found himself across from
the main gate to Alta-Qan, which stood open.

Well-dressed couples ambled out of the gate into the balmy night. Arm in
arm they meandered down the hill toward the sea walk along the coast.

Trevin sensed a silver light. Melaia. And Serai, apple green.

Out of the gates strode a circle of guards surrounding Melaia's eunuchs,
Serai, and Melaia arm in arm with Varic. The snake smiled, laughed, leaned
over and whispered in her ear. She returned his smile with hers.

Trevin shrank back into the shadows, squeezing the apricot in his fist, barely aware of the sticky flesh oozing through his fingers.

Then Melaia glanced his direction, her eyes scanning the street, but her group turned and followed the other couples down the hill.

Trevin knew she had sensed him. He told himself to leave. Now. It would be torture to follow.

But he couldn't pull away. From where he stood, he could see the first couples heading for a dock where a high-prowed boat waited. Caepio and his musicians stood at one end of the boat, playing their music into the night air.

Trevin retraced his steps to a side street and sprinted toward the coast, taking to the shadows again when he neared the dock. Couples boarded the boat, settling into place along the sides of the vessel. He crept around the dock house and crouched among the rushes, near enough to pick the pouch of the man who loitered there, murmuring to his lady.

Melaia's group halted a stone's throw from the dock, waiting for everyone else to board. Then they stepped up to the dock as well.

"Ow!" cried Melaia. She darted away from Varic and for a moment knelt outside the perimeter of guards. "A stone in my sandal," she said, looking in Trevin's direction.

Then her guards were around her. When she rose, she tossed the stone toward Trevin, and her group made their way to the boat. Trevin strained to see Melaia, but she was gone.

As the oars drew the vessel into the bay, Serai appeared at the side of the boat and scanned the shore. Trevin stepped into the moonlight long enough to give her a chance to see him.

Then he crouched, wiped his sticky hand across a patch of grass, and began his search for the stone at the side of the road. After a moment he saw a glint of moonlight among the pebbles. At first he thought it might be a coin, but when he picked it up, he saw a small ruby heart.

He looked out to sea. The oars had stopped, and the boat bobbed on the gentle waves, the music floating toward shore. He would give anything to be with Melaia in the moonlight on the waves tonight. But he held hope in his hand. She would wait. And he would make sure she didn't have to wait long.

∽☙∾

On Trevin's return to the Full Sail, he found Paullus out front, a pipe of pence-leaf between his teeth.

Paullus exhaled a wisp of sweet-scented smoke. "It's good to be away from the heat and noise of the tavern."

"Did Ollena send you out to wait for me?" asked Trevin.

"She followed you." Paullus nodded toward Alta-Qan.

Trevin hissed. He hadn't sensed her, no doubt because his attention had been focused elsewhere. But now he felt her approach. He crossed the street and leaned casually against the tethering post.

"Nice night for a stroll, hmm?" said Ollena as she passed. "Love this sea air." She nodded to Paullus and stepped into the tavern.

Paullus ambled over to Trevin and gazed into the sky. "It's my habit to come outdoors this time of evening and watch the stars. I try to remember how it felt to cross the stairway. My body's so earthbound now, I wonder if walking the lightbridge will feel like trying to get my sea legs."

"Or your sky legs," said Trevin.

Paullus coughed a deep laugh. "Aye, sky legs. That's what I'll need."

Trevin fingered the ruby heart he had slipped into his waist sash. "Do you know the coastline?"

"That I do. Sailed it for many a year before I opened the tavern."

"How long does it take to reach the Dregmoors by horse?"

Paullus eyed him. "Two days along the coast to Tigerre, the fortress at the mouth of the Davernon."

"And to cross into the Dregmoors?"

Paullus raised his eyebrows. "With your company? You'd never get in. Malevolents guard the border. They'd sense your angel friends crossing the river and run them through before they could set foot on the ground."

"No angels. Just me."

"You might get in, but it'll be a gamble getting out alive."

"My wager."

Paullus looked out to sea. "In that case you have choices. North of Tigerre there's a ferryman who can take you across the Davernon. That's one way. Another way is by boat, but any sailor worth trusting will take warning from the fire caves and stay away from the treacherous shoreline. It takes another day sailing east to find good harbor."

"Fire caves. That's a strange name."

"At night the Dregmoorians keep fires burning in the mouths of the caves to warn seamen of rocks and shoals." Paullus puffed on his pipe. "Superstition of late says there's another warning as well, a sound they call the Song of the Dead. It's said shipwrecked souls play the tune to keep others from the same fate."

Trevin's heartbeat quickened. "What kind of music?"

"I've never heard it myself, but one sailor described it as a lonesome, moansome lyre."

Or harp, thought Trevin. Two days to Tigerre, one to cross the Davernon and reach the fire caves. If the Song of the Dead came from the third harp, with quick, careful work he might return within a week. He looked east and smiled. Dwin wasn't the only one who could steal into the Dregmoors.

But first, Arelin's son, seed of wind and heir of fire, would depose a prince and clear his own name.

⌇⌇⌇

The next morning from his second-floor window at the inn, Trevin watched Livia and Jarrod eagerly walk their horses toward Alta-Qan while he turned the ruby heart over and over in his palm. He hated letting Jarrod and Livia go without him, but he couldn't risk running into Varic. Nor could Catellus, whose testimony about the forged scrolls was crucial. His son's life would be forfeit if Varic or Fornian spied him.

Trevin needed a private meeting with King Laetham, and Livia was going to arrange it. She had promised to let him know when and where it would take place. According to their plan, Jarrod would then bring two priests' robes with hoods to Catellus and Trevin, and all three would walk through the palace gates together.

Trevin slipped the heart back into his waist sash, paced his room, sharpened his sword, then went down the hall to play dice with Catellus and Pym in their room.

Near midday, running footsteps echoed in the hallway. Trevin felt Livia's clear blue presence and met her at the doorway.

"Varic's on his way," she panted. "I've alerted Paullus and Cilla. They're going to try to stall him when he arrives."

"How did he know I was here?" asked Trevin.

"Someone saw you. I'll tell you what I know as we go to the wharves."

"The wharves?" asked Catellus.

"Jarrod is booking passage for the four of you. It's the only way to leave the city. Varic has lookouts for you at every gate."

Trevin gaped at her. "Where—"

"We can talk on the way." Livia grabbed his arm and tugged him toward his room.

Trevin tugged back. "I can't leave the city. I have to clear my name."

"You can't clear your name dangling from a rope."

"King Laetham wouldn't go that far."

"King Laetham won't know until it's too late." Livia firmly drew him into his room and began stuffing his scattered belongings into his pack. "Varic has at least a dozen guards with him, several of them malevolents. They're talking of a hanging."

Ollena appeared in the doorway, her journey bags in hand.

Trevin buckled on his sword belt and took over Livia's frantic efforts to tie his pack. He made sure the harp was securely covered, then handed it to her. "Take the harp to the temple. Lock it away, and don't let anyone play it."

Pym and Catellus were already heading downstairs when Trevin reached the landing. He and Livia followed, Ollena behind them. As they slipped out the rear door of the Full Sail, the thud of horse hoofs and the calls of Varic's men resounded over the clamor of carts and laborers. Trevin sensed the oily, impure color of the malevolents and hoped the strength of Paullus's color and Cilla's would mask the Angelaeon in his own group until they could gain distance.

They sprinted east down a back road, then cut south toward the wharves, where they mingled with sailors, merchants, and fishmongers.

Livia craned her neck to see around the hulking dockworkers. "Keep an eye out for Jarrod," she said.

Trevin sidled up to her. "What about meeting with King Laetham? While Varic hunts us all over the city, we could be safely inside the palace, presenting our evidence against the jackal."

"I pushed for a private audience," said Livia, "but the king is in one of his downswings, seeing no one for a few days." She pointed to a dock where Jarrod stood beside a ship being loaded with casks and trunks.

Jarrod nodded when he saw them but kept scanning the crowds.

Gulls screeched. Waves slapped against the pilings. Trevin motioned to the others. Ollena crowded his elbow, and they all gathered around Jarrod. Except Pym.

Pym stepped back, pale and frowning. "I don't want to offend, but I'm not one for the sea. I'll go with you if you insist, Main Trevin, but I'll not be of use until we've put ashore somewhere."

"He's right to stay," said Catellus. "He's in no danger here. Pym can move freely around the city and keep searching for the comains."

"That I will," said Pym. "That I surely will."

"Agreed," said Trevin. "And help Livia and Jarrod protect Melaia."

"Done," said Pym, the color returning to his face.

Jarrod palmed the hilt of his dagger, alert to the swarm of activity around them. "I suggest you board as soon as possible," he said. "Varic will surely have the wharves searched."

Pym's words echoed in Trevin's head. *Until we've put ashore somewhere.* "Where is this vessel going?" he asked.

"To the fortress of Tigerre at the mouth of the Davernon," said Jarrod. "Across the river from the Dregmoors."

Trevin narrowed his eyes. "Did you talk with Paullus last night?"

Jarrod shrugged.

"They're here," said Ollena.

Trevin spotted two riders slowly making their way down the wharf road, eying the bustle around them.

Livia and Jarrod saw them too. They nodded farewell and went in separate directions, leaving Pym to see off his comain.

"Wait!" Trevin called after them. "When do we return?"

But neither angel heard.

"Probably when you've found a third harp," said Ollena, giving him a nudge.

Trevin shouldered his pack and followed her on board.

CHAPTER 21

Trevin turned his face to the wind and gripped the bulwarks, watching for the coastline to appear in the distance through the morning fog. It was their second day at sea, and he was trying to get the sea legs Paullus longed for. As wind whistled through the rigging, Trevin cocked his head, hoping to hear from Windweaver. But if the Archon was nearby, he wasn't speaking.

Ollena stepped up and handed him a round of bread.

"Was I right to leave Qanreef?" he asked. "Wouldn't it have been better to stand and fight?"

"Often the best way to win is not to fight at all," said Ollena. "You trusted Jarrod and Livia. I wouldn't say your trust was misplaced."

Trevin tore off a hunk of bread. Jarrod and Livia wanted the harps above all. Everything else was expendable. He had heard them say so the previous fall when they tried to get Melaia to forget that her father was king. They didn't care who the king was.

"A conniving schemer," muttered Trevin. "That's what Jarrod is."

"Oh?" Ollena brushed windblown strands of hair from her face.

"He intentionally sent me within spitting distance of the Dregmoors, knowing full well that I would be tempted to search for the last harp." Trevin chewed on the dry barley bread. Searching for the harp wasn't the problem. That had been his plan all along. He had just hoped to clear his name first and spend some time with Melaia. He felt like Jarrod had forced him to reverse his priorities.

"Doesn't Princess Melaia want all three harps?" said Ollena.

Trevin sighed. Although his first allegiance was to Melaia, her first allegiance was to the harps. There was no way around it. He glanced sideways at Ollena. "You're in on this, aren't you?"

"I *am* Angelaeon." Her face brightened, and she pointed at the fog. "Seaspinner."

Trevin squinted at the haze drifting lazily over the waves. At one spot it swirled and a figure emerged, pale with short white hair. She danced across the breakers and sank back into the fog. "Is that a good omen?" he asked.

"It means the Archon is doing her job." Ollena strolled on down the deck.

Trevin stared at the thinning fog, hoping to glimpse Seaspinner once more, but she had vanished.

At midday the dark gray cliffs of the Dregmoors appeared on the horizon. Draks grew more numerous as well, but the spy-birds kept their distance. Trevin tried to pick out a small one that might be Peron, but he saw several smaller draks and was never certain Peron flew among them.

At sunset they disembarked at the fortress of Tigerre, where Angelaeon presence was strong. Ollena discovered she knew the commander, a runty, stout angel named Rys, who appeared to have had his nose broken more than once. Rys gladly provided them with ample food and comfortable quarters for the night.

After everyone retired, Trevin and Catellus lit an oil lamp in the room they shared and bent over a rude map of the Dregmoors that Rys had loaned them. Trevin rubbed at the dull ache that had lodged in his right hand.

Catellus ran a finger north along the line that marked the Davernon River and tapped a spot. "Here's where Rys says we'll find the ferry."

"Nearer than I thought," said Trevin. "We'll leave the horses with Ollena."

"No you won't." Ollena stood in the doorway, her hands on her hips.

Trevin rolled his eyes. Every time he concentrated his attention on one issue, he missed the presence of angels. He couldn't afford such a lapse in the Dregmoors. "I need stealth," he said. "My instincts say it's best for you to wait for us here. You'll keep my sword and shield. Dagger and knife will serve me better in the caves."

"Leave your sword and shield here if you want." Ollena stepped into the room. "But I'm going with you."

"No you're not," said Trevin.

Catellus sat back and folded his arms, watching them.

Ollena scanned the map. "It's my duty to go with you, Main Trevin."

"Your duty is to protect me. If you go into the Dregmoors, every malevolent within sensing distance will be drawn our way. I value your skills and would welcome your company, but I cannot compromise my task."

Ollena bit her lip, her eyes on the map.

Trevin could see she was trying to think of a way around his reasoning. "Do you think malevolent guards can sense you from across the river?" he asked.

"Possibly."

"I want you to head north ahead of Catellus and me. Travel along the riverbank well past the ferry. Malevolents should sense you and be drawn upriver, away from us."

Ollena narrowed her eyes. "If anything happens to you, Queen Ambria will hang me."

Trevin chuckled. "I happen to know that only an angel or an immortal can kill an angel. Queen Ambria is very human."

"She'll find an angel to do the job for her, hmm?"

"I can't risk taking you."

Ollena scowled. "I'll patrol the riverbank."

"The Camrithian side."

Ollena exhaled slowly. "All right. The Camrithian side."

⤳❧⤳

After giving Ollena an hour to travel north the next morning, Trevin and Catellus trekked upriver. The recommended ferryman, a long-legged fellow, was touted as the only person with the skills to successfully cross the current. He seemed glad for the business, though his price was high. Trevin was grateful to have more than enough in King Kedemeth's pouch to pay for their passage. His right hand throbbed, so he used his left to select coins from the purse.

"Keep a lookout on the cliff face across the way," said the ferryman as he poled them into the swift current. "The Cliffs of Balemourne. A white-robed creature called the Ibex walks the cliffs on occasion. Not the top of the cliffs, mind you—the face of the cliffs. I've not seen the Ibex lately, so it's high time for her to show up again."

"Her?" asked Trevin.

"Rumor says it's a woman, but how a woman or a man could scale those cliffs, I've no notion. I say she's a specter sent to scare strangers like yourself from entering the land."

Trevin scanned the dark gray cliffs. Caves pocked the stone wall, resembling grotesque eyes and mouths. Varic's land.

A chill crawled along Trevin's spine. Melaia would never enter the Dregmoors. Not if he could help it.

Once they reached the rocky eastern bank of the Davernon, Trevin and Catellus followed the river south toward the sea. The ground was uneven and strewn with rocks, and more than once Trevin wished he had not left his staff with Ollena.

When they came within sight of the sea, they paused to rest beneath an outcropping of stone. Trevin studied the fortress of Tigerre, squat and solid on the far bank of the river. He had described Dwin to Rys, but the commander had not seen him. Even so, Dwin may have stood at this very spot and looked west.

"Drak droppings!" said Catellus. "I thought we'd lost the spy-birds, but they're everywhere."

Trevin gulped water from his flask and scanned the sky. Dozens of draks rode the wind currents, circling out over the sea, skimming the sparkling waves. One dived and came out with a fish, and the others chased it inland.

"I don't think they're following us," said Trevin.

Catellus pointed overhead. "What about that one?"

Trevin shaded his eyes. A lone drak. Small. He wondered if the salted beef in his pack would tempt the bird to his hand. If it came, how would he know it was Peron? Melaia could identify Peron by her hands, but he had never met the girl, never seen her hands.

The small drak banked in a high curve, then soared north along the cliffs alone. "She's homing," Trevin murmured.

"You think it's the little girl?"

"I want to think so."

"Who does she home to?"

"I wish I knew."

Trevin watched the drak duck through an arch in the rock and disappear. He opened and closed his right hand, trying to work out the pain. Then he headed across the scree, leading Catellus east along the ragged coast at the foot of the cliffs.

Boulders jagged out of the sea, treacherous islands in the crashing waves. Trevin edged as close to the cliffs as he could, pitying sailors who didn't heed the warning watch fires. He squinted up at the coastal caves. Eight, nine, maybe more. He doubted that they were guarded. Only the most determined intruder would climb these cliffs. Or a comain raised by a stonecutter and trained to climb. He was eager to nose around up there.

He scanned the rock face, searching for a path up the cliff. Over the swash of the sea and the rush of the wind, he heard a faint strain of music. He turned to Catellus. "Hear that?"

Catellus cocked his head. "The Song of the Dead?"

"Hope for the living." Trevin grinned. "That's the harp." He eyed the caves, hoping to glimpse the harp or at least discern which cave the melody came from. The caves gaped like eye sockets staring blindly out to sea.

Overhead, drifting clouds played with the sunlight, constantly shifting shadows across the cliff. In a moment's creep of light, a steep path appeared. Trevin clambered over the scree to reach it before shadows obscured it again.

"Look above," Catellus called.

The small drak had returned. Flying a zigzag course, it crossed in front of every cave. Trevin huffed. Peron or not, she was a distraction.

"Help me listen for the direction of the music," he said, climbing toward the lowest cave. He heard Catellus following.

Halfway there Trevin noticed the small drak dart from a ledge into a narrow crevice at the same level but some distance away. She flew out and crossed to the ledge again. Pausing to let Catellus catch up, Trevin watched the bird's back-and-forth flight between crevice and ledge.

Catellus reached Trevin and panted, "Sun's lowering. I'd rather not be clinging to this wall through the night. On the other hand, I don't want to be in a fire cave when the keepers come to light their blazes."

"Let's try the place the drak keeps flying into," said Trevin.

"That crevice? I doubt I can squeeze in. Besides, I'm not favorable to trusting a drak, even if she is your friend's friend. She's likely leading us into a trap."

The drak ruffled her wings as she eyed them from the ledge, which lay between them and the crevice.

"We'll have to risk it," said Trevin. "We can't search every cave before nightfall."

As he headed for the ledge, the drak flew west, out of sight. But the strain of music came clear now, the same sound he had heard from the trees in Eldarra.

He pulled himself to the ledge where the drak had rested. It was only a handbreadth wide, but where it met the cliff face, a cool draft flowed from a horizontal crack, carrying the hum.

Renewed energy surged through Trevin's tired muscles. He was close. Very close. If he were a beetle, he'd crawl straight in. He eyed the vertical crevice to his right a stone's throw away. Whether or not it was large enough to enter, he couldn't tell. He eased toward it across the face of the cliff.

The footing proved tricky. Trevin heard Catellus puffing behind him and turned to advise him to take his time, but before Trevin could speak, the rock beneath Catellus's foot crumbled. Shards skittered down the cliff.

Trevin grabbed Catellus's wrist and strained to hold him steady until, panting and hugging the mountainside, Catellus found a secure foothold.

Catellus grimaced and nodded.

Trevin eased himself to the crevice. Once he reached the narrow opening, he edged through it and sighed with relief when it opened onto a wide space.

Catellus hissed as he squeezed into the darkness behind Trevin. "You still here?" he murmured.

"Right beside you."

"I can't see a blasted thing."

"We're in a cave large enough to stable a horse." Trevin pointed deeper into the cave where the rock became striated. "It narrows into a tunnel that curves about five paces back."

Catellus eased to the floor and gingerly touched his right ankle. "I'm no good for going farther. That misstep twisted my foot."

"You're lucky you didn't plunge off the cliff into the waves," said Trevin. "And we're lucky the drak led us to an empty cave for the night."

"Or she's trapped us. We don't know the cave's empty farther in. Even if it is, we don't know it'll stay that way."

Trevin eyed the tunnel. He did sense something—or someone. Not Angelaeon. Not malevolent. Just—he frowned—life. He sensed life.

He sat down by Catellus and dug a couple of dried beef strips out of his waist pack. Catellus handed him some flatbread, and they chewed their salty supper in silence, listening to the hum of the harp.

⌒⌘⌒

During the night Trevin awoke with Catellus's hand across his mouth. "Your sleep is fitful," murmured Catellus. "You've been muttering, nigh onto crying out."

Trevin sat up, sweating, trembling, his aching hand drawn to his chest. His terror-dream had returned.

He took over the watch and centered his thoughts on Melaia—her smile, the way he sensed her silvery presence. As the light of dawn seeped into the mouth of the crevice, he whispered to her, "Wait for me. A few more days. Wait for me."

"Shades!" Catellus grabbed Trevin's arm and pointed at the walls. What Trevin had taken as striations in the rock were instead faded drawings, figures lining the cave wall. "It puts me in mind of Varic's art," said Catellus.

"Did you have to remind me of him?" Trevin grumbled. He studied the crowd. Men, women, sylvans, dwarfs. "Look at their clothes," he said. "Some are in skins; others are robed shoulder to toe."

"Robes were the style two hundred years ago during the Angel Wars." Catellus broke off a hunk of flatbread and handed half to Trevin. "These watchers knot my stomach."

The drawings made Trevin uneasy too. Maybe it was the way Catellus described them as watchers. He felt as if they knew he was present, as if their thoughts lay only a whisper beyond his hearing.

"How is your ankle?" Trevin asked.

"Swollen big as a melon." Catellus winced as he pulled back the cloak he had used as a blanket. "I'll be no good for nosing around in tunnels today. I'd be lying to tell you otherwise."

Trevin secured his knife and dagger. "Keep watch with these ancients, then. I'll be back with the harp."

"Try for some rope too. You may have to string me down the mountainside."

Trevin peered into the tunnel. Figures lined the walls as far as he could see. "If I don't return by tomorrow's dawn, try to get back to Tigerre," he said. "I'll meet you there." He headed toward the curve of the tunnel. He missed the reassuring sound of Catellus behind him, but he could move more quickly without the bulky mountain man.

Trevin intended to follow the hum of the harp, but it faded the farther he went, until finally he could not hear it at all. Instead, he felt as if a noisy crowd pressed in around him. He had never sensed such a thing before and attributed it to the cave paintings. They were flat, still, and silent but so realistic that he felt they could step out to join him at any moment. Whoever painted them had done a perfect job. He shivered. No wonder he felt as if their thoughts floated around him.

Ahead, the tunnel turned right. He paused. The music had come from the left. Unless he was turned around. He brushed aside the fleeting thought of turning back. He was not ready to give up on this path.

As Trevin followed the tunnel to the right, a faint light appeared ahead of him. After a few more paces, he saw that the light came from a larger cave.

Once again he heard the harp. He also sensed the presence of malevolents and smelled the sharp stench of gash. He rubbed his aching hand and crept forward, intent on sensing the direction of the malevolents as well as the music.

The larger cave turned out to be massive. Trevin peered from the tunnel, feeling as if he were looking out a tower window at Redcliff. Half the palace would fit in the cavern, towers included. Above him the rock walls rose to a high stone ceiling. The opposite wall held more caves. Below, the wall dropped to a floor that held row upon row of stone statues.

The ghostly snatch of a memory flitted through Trevin's mind, vanishing before he could catch it. He drew his aching hand to his chest and steadied his breathing. A shaft of sunlight fell from a break in the ceiling, slanting through the cavern and illuminating a figure dressed in flowing white striding across the wall. "The Ibex," whispered Trevin. He knew she was crossing a ledge, but she appeared to be walking on air a dizzying distance above the cavern floor. He picked out two caves above her, one to the left, one to the right, where he was fairly certain malevolents stood.

The hum of the harp caught him again, drifting from above. He scanned the rock at each side of his tunnel and realized that narrow stairs had been cut into the wall, leading from one level of caves to another.

He waited until the Ibex disappeared into a cave on the opposite wall and the aura of malevolents receded. The shaft of sunlight was vertical now. He breathed easier and sidled out of his tunnel.

The stairs on the wall had no railing, nothing to shield a misstep. Trevin wiped the sweat from his eyebrows and, avoiding a glance across or down into the open air of the cavern, he edged up step by step. Twice the stairs angled off in two different directions, toward different caves. Each time, he listened for the harp and followed the sound.

At last he reached the mouth of a tunnel where the hum of the harp seemed to originate. He slipped inside.

From where Trevin crouched, he could tell that the low-ceilinged tunnel ran straight, sloped gradually upward, and opened onto a chamber at the far end. He could also see an elongated shadow across the far wall of the chamber. The shadow wavered, suggesting a person standing before a flame. A hearth fire? A lantern? He sensed no malevolents, so he slipped out his dagger and crept closer.

A second shadow appeared, slanting across a gray marbled column. A few paces more brought a second column into view near the first, and between them a pedestal. Holding a kyparis harp. All was quiet except for its hum.

Trevin's right hand ached as he clenched his dagger, but his blood coursed like thunderlight through his veins. If the shadows were two guards, they were not malevolents. He could take down two.

He eased forward and spied the narrow rift he had seen from the cliff wall. It jagged high across the back wall of the cave, drawing a draft of air across the harp strings and carrying the melody into the outside world.

He also noticed a third shadow, this one across the floor. Three guards?

Pressing his back to the wall of the tunnel, Trevin inched ahead, then caught his breath. Not three guards, but five. All made of rock.

One drew him like a lodestone. He couldn't turn his eyes from its face.

"Melaia?" he whispered, chilled to the bone. The sight of the statue lured him into the chamber. He stood rooted before her, his arms limp at his side.

"It's Dreia." The man's voice sounded warm and weary.

Trevin spun on his heel and came face to face with a young soldier. An old shepherd. A seated woman. A robed girl. All carved of stone.

Then from the shadows beyond the figures came the rattle of a chain. A flesh-and-blood man rose from a bench.

Trevin hardly breathed. This was the picture in Melaia's book: the figures, the flickering torch, the cave—and the man. Dark hair. Square jaw. Intense eyes.

Benasin, the immortal Second-born.

Trevin stepped back, aware of the dagger in his hand. The last time he had faced Benasin, Lord Rejius was murdering him.

Benasin narrowed his eyes. "You? Rejius's apprentice? From Redcliff?"

Trevin sheathed his dagger and rubbed at the pain in his hand. "I serve the Angelaeon now."

"In that case I suppose you'll say you're here for the harp." Benasin wove his way through the stone figures until the chain around his ankle pulled taut, leaving him in the midst of his motionless company. "Hand me the key to my chain. It's on the pedestal. Behind the harp."

Trevin turned to look for the key but was arrested again by the statue. "Dreia," he murmured. "Melaia's mother." His chest tightened. He had last seen Dreia alive, carrying a harp. He stepped back and cleared his throat. "Why are the statues here?"

"These are tombs," said Benasin. "Their spirits live imprisoned within them. My dear brother, Dandreij—or Rejius, as you call him—has taken it upon himself to enshrine in stone every person I love." Benasin pointed to the soldier. "My best friend and comrade in the Angel Wars." To the old shepherd. "A treasured mentor." To the seated woman and girl. "My wife and daughter. Rejius calls them my idols."

Trevin felt numb. "And Dreia?"

"She's here because I loved her."

Trevin squeezed his eyes closed. His breath came shallow. He wished he could rewrite the past. "And Jarrod is—"

"Silence!" Benasin hissed. "Everyone I love ends up here. I've learned to avoid making my relationships obvious." He clanked back to his bench and sat. "Those who wanted to live died. I who want to die must live for all time." He raised his eyebrows. "The key?"

Trevin eyed the stone pedestal. The key lay at the back as if someone had casually set it down. He took it to Benasin. "Why isn't the key hidden?"

Benasin bent to the metal cuff around his ankle. "First, it's to taunt me—in sight but out of reach." One twist of the key, and his cuff clanked to the floor. Benasin massaged his ankle. "Second, my brother wants me to escape so he can start the hunt again. It's part of his game."

"I can get you out before he starts the hunt. The way is steep, but we can be in a safe place by nightfall." Trevin could hardly believe his luck. Not only would he bring Melaia a harp but also a treasured friend.

He dashed to the pedestal and grabbed the harp, but it resisted. A thin chain held it to the base. Easily broken. Trevin tugged on the harp, and the chain snapped.

A crack sounded within the columns. Before Trevin could move, a chain net dropped on him, pressing him to his knees.

Benasin tossed the key onto the bench. "I dare not trust you. For all I know my brother sent you to lure me into one of his deathtraps."

"I no longer serve Rejius." Trevin tried to raise his head, but the weight of the net held him down.

"Don't worry." Benasin swept up his brown cloak. "Rejius will find you and release you soon enough."

"Wait. I freed you. This is the way you thank me?"

Benasin slipped through a door in the far corner.

Trevin tried to move his arm. His hand. His foot. He couldn't. If this net was like Varic's, he would soon be fused to the ground, flat as the poppy on Melaia's chair. Flat as...

He groaned. Flat as the cave paintings. His throat knotted. They were real people, and he had felt their thoughts. By the time he was found, he would be painted to the floor, just as real and just as trapped.

Trevin felt the net growing hot, sucking at him, pressing him down. "Is this what you wanted, Jarrod?" he muttered. "Trade me for your father?" He crept his hand toward the edge of the net, then heard footsteps.

A serving maid carrying a tray stepped through the corner door. When she saw Benasin's unlocked chain, her eyes widened. Then she spied Trevin. She screamed, dropped the tray, and ran. Soup oozed across the floor and puddled around the feet of the seated woman.

Moments later Trevin sensed the approach of malevolents. Two men strode in, lean faced, dressed in leather vests and leggings. One had a heavy black beard and thick eyebrows. The other was fair faced and bore a red scar on his neck. Overlapping feathered wings etched their muscled arms. They raised the net and searched Trevin while he racked his mind for anything that might turn the situation to his favor.

"I served Lord Rejius in Camrithia." Trevin flexed his aching right hand.

The malevolents snatched his dagger and knife and the leather strap he had intended to use to fasten the harp to his back, which was now burning cold.

"I freed the Second-born for Lord Rejius so he can continue his eternal pursuit," said Trevin. "The immortals thrive on the chase."

The malevolents shoved Trevin to the bench and locked the metal cuff around his ankle.

Trevin stood. "I demand to see Lord Rejius."

"You'll see him when he's ready to see you," said the bearded one while the scarred malevolent replaced the key on the harp pedestal.

"I can be of use to him," Trevin called as they strode out.

He sighed. He had once used those words with Zastra, the queen mother at Redcliff, hoping she wouldn't throw him into the dungeon. It hadn't worked then either.

The pain in Trevin's hand became sharp and constant. He pressed his hand to his chest and paced the length of his chain from side to side, then toward the harp, then back to the bench.

He plopped down and eyed his stone companions. It was a wonder Benasin hadn't gone mad here. Maybe he had stayed sane because he was immortal.

How long would it take for a half human to lose his mind?

CHAPTER 22

T revin awoke screaming, sweating, and disoriented, at first thinking the stone figures were the image of his dreams multiplied. Then the chain around his ankle brought him back to reality.

To gain his bearings, he walked around. He passed the seated woman and confronted the soldier. "Have I been here two days, friend?" he asked the gray face. "Or three?"

He looked sideways at Dreia, three paces away. His chain wouldn't stretch that far, but he yearned to kneel at her feet, to somehow make amends. He rasped, "I'm sorry. I'm a fool, and I'm paying for it."

Trevin clanked back to the bench and reclined, rubbing his hand. "I guess a day or two doesn't matter to any of you," he murmured to the statues, "but it's been long enough for Catellus to give up on me and head back to the fortress at Tigerre. Though with a swollen ankle, he'll travel slowly." He imagined Ollena's reaction when she discovered her charge was missing. "May Catellus be strong enough to live through her wrath." He half smiled.

How long he could keep his spirits up, Trevin didn't know, but for now he refused to pity himself when his stone companions were much worse off. At least his chain allowed limited movement, while they stood frozen. They were free only in the motion of their thoughts, which he sensed as a constant flow of energy, almost a whisper, but without words, like the life he had sensed from the figures in the tunnels.

"The Dregmoors is one big trap," Trevin muttered.

The thought flow surged, then went silent.

Trevin sensed the approach of tainted light, oily, impure. He sat up, cradling his pained hand as the two malevolents strode in.

One stood by the door while the other unlocked Trevin's ankle cuff. Then they marched Trevin through hall after lanterned hall, each lined with flattened figures. The corridors grew wider and busier. Servants passed, silently going about their tasks. Trevin noticed that the women wore sandals decorated with small jewels like the ruby heart tucked in his waist sash.

The malevolents led Trevin down a flight of stone steps to a massive anteroom of black marble that reflected the torchlight. Guards swung open two tall, gilded doors.

"My lord," said the bearded malevolent. "The one you sent for."

"Grigor," came a deep, smooth voice that made Trevin's hair stand on end. "Bring him here."

Sweat beaded at Trevin's forehead as guilty memories crowded in. Spying, lying, cowing to the Firstborn's threats.

Grigor led Trevin into the center of a room studded with gems, then stepped back, leaving Trevin standing on a giant circular game board carved into the rock floor. Before him sat the immortal Firstborn, his gold-eyed gaze assessing his new guest.

A chill swept through Trevin. Lord Rejius had not fully regained his human body since Melaia had crushed his hawk form under her harp during the battle at Alta-Qan. Black feathers matted his head instead of hair. His nose curved, sharp and beak-like. Talons replaced his fingers.

Benasin had warned Rejius in the aerie that constant shape shifting would make him more hawk than human. Trevin had seen the Firstborn in both forms. This in-between state was hideous.

Hiding his disgust, Trevin bowed. "Lord Rejius. I offer you my services."

"Your services?" Lord Rejius stepped down from his gilded throne and circled Trevin, looking him up and down.

"Surely you remember me," said Trevin. "I brought you a kyparis harp."

"Then you fought me to deprive me of it again." Lord Rejius flicked Trevin's aching right hand with a talon.

Trevin clenched his jaw to keep from yelping.

"Deceit," hissed the hawkman. He turned to the door and yelled, "Orvis! Bring Stalia!"

The scarred malevolent swept out of the room.

Trevin rubbed his hand. Stalia, queen of the Dregmoors, Varic's mother.

Nothing good could come of her involvement. "Remember how I spied for you?" he told the hawkman. "I can do the same now. I've gained the trust of your enemies, but I serve you, the one who holds the greatest power." His gut burned with shame.

"The greatest power." Lord Rejius strutted, chuckling. "Yes, yes. Delicious power. My daughter must witness my power. Stalia. Oh, Stalia. Deceit and treachery." He tilted his head, studying Trevin. "I hope you enjoy games."

Trevin heard the door open behind him.

"My lord," a guard said, "Stalia has already left on her mission."

"That, I regret." Lord Rejius eyed Trevin. "I was going to invite her to play a game, with you as the pawn. And the prize." He motioned to a servant, who brought him a gold tray that held a die. "I suppose you will have to play in her place."

He strode around the game board, pointing to the sections. "Each has a symbol on it," he said, "depicting my successes: gash, the silver net, draks, idols, bloodletting, mines, leatherwings." He tossed the die to Trevin.

Trevin caught it in his sweaty palm. A cube. Dots on each side. One to six. "What are the rules?"

"You roll the die. From where you stand, you may choose any section as your first step. The die will tell you how many sections to move. The game ends when you throw a six. With a six you make no move; the section you stand in is your reward." Lord Rejius rubbed his palms together. "Begin."

Trevin could feel his pulse in his temples as he rolled the die. A four. He could work mines, perhaps survive bloodletting. The net he wanted to avoid. He started there so he could move away from it. But the game board was a circle. If play lasted long enough, he would face the net again.

He took his four steps: net, draks, idols, bloodletting.

Lord Rejius scooped up the die and rolled it between his palms. "This is not the real game, you know. The real game is played upground. You've been part of it for a long time. In your last move you released my brother, and he ensnared you. Delightful twist of the game."

"I thought you might be pleased," said Trevin.

Lord Rejius tossed Trevin the die. "Roll!"

The die landed with a three on top. Trevin stepped to gash.

Again Rejius snatched up the die. "Varic is part of the game too. He thinks I don't know who you are. I allow him to hold you as his valuable secret. He wants the throne, you see." He tossed the die to Trevin.

The next roll was a two. Trevin moved past the net and stopped on draks.

The hawkman picked up the die. "Stalia is also part of the game. Forever. Just like Benasin. I have Stalia in a double bind, for I suspect she's holding more than one secret from me. Yet I hold secrets from her as well." He tossed the die to Trevin.

Trevin rolled. A six.

Lord Rejius crowed.

"Draks!" Trevin grabbed at a glimmer of hope. "Let me prove my loyalty to you as a drak-keeper. I was good with the draks. Your talonmasters said as much. I was on my way to becoming a skilled talonmaster myself."

Lord Rejius folded his arms. "Plead for my forgiveness."

Trevin gritted his teeth and bowed his head. "Please forgive me, my lord."

"On your knees!" shouted Rejius.

Trevin knelt. His naming would mean nothing after this. "My lord, please forgive me."

"On your face, worm. Beg me. Beg me for mercy."

Trevin lay prostrate before the hawkman, burning with shame. Arelin's sword had lied. He was not a confident, wise man. He was a coward and a fool. "I beg you, my lord," he said. "I beg you for mercy. Please forgive me."

Lord Rejius grabbed Trevin's hair and yanked him to his knees. Trevin inhaled sharply, his eyes watering, and the hawkman swiped his talons across Trevin's forehead.

Trevin bit down on his lip. The scratches stung like fire, and he could feel blood trickle down his face, but he held himself steady. He was now in Lord Rejius's service, and the hawkman had no use for whiners.

"Beggars usually forfeit their right to choose in this game," said Lord Rejius. "Why should I treat you any differently?"

Because I don't want to die a stupid, worthless death, thought Trevin. But he said nothing.

"This could be part of our game." A cruel smile crept across Lord Rejius's face. "You want to work with draks? Come."

Trevin scrambled to his feet and followed the hawkman out the door, flanked by Grigor and Orvis. He tried to ignore the pain in his hand and the oozing blood on his forehead. At least if he was caring for draks, he would be free. Maybe he could find Peron.

They marched a confusion of corridors, then climbed two long flights of stone stairs that ended in a windowless room filled with the sharp odor of bird droppings. The only fresh air entered through two holes in the ceiling. Cages lined the walls, all of them occupied by fidgeting draks. Trevin could see fear in their eyes. The thought of cleaning their cages disgusted him, but he told himself the job would be temporary. He would escape at the first opportunity.

"Let's see if you still have your talent," said Lord Rejius. "Transfer one of the birds to another cage. Any cage you like."

Trevin eyed the draks and chose one that appeared calmer than the others. The human hands that served for its feet looked older, less likely to fight. He plucked a piece of raw meat from a bucket and slowly approached the bird. Speaking softly, he unlatched the cage and held out the meat in his aching right hand, ready to clamp the bird's legs with his left. The bird retreated, its gray eyes wary. Trevin leaned into the cage, gently coaxing it toward him.

As soon as he felt brawny hands on his back, he knew his mistake. He jerked around but too late. Both malevolents shoved him in with such force he smashed into the back of the cage. The old bird squawked and flapped in his face.

Trevin dived at the closing bars, but they latched and held. Orvis added a lock and smugly stepped back.

"What are you doing?" Trevin yelled. "I can help you. I can be of use."

"Of course you can," said Lord Rejius, "and you will. But I'm no fool, a fact my daughter must learn. I'm eager to see Stalia's face when I present her with a drak with *your* hands." He strutted out, followed by his malevolents.

The door shut, the bolt clanked, and the draks moaned. Trevin had never heard such a sound from draks. It curdled his stomach to think that perhaps only a week before, maybe even a day before, they had been fully human. When he had worked with draks at Redcliff, he had avoided asking how the transformation happened. Was it painful? How long before the drak-makers came for him? Who would he home to?

His hand flew to his harp pendant, then to the heart-shaped ruby tucked in his waist sash. Draks usually homed to someone who held a treasured possession of the soul within the bird's body. He drew out the pendant. Where could he hide it? Maybe he could toss it into the back corner of the room. Or even slide it under the straw in the cage.

But he couldn't bear to part with the pendant or the ruby heart. As he clutched the small harp, he realized he wanted to home to the treasures. It didn't matter who held them. They might be his only path to memories of Melaia.

The room dimmed as the sun angled away from the holes in the ceiling. All the old accusations pressed in. *Thief. Deceiver. Turncoat.* And the one crime he had kept at bay that now refused to be ignored.

He eyed the old drak. A bird was a poor confessor, but Trevin yearned to come completely clean before his voice turned into a squawk.

"I ask forgiveness." His throat tightened. "I was the spy who told Lord Rejius where Dreia's caravan was. It's my fault she was murdered."

The drak merely blinked at him and stayed aloof.

Chilled to the bone, Trevin rubbed his arms, leaned his head back against the bars, and tried not to retch at the stench around him. Soon he would receive his well-deserved punishment.

CHAPTER 23

Shortly after a shaft of sunlight shot through the holes in the roof of the aerie, the two malevolents dragged Trevin from the drak cage and bound his hands behind him. With Grigor leading, Orvis following, Trevin trudged down a dim corridor that ended in darkness.

He concentrated on the last steps his feet would take, tried to inhale a deep breath, one of the last his human chest would feel. By this time tomorrow how would he think? What would he remember? In Flauren, Pym had told him to stride to his death tall and confident. But this was worse than death. Sweat trickled into Trevin's eyes, and he blinked back the sting.

A maid carrying a basket on her head entered from a side hall in front of Grigor and swayed down the corridor ahead. Trevin thought of Melaia, and his throat thickened.

"Out of our way," snapped Grigor.

The maid picked up her pace but tripped, spilling her basket. Spindles and balls of yarn rolled across the floor.

As Grigor shoved the woman aside, a hooded figure in a brown cloak leaped from the side hall and plunged a dagger into him. At the same time, Trevin heard Orvis grunt. He turned to see the wide-eyed malevolent on the floor, blood pooling around him, his attacker gone.

The cloaked man helped the young woman stuff the yarn and spindles back into her basket. Then she scurried off one way as the man tugged Trevin the other direction.

They dashed through a maze of hallways. Then the man pulled Trevin into an alcove and cut through the rope that bound his hands.

Trevin peered into the shadow of the man's hood. "Benasin!"

Benasin put his finger to his lips. "We're not out yet." He thrust the hilt of a dagger into Trevin's hands and motioned for him to follow.

They took a descending corridor, which didn't make sense to Trevin, but he followed. If anyone knew a way out, it was Benasin.

At last the path leveled, and they headed toward light. Benasin ducked into a storage niche. "A short rest," he panted. "I've not used my feet this much in months."

Trevin dabbed his forehead with his sleeve. Sweat stung the talon scratches. "Why did you come for me?" he asked.

"I ran into the Asp."

"Why would he be interested in me?"

"Your brother was with him."

Trevin's mouth fell open. "Dwin?"

"You didn't recognize the young woman in the hall?"

"That was Dwin? What about the person behind me—was that the Asp?"

Benasin nodded. "If they're doing their job, our way out will be clear. For now we should be safe. Guards will expect us to run out, not in." He took a deep breath. "Rested?" He didn't wait for an answer.

Together they ran down the hall toward the light, which turned out to be the enormous cavern of statues Trevin had viewed from above. Benasin led him through the statues, staying in the shadows, gliding from figure to figure toward the far side, where Trevin saw several tunnels to choose from.

Again Trevin sensed streams of thought in the air as the statues watched them flee across the floor.

A light flashed in one of the tunnels, and they headed toward it. As they ducked in, a hand grabbed Trevin's arm and pulled him aside.

"Dwin!" Trevin whispered, embracing his brother. Dwin was taller, thinner—wiry. By the feel of it, he wore a knife tucked into his belt. Trevin tapped it. "So the maid was armed!"

Dwin drew the blade, the thinnest Trevin had ever seen. It reminded him of a needle. "All maids should carry knives, don't you think?" asked Dwin. He slipped it back in place.

Trevin grinned. "You were convincing dressed as a maid."

Dwin ran his hand through his black curls. "Don't laugh. You were almost dressed as a drak."

"Are we gabbing or getting out of here?" asked Benasin.

"This tunnel is clear," said Dwin. "Most of the guards have gone to help with the rock slide that blocked the stairway leading to the throne room."

"Courtesy of the Asp, no doubt," said Benasin. "Let's not waste the time he bought us." He headed through the tunnel.

"Wait!" said Trevin. "I have to get the harp."

"Don't be a fool," said Benasin. "If you're recaptured, you won't live the night."

"Dwin can help. We'll not get caught."

Dwin rolled his eyes. "I'm not invincible. Besides, I'm on the way out too. I have reports to make." He swatted Trevin on the shoulder. "Race you."

Trevin sighed and dashed after Dwin. The race was not swift, for the tunnel twisted and turned and sloped upward, but at last they stood panting at the mouth of the passage on the cliffs facing the sea.

A heavy fog bank grayed the waves. Over the soft slap of water, Trevin could hear the faint hum of harp strings. A heaviness settled on him as if a net of chains weighted his heart. He had failed.

"The Asp said he arranged for a boat to meet us," said Dwin.

"They'll not find us in this fog." Trevin rubbed his hand. The pain had eased.

Dwin studied the coastline. "They'll see the fires in the caves."

"Warning them away," said Trevin. "If they try to come close, they'll be dashed on the rocks."

Benasin squatted and eyed the fog. "Part of the sea smoke is shifting." He pointed. "Unnaturally. How does it appear to you?"

A swirling mist danced toward the shore and disappeared into the cloud bank. "Seaspinner," said Trevin. "Do you think she brought the fog?"

"That I don't know." Benasin edged out onto the cliff. "But as long as she stays there, she'll see us climb down. Once we reach the sea, perhaps she'll help us."

A ledge sloped across the cliff, providing a narrow but firm toehold. They edged along it as quickly as possible, hugging the mountainside. Near the bottom the fog thinned, revealing a shadowy bulk offshore.

"There's the boat." Benasin wobbled over the rocks toward the waves, shedding his cloak. Trevin and Dwin scrambled after him.

Benasin bundled his cloak and was tying it around his waist when a cry came from above.

"Halt!" An arrow slammed into a crack at Trevin's feet. He fell back against Dwin. They were completely exposed.

The bowman took aim again. An arrow whistled through the air—and hit the bowman full in the chest. He stumbled back into the cave as his bow and arrow rattled down the side of the cliff.

"Ollena." Trevin grinned.

Dwin tugged at him, and they sloshed into the rocky surf with Benasin.

Wisps of fog fingered the water and shielded them from view as they swam, but within a few strokes, they left the fog behind. A small ship bobbed ahead in the waves with Ollena standing at the prow like a warrior goddess, her bow aimed at the barely visible cliffs.

Catellus waved Trevin to a rope ladder and tugged him in as he reached the top. Dwin followed, then Benasin. They lay on deck, dripping and panting.

Ollena squatted beside Trevin. "Are you all right?" The wind ruffled her long hair.

"You're amazing," he said. "You saved our lives, and I'd hug you for it, but I'm soaked with brine."

Ollena cocked her head. "And I'm soaked with the smell of the fish these sailors catch for meals."

"You smell of sandalwood," said Trevin.

"You smell of seaweed," said Ollena.

He took her hand. "Thanks."

She slipped her hand from his. "You need dry clothes."

Under the first star of evening, the ship plowed through the waves, its sail bulging in the wind. Trevin sat on deck, leaning against a coil of rope, his legs stretched out. Benasin dozed to his right. To his left Dwin picked raisins out of a bowl and popped them into his mouth.

Trevin stared at the darkening sky and mulled over Catellus's report. The Asp had discovered him hobbling toward the river and had taken him to the ferry with instructions to hire a boat to wait offshore near the fire caves. Ollena met the ferry when it docked and was livid that Trevin had been left behind. She would have entered the Dregmoors then and there if Catellus had not convinced her of the wisdom of the Asp's plan.

Dwin shoved the bowl toward Trevin.

Trevin shoved it back.

"You hardly ate supper," said Dwin. "You have to be starving. I wager you got only rancid chunks of raw meat in the drak cages."

Trevin groaned. "*That* awakens my appetite."

"You're on the way to Qanreef, back to a princess," said Dwin. "You should be cheering. What's wrong?"

"The stars are aligning."

Dwin looked askance at him. "Are you sure they didn't start the drak process on you?"

"The stars of the beltway align in a certain way only once every two hundred years," said Trevin. "Those stars are reception points for the stairway that's supposed to connect this earth with heaven."

"So?" Dwin shoved the bowl back to Trevin.

"So I failed." Trevin fingered a raisin. "Melaia needs the third harp to restore the Tree, but I'm returning empty handed. I've let the Angelaeon down. Dash it, Dwin, I might as well take this boat to the southern isles."

"Run from your failure?" Benasin stretched. "I've been running all my immortal life. I don't know about you, but it's time I stopped."

"You have good reason to run. But me? I've been running from myself. From my own guilt." Trevin tossed the raisin back into the bowl. It had been easier to confess to a drak.

"Don't blame yourself. Blame me," said Benasin. "You've been swept into my maelstrom. Rejius and Dreia and I are at the center of it. Unfortunately, with Dreia's death—"

"Dreia's death is my fault," blurted Trevin. "Rejius sent out spies, and I was the one who discovered where she was. *I* informed Rejius about the caravan headed south."

Benasin rose and paced to the side of the ship. For a long time he gazed into the darkness.

Dwin shuffled raisins around the bowl and said nothing.

Trevin rubbed his right hand. The pain was gone, but he would have it back if he could trade it for the pain of his guilt.

Benasin turned to Trevin. "Is that why you serve Melaia? Is that why you support the Angelaeon? To atone for your guilt?"

"Trevin didn't kill Dreia," said Dwin. "He was at Redcliff when it happened."

"But it was my information that sent the malevolents after her," said Trevin.

"Did you know they intended a massacre?" asked Benasin.

"Does it matter?" asked Trevin. "There were at least a score of people in that caravan, including Dreia. All of them died. Because of me."

"All of them died because of Rejius," said Benasin.

Trevin shook his head. "I knew he wanted a harp."

"But you didn't know he would murder to get it," said Dwin.

"I knew what he was capable of." Trevin stood and steadied himself on a wooden crate.

"I don't hold you responsible for my brother's sins," said Benasin, "but I wager you'll have to tell Jarrod and Melaia before the guilt will loose its choke hold on you."

Trevin swayed toward the prow. He knew Benasin was right, but he dreaded facing Jarrod and Melaia.

A husky voice spoke from the shadows. "I would have done the same myself if I had been—"

"The fool that I am," Trevin finished.

Ollena grabbed his upper arm with a grip that could have dislocated it if she had tugged.

Trevin glared at her.

"You interrupted me," she said. "Stop beating yourself up, or we'll be down one more man, and that will only make the enemy's job easier." She eased her grip. "As I was saying, I would have done the same if I had been in your situation. I am loyal to the one I serve. I follow her orders. You did the same. It just happened you were on the wrong side."

"And I knew it," said Trevin. "There's the difference."

"It's also the reason you changed sides, hmm?"

Trevin stared out at the endless sea as Ollena headed toward the back of the ship. *Is that why you serve Melaia…support the Angelaeon? To atone?* He clenched the side rail. He could answer the first question. He had loved Melaia long before he knew she was Dreia's daughter. As for supporting the Angelaeon, he had no answer for that.

Dwin swayed up beside him. "Now I see why you were upset when I told you I wanted to be a spy."

For a moment they stood in silence. For the first time Trevin sensed that he and Dwin were peers. It felt oddly comforting.

"There's something you should know," said Dwin. "In the Dregmoors I discovered you can claim an angel as your father."

"I know. I learned about Arelin in Eldarra. He died rescuing Windwings."

Dwin snorted. "Arelin didn't die. Arelin is the Asp."

CHAPTER 24

Winds remained steady throughout the night and into the next day. The ship captain sent word that he expected to make Qanreef by late afternoon or early evening.

Trevin paced to the stern. As sailors adjusted the steering oars at the sides of the vessel, he watched trails of white foam scatter in the waves. The Dregmoorian coast was long gone. So was the harp. So was the opportunity to meet his father.

Although Trevin had plied Dwin with questions about Arelin, Dwin had been tight lipped. He would say only that Arelin was a good, astute angel, crippled from the battle for the Windwings.

Trevin flexed his right hand, free from pain. He had always thought missing a finger made him less than whole. All the while his crippled father had been traveling the tunnels of the Dregmoors like any able-bodied man.

Benasin placed a hand on Trevin's shoulder. "Thinking of the harp—or the Asp?"

"Did you know he was my father?"

"Not until Dwin told me last night. I see the resemblance now. How I missed it before, I'll never know."

"He was so close in the corridor," said Trevin. "Didn't he want to meet me?" The boat pitched, and Trevin gripped the top of the bulwarks.

Benasin grabbed a guyline. "I wager Arelin stayed aloof for the same reason I keep my distance from Jarrod. My presence exposes him to danger. Your father probably wanted to make sure you left the Dregmoors alive."

Trevin hoped that was the reason. Being a spy, his father probably knew how shamefully his son had bowed to the hawkman and how he had been duped into entering a drak's cage. "What do you know about Arelin?" he asked.

"It's ironic. The Asp probably knows all there is to know about me and my brother, but I know very little about the Asp."

Trevin studied Benasin's profile, set in a determined gaze eastward, and said, "I know a half-truth when I hear one. I've told enough of them myself."

Benasin shot a startled glance at Trevin, then chuckled. "The Asp will enjoy you. But I'm not at liberty to divulge his closely guarded secrets."

"Even to his son?"

"Even to his son."

Trevin huffed. "All right, then. Tell me about yourself."

Benasin turned and swayed toward the bow.

Trevin followed. "You asked me last night if I serve Melaia to assuage my guilt. The answer is no. I'm involved now, Benasin. I mean to support Melaia to the end—and my father too. What should I know?"

"What will be of use to you?"

"Anything about the Dregmoors and Rejius," said Trevin. "What should I expect when I return for the harp?"

"Trouble." Benasin tapped his fist on the bulwarks. "I foresee nothing else in the Dregmoors."

"Then tell me about Rejius's past."

Benasin scratched his beard. "You know the story of the Wisdom Tree?"

"I do."

"Then you know that Rejius, Stalia, and I ate the seeds of the Tree." Benasin leaned against a barrel of nets. "At first we had no notion that we were immortal. We knew only that the souls of the dead were gathering at the site of the Tree, grabbing at us, asking where the stairway was. We knew of nothing to do but lead them into the caverns of the Dregmoors."

Trevin sat on a cask. "Isn't that Earthbearer's domain?"

"It is. Earthbearer welcomed the spirits, but he made it clear that Rejius and I were responsible for them. He said his duties as Archon did not include playing nursemaid to the souls of the dead. Besides, it was our fault they couldn't cross the stairway. So Earthbearer allowed us the Shallows and gave us limited access to Mid-Realm as well. Not the Deeps, though. The Deeps are his dwelling place."

"What about Stalia?" asked Trevin.

Benasin lifted the corner of a net and fingered a frayed knot. "Poor girl. Stalia was the first to realize we were aging so slowly you could hardly call it aging at all."

"The gift of the seeds."

"Or the curse. We outlived family and friends. Their souls entered the Shallows, and what could we do but let them wander? But a wandering shade is a misery to behold. We got the idea that we, being immortal, might be able to restore life to the spirits, so we began exploring earth elements, experimenting with alchemy."

"You and Rejius together?" asked Trevin. "I thought you were always enemies."

"We weren't friends. For a time we lived under a tense truce, but we could never overcome our old rivalries. We tried to outdo each other. I created the draks and leatherwings as a way to free the spirits of the dead. Rejius turned them into prisons for the living." Benasin dropped the net back into the barrel. "Feel free to push me overboard."

Trevin looked away. "If I pushed you over, I'd have to take the leap myself. You heard my confession last night. I'm in no way pure enough to condemn you."

"Nor I you," said Benasin.

The wind sang through the rigging. Gulls shrilled and skimmed the waves. The Camrithian coastline sprawled low and gray across the horizon.

Trevin cleared his throat. "Who decided to entomb spirits in stone statues?"

Benasin blinked as if his mind were returning from far away. "The statues were Rejius's creation, as well as the nets that fuse souls to rock."

Trevin shuddered at the memory of the cave paintings.

"Rejius did it to keep the souls from wandering, to maintain control," said Benasin. "You can't imagine it. The dead never stop coming."

"What about gash?"

Benasin snorted. "I suggested we might reduce the number of dead if we found a way to extend the lives of the living, maybe give everyone immortality. That's what inspired Rejius to concoct gash."

"I've seen gash-drunks."

"A few drinks and you crave it. You'll do anything to get it. Many serve Rejius for the drink."

Trevin clenched his jaw. The relationship between Varic and his grandfather Rejius was dangerously clear. Melaia could not, would not marry into the tyrant's dynasty.

"You're turning red," said Benasin. "You might try to breathe deeper."

Trevin inhaled the brine-laden air, but his fists remained clenched as he scanned the horizon. Nearer now. One hour more? Two?

Dwin sauntered up with a flask. "I heard you speak of gash. Thought you might be thirsty."

Trevin narrowed his eyes. "Tell me that's not what you're holding."

Dwin saluted with the flask. "It's the captain's best wine. In honor of smooth sailing all the way."

"We're not home yet," said Trevin.

"Near enough." Dwin handed the flask to Benasin, who took a swig. Dwin lolled against the bulwarks, watching the immortal. "I thought you had always been running from Rejius. The Asp said I was wrong."

Benasin corked the flask and handed it to Trevin. "I tried as long as I could to live peaceably with my brother and Stalia. But I couldn't stomach Rejius's experiments. What's more, his grudge against me only grew. As I said before, I learned early on that he would take from me anything I loved. I was desperate for a way out and could think of only one who might provide it."

"Dreia." Trevin sipped the spiced wine.

"She was my last hope," said Benasin. "I left the Dregmoors for good—or so I thought—and searched for Dreia. But Rejius hunted me. Tracked me with draks. He dragged me back to the Dregmoors more than once before I became skilled enough to evade him."

Trevin held out the flask to Dwin.

Dwin shook his head. "I've had enough."

Trevin raised his eyebrows. "I never thought I'd see you turn down wine. Especially the captain's best."

"The Asp says a spy needs a clear head. Your life can be at stake."

Trevin grinned. He could have told Dwin the same. In fact, he *had* told him. The life-or-death part had obviously become reality for Dwin.

"So, Benasin, you found Dreia?" prompted Dwin.

Benasin nodded. "I hadn't seen her for more than a hundred and sixty years."

Dwin's jaw dropped. "A hundred and sixty years! What kept you in the Dregmoors that long?"

"Guilt," said Benasin. "I believed the destruction of the Tree was my fault and the dead were my responsibility—facts Rejius relentlessly brought to my attention. Besides, I thought I could be a moderating influence on my brother's excesses."

"What about Dreia?" asked Trevin.

A sense of wonder softened Benasin's face. "I swear I'll never know why, but she forgave me and told me the debt could be repaid. She had been journeying, mostly dividing her time between the Erielyon in the north and the western tribes, which is where I found her, just as beautiful as the day I first saw her. She showed me three harps she had hired a craftsman to create from the wood of the Wisdom Tree—kyparis wood. She had saved a few pieces when the Tree was felled. She told me that the three, when united, would restore the Tree. I asked her why she hadn't united them."

"Because the stars must be aligned," said Trevin. "Which happens only once every two hundred years." He watched the coastline draw nearer.

"That's one reason," said Benasin. "The other reason is that no angel can unite the harps. Nor can any human. Dreia was the angel at fault for giving me the fruit of the Tree. I was the human to blame for failing to return the seeds. So the debt must be repaid by one who is both angel and human."

"Breath of angel, blood of man,'" said Trevin.

"Just so," said Benasin. "And who but Dreia and I should bear the child, we thought. So we bore a son for that purpose. But we failed to take my immortality into account. We had hoped that when our son came of age, the kyparis harps would resonate in his hands as they did for Dreia. By the time he was sixteen, we knew our hopes were in vain. Jarrod is a new breed: breath of angel, blood of immortal."

"So you lived with Dreia and Jarrod for a while," said Dwin.

"Oh no," said Benasin. "I had to stay on the move. I feared Rejius would find Dreia and Jarrod. They journeyed. I journeyed. We met a few weeks a year at secret locations."

"And the harps?" asked Trevin.

"I advised Dreia to hide them well."

"But you kept one in your quarters at Navia," said Trevin.

"Dreia insisted on it," said Benasin. "She hoped one day to send the chosen 'breath of angel, blood of man' to fetch it." They ambled toward the prow. "It was in Navia that I was able to settle for a time before Rejius started hunting me again."

Trevin ran his hand along the bulwarks. "Do you think Rejius will tire of immortality as you did?"

Dwin laughed. "Rejius thrives on immortality. He loves the power. Even the malevolents are in awe of him, because when he dies, he returns to flesh. When they die, they're entombed in stone like any other spirit."

Trevin stepped out of the way of a deck hand carrying a rope. Sailors scurried about, preparing for their arrival at Qanreef.

"Rejius is disgusted with me," said Benasin. "He thinks I've backed down and become weak." He looked to the open sea. "Perhaps I have. I'm weary, friends. I'm weary."

Trevin felt he should offer an encouraging word, but he had none. In Benasin's place he would be weary too. They stood at the bow in silence, watching Alta-Qan appear, looming up from the chalk bluff.

"I've never viewed Qanreef from the sea," said Dwin. "I didn't realize the whitewashed buildings were so bright."

Trevin shaded his eyes. The white of the city wavered. "That's not the buildings," he said. "It's flags and drapes."

The city was festooned in white. For a wedding.

⊱⊰

Trevin stood beside the tethering post across from the Full Sail. He and his company had disembarked after nightfall and made their way straight to the tavern. Paullus had told them that while they were gone, Pym spent his days searching for news of the comains, keeping his ear to the talk, following threads of rumors. In the evenings he dined with Jarrod at the temple, then returned to the tavern for the night, bringing the daily gossip with him.

Hungry for news, Trevin watched for Pym to shamble down the street from the palace. He took some comfort in knowing Jarrod and Livia were at

Alta-Qan. On the other hand, being ultimately loyal to the Angelaeon, they may have convinced Melaia that marriage to Varic was the way to reach the third harp.

Trevin dug his staff into the dirt at the foot of the post. His stomach felt like one big knot. The local chatter, according to Cilla, centered on guessing the date the wedding would take place. White silks had adorned Qanreef for three days, and the whole city waited for the presentation of the bride and groom. No one knew if the wedded couple would be King Laetham and Lady Jayde or Princess Melaia and Prince Varic. Possibly both.

A bandy-legged shadow approached, picking up his pace as he neared. "Main Trevin!" called Pym. "You're back. News of you hadn't reached the palace."

"Good. I'd rather lie low until I have a plan. Am I still a wanted man in the king's eyes?"

"That's a concern, it is." Pym ran a hand through his disheveled hair.

"What about the wedding?"

"Hasn't happened yet."

The knot in Trevin's stomach eased. "Any news of the comains?"

"Plenty of rumors but nothing of value. I wormed about the docks, trying to learn of any men who were shipped out—or boys, in the case of Catellus's son—but the search proved as hollow as a drained barrel. Except for one thing I learned by accident. I mentioned Lady Jayde to a sailor from the southern isles. He claims he hears the scuttle that goes on in the islands, but he's never heard of Lady Jayde."

"Then who woos the king?"

"Jarrod's asking the same question."

Trevin poked the road with his staff. "Do you think Jarrod can arrange for me to meet privately with Melaia before I request an audience with King Laetham? She may be able to get me in to see him."

"I've seen nothing of the princess for days. I hear she's confined to her quarters, but if anyone can arrange it, Jarrod and Serai can. You sit tight here. I'll speak to them first thing in the morning and let you know what's possible."

Benasin strode out of the tavern. "Arme Pym! Just the man I need. I'm leaving at daybreak. Can you procure a mount for me, one for swift riding and long distance?"

"I know the right horse," said Pym. "She's at a stable down the way. You have coin for her?"

Benasin patted his side, and his pouch clinked.

"I'll see to it." Pym trotted down the street. "Save me a mug in the tavern," he called over his shoulder.

Trevin eyed Benasin. "I thought you planned to stop running."

"I'm not running but leading. Rejius will be after me, and it's to your advantage that I take him far from Qanreef."

"Then take this." Trevin handed him the staff. "From Jarrod. He asked me to give it to you."

Benasin flexed his fingers around the staff. "Timely."

"Before you leave, maybe you can answer a question," said Trevin. "Rejius changed Melaia's young friend Peron into a drak."

Benasin hissed.

"Can the process be reversed?"

Benasin rubbed his brow. "I've never tried to undo the transformation. But I suppose it's possible, though it wouldn't be without pain for the girl. If it failed, her spirit would be subject to my brother's whims."

"At least now she flies free," said Trevin.

"A point to seriously consider." Benasin sighed, then squared his shoulders. "Arelin's son, I hope we meet again."

"I'm sure we will." Trevin studied the lights of Alta-Qan. Why not stand up to Varic as an equal? He eyed Benasin. "Will you travel north?"

"As far north as I can, and quickly."

"Will you carry a message to Eldarra for me?"

"Easily done."

"Tell the king and queen of Eldarra that I accept."

Benasin raised an eyebrow but asked no question. Trevin gave no explanation, preferring not to risk the circulation of rumors until he chose to reveal the Eldarran offer.

"I'll convey your message." Benasin studied his staff and smiled sadly. "Tell my son you've seen me." His eyes grew moist. "Tell him I wish him well."

"Gladly," said Trevin. He just hoped he wouldn't have to deliver the message at a wedding celebration.

revin spent the morning waiting for Pym to return from the palace. He circled the common room until Cilla sweet-talked him into sitting still for breakfast. Then he paced the cellar, where he recalled a morning almost as tense as this one, when he inadvertently told Melaia the king was her father. If he had kept his mouth shut that day, events might have unfolded differently.

When he heard voices overhead, he sprinted upstairs, only to find a couple of sailors ordering their morning grub. He continued up to the chamber he shared with Catellus and paced the room while Catellus sharpened and polished his dagger, his knife, his sword.

"Land somewhere, would you?" said Catellus. "You're nervous enough for both of us."

Trevin plopped onto a stool and slipped his sword from its scabbard. Pym had kept it perfectly polished. He wrapped his hand around the hilt. His father had held this sword. Arelin. The Asp. Trevin sighed. If only he had turned faster in the corridor, he might have seen his father. They had been close enough to touch.

He studied his reflection in the blade. Wise, confident—the image had not changed. Neither had he—a fact he knew well after groveling before Rejius. But for the first time, he saw in the reflected eyes a resolve that resonated in the core of his being. He would become that man whatever the cost.

At noon the door banged open. Pym leaned against the doorframe, hands on his knees, panting. "Jarrod says…if you want to see Melaia…you'll come now."

Trevin shot to his feet. He and Catellus buckled on their sword belts, secured their daggers, and grabbed their shields and cloaks. Moments later they followed Pym down a back street toward the citadel. Trevin realized he hadn't bothered to tell Ollena he was leaving, but he suspected she had heard.

"Why the hurry?" asked Catellus.

"Don't know," said Pym. "Jarrod will have to tell you. He's waiting at the temple by the burial door."

"Are malevolents about?" asked Trevin.

"They are. They're aware of Jarrod, Serai, and Livia. So far the one side's keeping a fair distance from the other, but they're all wary."

"And King Laetham is oblivious," said Trevin.

"Or pretends to be," said Pym. "He lives by the old saying 'Ignore trouble, and it will ignore you.'"

Catellus snorted. "More likely it'll become your bedmate."

Jarrod opened the Door of the Dead as they approached, and waved them in. He pulled Trevin aside. "Melaia will join you on the roof as soon as she can. It's draped with white tenting, so you'll not be visible to onlookers, but Melaia hasn't much time. Her wedding is midafternoon."

"Midafternoon?" The word stuck in Trevin's throat.

"Melaia persuaded the king to allow her to come to the temple to pray before the ceremony." Jarrod held his torch high as they swept through the burial vault with its death masks, gravestones, and statues, an eerie reminder of the stone figures in the Dregmoors.

"Condemnation!" said Trevin. "Are you taking their vows, Jarrod? Can't you prevent the marriage? At least postpone it."

"Lady Jayde brought her own priest," said Jarrod. "A round, mealy, completely obsequious puppet."

They sprinted up the stone stairs to the main floor. "Pym," said Jarrod, "I suggest you and Catellus stay in my quarters." They nodded and dashed away as Jarrod and Trevin headed for the stairs that led to the roof.

"I saw your father," said Trevin. "Traveled with him from the Dregmoors."

"Dwin told me."

"He asked me to give you his greeting and wish you well."

"He couldn't find a way to give me the message himself?"

"He's traveling north to distract Rejius from us."

"Why am I not surprised?" asked Jarrod.

Now that Trevin longed to see his own father, he recognized the same in Jarrod. But a bitter anger coiled beneath Jarrod's pain.

Jarrod pointed to the stairway ahead. "As soon as Melaia arrives, I'll send her up."

"Does she know I found the second harp?" asked Trevin.

"She does, but she asked me to keep it hidden in the temple. She also knows you went into the Dregmoors."

Trevin gazed up the stairs. The roof door stood open, and the sea breeze flowed down the steps, along with a slant of sunlight.

Jarrod caught his sleeve. "Be wise, my friend. Make your farewell in such a way that you don't regret it later."

Trevin trudged up the stairs, numb. *Make your farewell.* After this day Melaia would be at a distance he could not cross.

As he climbed, the door and its slant of sunlight blurred into one image. He wiped his eyes and stepped from the door in the dome of the temple onto a rooftop pavilioned in white. The breeze-billowed silks stretched from the dome across the wide walk around it to the parapet.

Trevin set his cloak, sword, and shield on a bench by the north wall and gazed through the gap between the silk and the ledge of the parapet to the burial ground below. Today might be his only chance to tell Melaia about his role in Dreia's death and beg her forgiveness. At least they would have their own private pavilion. But how much time would they have? He sighed. No matter. He wouldn't waste a minute.

Footfalls echoed in the stairwell, and Trevin sensed Melaia's silver light. He turned as the most beautiful being he had ever seen stepped onto the roof. She wore a fitted blue gown with a sheer white over-robe. Her dark-honey hair flowed loose across her shoulders. She studied him with her rich brown eyes, her smile wavering, uncertain.

"Princess." He bowed.

Melaia laughed. "Enough, Trevin. You know I've never really been a princess to you."

"You're right. To me you've always been an angel, and you ever will be." He stopped before his voice cracked.

Melaia blushed and strode regally to him. "You're changed. You're—"

"Better?" He tried to be inconspicuous as he inhaled her lavender scent.

Melaia placed her hands on her hips. "How can the best get better?"

"Wiser, I hope. More aware of what I have—and what I don't."

Melaia took his hand and drew him to the bench where his cloak and shield lay. She still wore her harp pendant. "Trevin, I'm sorry."

"I'm the one who should apologize." His throat felt thick. Heavens, how he loved her.

"I didn't know you would return," she said.

"You didn't trust me?"

"That's not it." Tears welled in her eyes. "I saw you in my book. Through the harp. I saw you chained. I was so afraid that I couldn't sleep, I couldn't eat. Not until I had a way to get into the Dregmoors. I thought as Prince Varic's wife, I might have some influence in freeing you."

Trevin tensed. He couldn't bear to see her cry. "Benasin helped me escape."

She perked up. "You found Benasin!"

"He escaped with me, but I couldn't bring the harp. I've failed you."

"You've not failed me."

"I failed you long ago."

Melaia frowned.

Trevin wished he could kiss away that frown instead of making it darker. He looked down at their clasped hands, his rough and scarred, hers soft and scented. There was no easy way.

He took a deep breath. "I should have confessed long ago. I'm responsible for your mother's death."

She stiffened but did not pull away. "In what way?"

"You know I was a spy for Lord Rejius," he said.

"Yes," she whispered.

"He sent me to confirm a drak sighting of a woman with a harp in the Aubendahl hills. I found her and told Rejius where she was. My report led to the massacre of the caravan. And the stolen harp. I'm sorry. I hoped bringing the harp back from the Dregmoors might atone for part of what I've done, but I can't make up for Dreia's death."

Melaia cupped his face in her hands and looked into his eyes. He wished time would stop then and there.

"I forgive you, Trevin." She blinked back tears. "I forgive you for the past, completely and forever. Can *you* ever forgive me for what I've done to our future?"

"Oh, Melaia." Trevin kissed her hands.

Shouts rang from the stairwell. Varic emerged, wearing a tunic the same blue as Melaia's gown. A gold band crossed his forehead and snaked beneath his wavy, dark hair. His beetle-black eyes glared, and he roared, "Get away from my wife!"

Serai dashed through the door, Jarrod behind her. They froze, tense as wagemongers at a cockfight. Trevin expected no help from them unless they decided to interfere in human will for once. He dropped Melaia's hands.

Varic halted three paces away. "You cripple-handed deceiver," he snarled. "I should have known better than to leave your fate to the Eldarrans. Idiots, all of them. I should have netted you the moment I first saw you." He deftly slipped off his silver waist sash.

Melaia stepped between them, her fists clenched at her side. "Put that away, Varic. I'm marrying you. Trevin and I are simply saying our farewells."

"I intend to make sure they're final," said Varic.

Melaia stepped toward him. "This is our wedding day." Her voice was soothing. "I'll have no fighting on our wedding day."

Varic grabbed her arm and flung her aside.

Trevin started toward her, but Varic whirled his net, and Trevin retreated to keep the snare away from Melaia. Watching Varic's every move, Trevin edged toward the bench where his sword lay.

Varic's net widened as it spun. Trevin glanced at the bench and silently cursed his luck. His sword lay beyond his cloak and shield.

The flick of Varic's wrist was almost imperceptible. As the net shot from his hand, Trevin snatched his shield and swung at the mesh, deflecting it. But the net swept the shield from his hands and took it clattering to the rooftop.

Varic drew his sword, and Trevin lunged for his.

"No fighting, Varic," shouted Melaia. "I'm marrying you for peace. Fighting will do no good."

"That's how little you know, Princess," Varic hissed. "I mean to assure my future." He lunged.

Trevin twisted sideways, drawing Varic from Melaia, who backed away with Serai at one hand, Jarrod at the other. Trevin's move also ensured that the parapet was not at his back so he had room to retreat. But he found his right side now hampered by the temple dome. He would also have to avoid two stools and a lamp table by the stairwell door.

Varic swung. Trevin parried, his mind swirling with Ollena's drills. *Evade, body first.* Varic had the longer reach, so Trevin knew he would have to stay out of range until he was certain his sword would find its mark.

Varic kicked a stool at Trevin, and it hit him in the shin. *Balance.* He sidestepped as the stool clattered to the parapet.

Varic's next swing was high. Trevin ducked and cut back, slicing Varic's sleeve. *Breathe.*

"Cur," Varic growled. "I shall have the throne. Not you." He cut across the middle, catching Trevin's tunic, which ripped as Trevin parried the blade away.

Control. Trevin advanced, cutting toward Varic's weak right.

Varic slashed the silk tenting, sending it fluttering toward Trevin.

Ducking under the silk, Trevin kept advancing. *You were born to this.* He could tell Varic was tiring, so he cut again toward Varic's right. And again. Then he realized the move had placed his back to the parapet, hindering a full retreat. What's more, Varic's net lay close enough to trip him if he wasn't careful.

Varic's eyes brightened as he saw his advantage and prepared to lunge.

Serai yelped; Jarrod shouted. Trevin sensed Melaia's silver light flaring toward him and knew she would throw herself between him and the Dregmoorian prince.

Varic lunged. Dropping his sword, Trevin leaped sideways and shoved Melaia into Serai's arms.

Varic swerved to shift his aim, but his feet tangled in the silver net. He stumbled over the bench and into the silk tenting, which snapped free of its moorings, spilling him over the parapet.

His scream ended in silence.

Trevin scrambled to his feet and looked over the half wall. Jarrod joined him. Below, Ollena, sword in hand, strode to Varic, who lay crumpled at the base of the temple.

"Is he dead?" called Trevin.

She nudged Varic with the toe of her boot. "Is he your friend or your enemy?"

"Enemy," called Jarrod.

Ollena plunged her sword into Varic's chest. "He's dead," she called.

Trevin gaped at her. "He was the prince of the Dregmoors."

"Not to me," called Ollena. "He was Rikin the Betrayer."

Jarrod headed down the stairs, and Trevin turned to Melaia, rubbing his sword arm. "I'm sorry," he said. "I didn't mean for it to turn out this way."

Melaia trembled. "Varic didn't mean for it to turn out this way either. He meant for *you* to die."

Serai dusted off Melaia's gown. "Guests are assembling in the great hall. I warrant the whole court will be seeking both you and Varic soon. Do you want me to go and make an excuse for you?"

The color was returning to Melaia's cheeks. "I'll go," she said.

Serai smoothed back Melaia's hair. "What do we say about Varic?"

"I don't know." Melaia looked at Trevin, her eyebrows raised in question.

"Say nothing," he said.

"What if someone asks?" Serai tugged Melaia toward the stairs.

"Then say Jarrod's offering prayers for him."

Melaia rolled her eyes. "Prayers and Varic don't go together."

"Then try to avoid people who would ask," said Trevin. "I'll come to the great hall after I clean up. I'll tell the king about Varic, but I'll leave you out of it." He examined Arelin's sword. Barely nicked.

Melaia pulled away from Serai, ran to Trevin, and kissed him on the cheek. "Hurry," she said. Then she dashed down the stairs after Serai.

The loose tenting snapped in the wind. Trevin peered over the wall and watched Jarrod and Catellus help Ollena haul Varic's body through the Door of the Dead. He turned back to the rooftop. Jagged white silk dangled from the slashed pavilion. The stools were toppled, and one lay near the net, now bunched in a pile where Varic had stumbled. Beside the net, Trevin's shield lay fused to the rooftop as if it were painted on.

"Disgusting." Trevin crouched and stroked the frost-cold image.

Then he felt heat radiating around him, and a small flame appeared beside the net. Trevin scooted back as the flame grew, swirling into a figure.

"Flametender," he whispered.

She nodded. Heat swelled, and sweat dripped from Trevin's forehead. His hands felt blazing hot.

Flametender knelt and slid the silver net over the shield. Then she held out her hands to Trevin as before. When he placed his palms on hers, she guided them to the net and pressed them to the shield. Then she backed away with a satisfied smile, fading into a flame that shrank until it vanished.

As she left, Trevin felt the net bulge under his hands. He swept the net aside and found his shield whole. He stared at his cooling palms.

"Main Trevin!" Pym's voice echoed up the stairwell.

Trevin grabbed sword, shield, and net and sprinted downstairs.

Pym met him at the bottom. "Ollena told me Varic is dead," he said. "What happened?"

Trevin didn't break his stride as they headed to Jarrod's quarters. "Varic found us on the roof and insisted on fighting. He fell over the wall."

"Ollena is cleaning her sword."

"She made sure Varic's death was a swift one."

Jarrod was not in his quarters. Trevin shoved the net under a stool in the back corner, poured a pitcher of water into a basin, and splashed his face clean.

Jarrod entered and pointed Trevin to a towel. "We've laid the body among the tombs below."

"Ollena sent this." Catellus plopped Trevin's pack on the table.

Trevin dried his face and dug through the clothing Ambria had carefully folded and packed. "I'll want the harp," he said, "in case I have to justify my presence by showing evidence of my 'successful' quest."

He pulled a noble-looking tunic and leggings from the pack and dressed as quickly as he could, thinking he might as well appear to be a success, even if the quest itself had largely failed. The Eldarrans were allies, to be sure. But for all his searching, he could present only one comain, one harp, and himself as the Oracle's sign. Pitiful.

Jarrod brought out the harp. "Varic's death kills the peace treaty," he said.

"Which means the king is likely to kill me," said Trevin. "Unless Fornian reaches me first. It's the third death I could be blamed for, including Nash and Resarian."

Actually four, he thought, remembering Dreia's statue as he combed through his hair with his fingers and tried to bind it at his neck. He fumbled with the cord, and Jarrod tied it for him.

"I'm walking straight in," said Trevin. "I'm tired of skulking along the back streets."

"Wear this, then." Jarrod tossed him a blue priest's cloak. "Hood up. I'll go with you."

"And I." Ollena stood outside the door, her palm on the hilt of her sword.

Pym and Catellus rose to join them.

Trevin tugged on the cloak, tied a sash around the harp frame, and slipped it across his back. Then he pulled up his hood and followed Jarrod out of the temple, flanked by his friends.

Colorful ribbons fluttered from every pole, post, and column around the courtyard. From the rooftops, white tenting billowed in the sea breeze, creating a bright backdrop for the small black drak that swooped in and landed on a window ledge high above.

Dwin emerged from the palace door and met them halfway. "There's plenty of mumbling in the great hall. Guards are allowing no one to see Varic, not even his friends."

Trevin didn't break his stride. "Varic is dead."

Dwin's jaw dropped. "How—"

"We fought on the temple roof. I ducked as he lunged, and he went over the edge."

"Does Melaia know?"

"She saw it, but I'm to announce it."

Dwin sucked air through his clenched teeth. "I don't envy you today. Varic wasn't the most loved among the people, but he was the king's hope for peace and a favorite of Lady Jayde. It's good that you have your legion with you."

Together they strode up the front steps of the palace.

"I bring special guests with me," Jarrod told the guards. "Visitors from our Eldarran allies."

The guards waved them in, casting their most wary looks on Ollena.

At the arched doorway to the great hall, Jarrod spoke with guards again and gained entrance into a room draped in white silk and colored ribbons. Aromas of the coming feast drifted through the air along with the happy hum of conversation from well-dressed guests who crowded the benches arranged on the north and south walls.

A wide center aisle crossed from the main door on the west to the dais along the east wall, where the shields of the missing comains hung, each bearing the image of a different animal in a regal pose. A round, bald, gold-robed priest was placing two white cushions on the floor before the throne on the dais while Caepio strolled along the front of the room, playing his lyre.

Dwin sauntered in to sit by the priestesses Nuri and Iona on a bench along the north wall, which held four tall windows and a gallery above. Nearby, Hanni, the high priestess, chatted with Livia and Lord Beker, the king's blond-bearded advisor. Pym scooted onto a bench near the entrance. Catellus stayed in the corridor, hidden from Varic's friends.

Too restless to sit, Trevin opted to stand with Jarrod against the back wall. Silks and ribbons had transformed the hall, but they could not mask memories of Lord Rejius trying to claim the kingship there last year.

A tainted aura drew Trevin's attention to the south wall, which held four windows that looked across the lip of the bluff to the sea beyond. Two couples casually conversed beside one window. Malevolents, all of them. At the next window stood Fornian, arms folded, eying the guests. Trevin angled his head so his hood would shadow his face.

Ollena strode into the hall, and Fornian studied her as if trying to place her.

"Orin the hunter," Ollena murmured, passing Trevin on her way to a nearby bench.

Serai slipped in and motioned for Trevin. He joined her in the corridor.

"We stationed a guard at Varic's quarters," she whispered, "to tell anyone who asks that he doesn't want to be disturbed."

Trevin sensed Melaia's approach and looked up. How she managed to look more beautiful than on the rooftop, he didn't know. He stared, barely breathing. Her hair was gathered atop her head, her face framed with a veil, folded back. The only thing missing was the wedding-day radiance of the perfect bride.

Melaia stepped up to Trevin, while her bodyguards halted a few paces away. Her worried eyes searched his. "After my father takes his place on his throne, I'm to enter," she said. "When I reach the dais, I'll turn, kneel, and face this archway. Then Varic is—was—to walk in. I don't know what to do at that point. I've not told anyone. I've not even seen my father."

Trevin peered into the great hall, where Fornian paced the length of the south wall, visibly disturbed. Then the hall quieted, and Fornian halted.

A dark-haired woman in a revealing white gown entered from a door behind the dais. Her sheer white cloak looked like a full veil, though instead of covering her heart-shaped face, it swooped back from her shoulders, displaying a sapphire pendant. She reminded Trevin of a white lion on the prowl, ready to pounce.

"Lady Jayde," murmured Serai.

The lady swished to a chair beside the king's throne and remained standing as a page entered and announced the sovereign. Everyone knelt, including the lady, as King Laetham strode in with a magnanimous smile.

Trevin's stomach twisted at the thought of what would happen to that smile in only a matter of minutes. He turned to Melaia. "Just do your part."

She nodded, veiled her face, and squared her shoulders. Serai walked her to the archway.

"The shields," Catellus whispered over Trevin's shoulder. "I see it now. We have to get the shields."

"Which was yours?"

"The white stag."

Trevin nodded, realizing Catellus had not seen his shield since he sent it away with his son. Viewing it now had surely reminded him of his son's captivity.

Melaia was halfway to the dais. Lady Jayde leaned seductively toward King Laetham and whispered. The king's grin broadened. When Melaia reached the front, she bowed to her father, then turned and knelt on one of the white cushions, her eyes on the archway.

Trevin's heart drummed in his chest. He slipped off the priest's cloak, handed it to Catellus, and repositioned the harp on his back.

In the great hall the guests shifted uneasily. The king's smile stiffened. Fornian leaned forward, scowling.

Trevin strode through the doorway.

CHAPTER 26

The great hall sizzled with whispers, and the king's smile froze. The priest opened and closed his mouth like a frog. Lady Jayde glanced at Fornian, who nodded. She turned her glare to Trevin.

As Trevin strode down the aisle, he felt a twisting pull of power from Lady Jayde, but he did not sense her as a malevolent. Four paces from the dais, he went to one knee.

"Main Trevin!" boomed the king. "Explain yourself. Where is Prince Varic?"

The entire room lay silent. Trevin felt all eyes watching him as he rose. "This afternoon I was welcomed to the temple by Prince Varic's sword."

The king narrowed his eyes. Lady Jayde drew her hand delicately to her throat.

"Varic attacked me on the temple roof," said Trevin. "I ducked, but he couldn't pull back. He fell over the parapet. His body is at the temple." Out of the corner of his eye, he saw Fornian slip out of the hall.

Lady Jayde's face paled. "How do we know *you* didn't send Varic to his death?" She turned to King Laetham. "Isn't this the man who murdered the Eldarran prince and brought your personal servant to a cruel end? Now he has killed the prince of the Dregmoors and has the insolence to announce it in front of the bride on her wedding day."

Trevin wondered if anyone else noticed that the bride did not seem particularly upset. "Sire," he said, "Varic killed the Eldarran prince, and I have good reason to suspect he murdered Nash *and* arranged for the disappearance of your comains. I'm prepared to give you a full report."

The king opened his mouth to speak, but Lady Jayde blurted, "We're here for a wedding, and he wants to make a report! To shift the blame, no doubt."

Melaia rose from her cushion and folded back her veil. "Trevin is not a murderer. He's telling the truth. I saw Varic fall."

Lady Jayde clenched her fists in her lap. "*You* were there? Perhaps you two conspired to murder the prince and invented this tale to cover your crime."

King Laetham scowled at Lady Jayde. "I do not believe my daughter is a murderer, and I'll thank you to let me handle this." Red-faced, he turned to Melaia. "It's understandable that Lady Jayde is upset. She and I meant to marry today as well. After your wedding."

Melaia gaped at her father. "You kept this from me?"

"We didn't want to eclipse your own anticipation," said Lady Jayde. "But this! This destroys not only the wedding but the Dregmoorian peace offer as well!"

The king shook a jeweled finger at Melaia. "If it's true that you've wittingly destroyed the hope of peace for Camrithia, I'll hold you personally responsible for any ensuing hostility by the Dregmoorians." He glared at Trevin. "As for you, *you* will be held in chains."

"If I may, Your Grace." Lord Beker strode to the center of the hall. "We're all stunned at the news of Varic's death, having gathered for something far more pleasant."

Trevin glanced at Melaia. He doubted either of them would have found the wedding ceremony any more pleasant than murder charges.

"However," said Lord Beker, "since we are gathered, I request that we hear more. It seems to me that if Main Trevin were truly guilty of murder, he wouldn't be fool enough to walk in here before us all. I suggest we consider his report. As for the princess, though it's no secret that she felt less than elated about this match, I do not consider her a liar."

Lady Jayde placed her hand on the king's shoulder. "Laetham, this is not the time to discuss these distressing matters. Our guests came to see a wedding. The priest is here. Send this murderer to a cell, and *we* can be wed. You'll have time later to consider your next steps."

"Our next steps are to prepare to defend our borders," growled King Laetham. "The Dregmoorians send their prince with a peace offer; we return him in a shroud."

"Please, Father, you need to hear Main Trevin's report," said Melaia. "He gained an alliance with Eldarra."

Trevin slipped the harp from his back. "I bring greetings from King Kedemeth and Queen Ambria, I found one of your comains alive and well, and you can see that I have one of the harps Melaia wanted." He handed the harp to Melaia. "I've completed my tasks, and I return in peace." He raised his empty hands to indicate that he held no malice.

Lady Jayde's eyes narrowed. Trevin sensed something festering beneath the surface of this woman. He wished he could draw his sword and glimpse her character in the reflection, but he had declared peaceful intentions.

"Liar!" Fornian stormed through the doorway. "Varic didn't fall. He was run through with a sword." He drew his dagger and headed for Trevin.

Half of the guests on the north side of the hall rose. Swords hissed from their scabbards, echoed by blades drawn along the south wall. Catellus entered, his dagger in hand.

Ollena stepped in front of Trevin, her sword poised. "I ended Varic's life," she told Fornian. "I'll do the same for you if you insist, hmm? Varic fell from the roof of the temple. His neck broke, and he would have died slowly. I spared him the pain."

Fornian glared at her, fuming, and Ollena stared back, both daring each other to strike first.

Trevin turned to King Laetham, an idea taking hold. "I swear you've heard the truth. I come in peace. As proof, I lay down my sword."

Slowly he drew Arelin's sword and lowered it to the floor, tilting the blade to catch Lady Jayde's reflection. But when he saw her image, he could hardly make sense of it. An ancient, shriveled face lined with fear, recklessness, and desperation sat atop a child's body.

Then, over the child's shoulder, he glimpsed the reflection of one of the shields on the wall. He caught his breath. The shield bore not the image of an animal but the likeness of a man.

That's what Catellus was trying to say, thought Trevin. Varic had reduced the comains to images, trapped them within their own shields.

He set the sword on the floor, his mind racing. Who was Lady Jayde?

King Laetham paced the dais. "Perhaps, Main Trevin, if you are such an envoy of peace, you should take the true murderer, this warrior woman, into the Dregmoors to stand trial for the death of the prince. She confessed murder. You could be witness." He turned to Lord Beker. "Might that appease the Dregmoorians?"

"Possibly," said Lord Beker.

Lady Jayde huffed. "Even if the Dregmoorians exact justice for the prince's death, they will have no marriage ties, no incentive to guarantee further peace. I suggest you send the harps as a substitute for the princess."

"Impossible," said Melaia.

King Laetham looked askance at Lady Jayde. "Why would the Dregmoorians accept these harps? Are they truly that valuable?"

"There's only one way to find out," said Lady Jayde.

"The harps stay here with me," said Melaia.

Lady Jayde and Melaia began arguing the matter. Trevin was aware of their voices, but his mind had turned to the image of the ancient child. Only two other people would appear that old in the eye of the sword. Benasin and Rejius.

This lady was the immortal girl. Benasin's niece. Rejius's daughter. Stalia. Queen of the Dregmoors and—wedding be cursed!—Varic's mother, here to make certain the Camrithian throne was transferred to the Dregmoors through Varic or herself or both. She would love to return to Lord Rejius with both harps.

Melaia and Lady Jayde fell silent and glared at each other. King Laetham sank to his throne, rubbing his forehead.

"Will there be a wedding or not?" the priest asked sheepishly, his round face white as the moon.

"The harps stay with Melaia," said Trevin. "The warrior woman and I stay as well, Queen Stalia."

Lady Jayde stiffened. "You play a fool's game, young man," she growled.

"I believe the fool's game is carved in stone before Lord Rejius's throne," he said. "He called for you but was told you had already left on your mission, so I played the game in your stead."

King Laetham leaned forward. "What are you saying, Main Trevin?"

Lady Jayde paled but held her chin high. "He's babbling nonsense to avoid being sent to the Dregmoors," she said. "He's afraid they'll find him as guilty as his warrior friend."

Trevin glanced back at Ollena, who still held Fornian at bay. Verbal sparring was akin to sword fighting. *Cut to the inside.* "Maybe the lady will tell us how to release our comains," he said. "They're here, imaged in their own shields."

Lady Jayde snorted. "Madness! Have you ever heard of such, Laetham?"

Look for an advantage. "Your father said he had you in a double bind."

Stalia's expression hardened. For a moment she looked around the room, opening and closing her hands. Then in one swift move, she leaped at the king and pressed a needle-like knife to his throat.

Two guards had started across the dais, but they halted halfway as the entire room froze.

Trevin stepped back, horrified. He had meant to make Lady Jayde admit her true identity but not like this. Crimson-faced, King Laetham gripped the arms of his throne.

Stalia nodded at Melaia. "Bring me the harp. Have your maid fetch the other."

Melaia motioned to Serai, who hesitated for only a moment before slipping out. But Trevin could see Melaia wrestling with herself. She would do anything to keep Stalia from taking the last two harps to the hawkman. Anything but watch her father die.

Trevin sensed malevolents arriving at the entrance and the doorway behind the dais. As Melaia started toward Stalia with the harp, he made the only move he saw that might shift the advantage.

"Play the harp," he told Melaia.

"Bring the harp to me," ordered Stalia, pressing her knife to the king's throat.

Melaia winced with the king, but she had already positioned the harp, and by the time Stalia made her third demand, a tune was in the air.

The floor shivered. Hanging lamps swayed. Guests shared uneasy glances. The priest grabbed the two white cushions and scuttled away.

"No music!" shouted Stalia.

One of the malevolent couples Trevin had seen earlier approached the dais. The king's guards stepped closer.

Melaia shot Trevin a questioning look.

He flexed his fingers, tense and unsure, but nodded, and she kept playing. The floor lurched, and the king's chair slid back, throwing Stalia off balance.

Trevin snatched Arelin's sword and rushed Stalia as the king's guards and Lord Beker engaged the two malevolents. But the dais cracked, throwing Trevin to his knees, and Stalia swept past him, nimbly edging the fissure, headed for Melaia.

Trevin scrambled to his feet, yelling, "Melaia! Stop playing!"

But she had stopped. Wide-eyed, she hugged the harp, retreating from Stalia, her bodyguards shielding her.

Still the floor shook. Cracks widened. The entire hall erupted in a confusion of fighting and fleeing. Angelaeon, malevolents, guards, guests—everyone scrambled for balance as the floor bucked. Catellus engaged Fornian. Ollena lunged at one malevolent, and Jarrod took on another. Pym was swiping with his dagger and dodging. Dwin held a menacing stance as he guarded Hanni and her girls, who had fled into a corner.

"Main Trevin!" King Laetham called. His throne had tilted to one side, pinning him against the wall. He struggled to escape his chair as, one after another, the king's guards fell to the two malevolents.

Lord Beker reached the king first and tried to fend off the malevolents. Trevin drove one of them back, ducked falling plaster, and grabbed King Laetham's arm.

Ollena's fierce yell cut through the mayhem as she sprinted to the dais. Her sword cut down one malevolent. The other retreated as Ollena laid into her.

Trevin helped Lord Beker haul the king out from under his throne.

"Cursed witch!" snarled King Laetham, grabbing one of his guards' swords. He stumbled after Stalia with Lord Beker at his heels.

Catellus dashed up to Trevin. "Help me with the shields." He sheathed his dagger and leaped onto the king's tilted throne. Plaster showered down around him.

"Catellus, get back!" shouted Trevin.

Catellus reached as high as he could, clawing at the wall.

Trevin seized him by the collar and yanked him away as chunks of wall crashed down.

"They'll be buried," cried Catellus, twisting out of Trevin's grip.

Trevin turned to see a malevolent spear one of Melaia's bodyguards. Jarrod pressed the malevolent into a retreat, Livia met the advance of another, and

Stalia stalked toward Melaia's last bodyguard. Behind him, Melaia backed away with the harp, her face ashen.

Trevin began fighting his way toward Melaia, sensing Ollena close behind him.

King Laetham bellowed for the fight to halt, but two malevolents swept toward him and Lord Beker. Ollena dived between them with a shout.

Trevin ducked the wild swing of a sword, ran his attacker through, and stumbled across the upturned floor, desperate to reach Melaia. He saw Jarrod finish off a malevolent. "Jarrod!" he yelled. "Get Melaia and the harp out of here!"

Jarrod nodded and reached for Melaia, and Trevin lunged for Stalia and grabbed her just as another tremor hit. They both fell.

Stalia wormed out of Trevin's grip, scrambled over a pile of roof tiles, and headed for a breach in the south wall.

Trevin stumbled after her. A lampstand toppled, and flames shot up the white drapery. Walls wavered. Shouts rang from every direction.

Stalia slipped through the breach in the wall.

Trevin sidestepped widening cracks, ducked to avoid falling timbers, and swerved to miss tumbling tiles.

At last he gained the breach and edged out into the brine-laden breeze. Into the red of sunset. Onto the promontory of the chalk bluff that ended in a sheer drop to the sea below.

Stalia stood calmly at the edge of the cliff, facing Trevin with her needle-sharp knife, her white cloak billowing in the sea breeze.

Holding his sword with both hands, Trevin eased toward her, determined not to fail this time.

"You're making a grave mistake," said Stalia. "I'm not who you think I am."

"I know." Trevin tightened his grip. Pain numbed his right hand. "You're a decrepit old child."

"Old, I am. Decrepit child? I think not. I'm on your side. I waited here for you."

"Liar. You're here because you're trapped."

"Am I?" She sheathed her knife. "Put away your sword and come with me. We can help each other. I have what you want, and you have what I want."

"I'll see that you never get it." He kept his blade aimed at her heart. As long as he lived, she would not touch the harps. Or Melaia.

"You're wrong," she said. "We're all in the game. But you and I, we're on the same side, Son."

Trevin gritted his teeth. Lord Rejius, too, had called him *son* to taunt him. He narrowed his eyes. "Don't try to manipulate me."

Stalia's eyebrows arched. "How like your father you are. I should never have doubted him when he told me you were safe." She raised her hood.

Trevin caught his breath as the memory flooded in. He stood in a cavern. A cloaked figure rolled him a green ball, large and smooth. He had never seen such a grand bauble. His right hand reached for it, touched it. A dagger flashed. Strong arms grabbed him, pressed his hand, pressed the blood, pressed the flame-hot pain, pressed his mouth to stifle the screams.

As other images surfaced, Trevin struggled to hold his sword steady. He remembered trundling through a long lanterned corridor, clutching his father's big hand, reaching for a carved toy horse on a stone shelf, crawling into his mother's warm lap in a cold, lamp-lit cave. And glancing up from the green ball to see her—it *was* her—cloaked and hooded, attacking him with a dagger.

Trevin stared at Stalia. Her eyes. He remembered her eyes. His hand throbbed.

She was the figure from his terror-dream.

She was his mother.

"You," he growled. "*You* maimed me."

"I saved you," she hissed.

A sea of thoughts crashed over Trevin. He was the son of Stalia and grandson of Rejius, who knew exactly who his game piece was. Every shameful failure, every misstep, every wrong choice washed over Trevin. He was the heir of treachery and deceit and cruelty. He swayed, a wave of nausea weakening his legs.

Stalia's voice drifted around him like a soothing song. "You can help end all this. Come with me. Bring the harps. Bring Melaia."

Melaia's name anchored him. *I forgive you for the past, completely and forever. Can you ever forgive me for what I've done to our future?*

If she could forgive him, and he could forgive her, then he could forgive himself. He could face the whole of his rotten, damnable past.

"It will not control my future," he muttered, gripping his sword.

"Bring the harps," Stalia crooned. "Bring Melaia."

"No!" Trevin shouted. "You will not control my future!" Yelling like a warrior, he lunged.

Stalia turned and stepped off the cliff, the flutter of her cloak the only sound as she dropped out of sight toward the sea.

Trevin stumbled and fell to his knees, gasping, numb. He stared at the spot where Stalia had fallen, half expecting her to reappear. But she didn't. She had vanished, as if she truly had been a dream.

Then he glimpsed movement along the face of the cliff to the east, a white figure gliding swiftly along a ledge only a goat could tread. The Ibex paused and glanced back, her face hidden in the depths of her hood, then disappeared around the curve of the bluff.

Trevin rose slowly, stunned, his breath trapped in his throat.

Then a crash exploded behind him, and he turned to see the entire palace collapse.

"Melaia!" he cried. "Dwin!"

He ran toward the crumbled wall, then staggered back, the blistering flames that licked at the rubble keeping him at bay.

Fool! he railed at himself. Windweaver had told him to use the harp wisely. *Fool!*

Trevin's knees buckled. Trapped between the fire and the cliff, he fell to the ground, exhausted, alone, completely and utterly broken.

CHAPTER 27

A ll night Trevin fought sleep but was too weary to keep his eyes open. He dozed, restless, with flames crackling on one side and waves crashing on the other. He dreamed that Stalia had returned to kill him by stabbing him again and again with her needle-sharp knife.

When he awoke, he discovered a small drak pecking at the harp pendant that lay on his chest.

"Peron!" Trevin grabbed for her, but she squawked and flapped away. "I'm sorry," he called. "I won't hurt you."

She shrank to a speck over the eastern horizon and disappeared.

Trevin closed his hand around the small harp and stared at the smoldering ruins of Alta-Qan. Only a corner of the temple stood whole. The rest was rubble. And undoubtedly a grave.

But whose? It was the one pain he was not prepared to face. He had only just confronted the pain of his past. How could he face a future of agony? And once again, his fault.

He wiped his eyes. How could he survive if—

A shout split the air. His name.

"Here!" he cried, leaping to his feet. He slipped his sword into its scabbard and ran to the edge of the rubble. "Here! On the bluff!"

Picking a path through the smoldering rubble, he slowly made his way to the top of the mound. On the other side, a line of searchers crept across the debris: Caepio, Paullus, Jarrod, Livia, Pym. And Melaia.

Trevin waved and shouted, "Here! Up here!"

As they cheered, Trevin ran, leaped, slid, and slipped down the pile of rubble. The others, Melaia in the lead, scrambled toward him over the debris. She grabbed him, and he pulled her into a tight hug.

"I'm not letting go ever, ever, ever," she cried into his torn tunic. "I thought you had been crushed, and it was my fault."

"Your fault?"

"It was the harp. I began the earthquake by playing the harp."

"I told you to play. If anyone is at fault, it's me." Trevin stroked her hair and looked at the group before him, hanging back. "Where's Dwin?" he asked.

"He's not with you?" asked Jarrod.

Melaia looked up, tears spilling down her cheeks. "We haven't found Dwin or my father or Ollena. But we thought *you* were gone, and here you are. Maybe we'll find the others alive too."

"Hanni and the girls?" asked Trevin.

"With Serai," said Livia. "They've set up a place for the wounded outside the burial grounds."

Trevin held tight to Melaia. She was trembling like a scared rabbit. "Catellus?"

"He's working with the shields." Pym raked his hand through his hair. "He's trying to find a way to release the comains. He's desperate for it, he is."

"And the harps?" asked Trevin. "Did you get the harps out?"

"Both," said Melaia.

He looked toward Qanreef sprawling across the coast, its whitewashed houses glinting in the sun. "What about the city?"

"Cracks in every wall," said Paullus, "but here on the bluff is where the ground split."

With Melaia beside him, Trevin joined the searchers. They tossed aside charred wood, roof tiles, and chunks of clay. As they dug through layer after layer of debris, they called out and listened for signs of life.

They found Fornian and Melaia's bodyguards, all three dead. Each body was carried to the burial grounds.

It was late morning when Jarrod shouted, "Over here!"

Trevin and Melaia staggered through the wreckage to where Jarrod, Caepio, and Pym were tugging away timbers. When Trevin neared, Jarrod pointed into a small chasm. A hand was visible beneath shards of tile. A hand wearing a large ruby ring.

They yanked aside piece after piece of tile and stone. The first body they reached was Ollena's, a dagger protruding from her chest. The king groaned beneath her.

Trevin knelt and helped raise her out of the chasm. He thought he caught a whiff of sandalwood, but where was the light, the sunset red? She would open her eyes, wouldn't she? She couldn't be gone.

Breathe, Ollena. Breathe. You were born to this. You were born to this. You were.

Trevin bowed his head.

A soft hand swept back his hair. "She saved my father's life," murmured Melaia.

"It's what she was born to do," said Trevin.

Livia knelt beside him. "Do you want to help carry her to the burial grounds?"

Trevin wiped his eyes and shook his head. "I have to find Dwin."

He watched as Livia, Pym, and a group of townsmen carried Ollena and the king toward the grounds beyond the temple wall, which had become a field of the dead and wounded. Melaia walked with them, holding the king's hand.

Trevin wiped his brow on his sleeve and turned back to the search, calling for Dwin. Now and then he paused to eye the city streets below, hoping to see his brother among the milling crowds. A call from Jarrod or Paullus or Catellus, who had joined the search midafternoon, would take him scrambling their direction, dreading what he would find.

As the sun lowered, a cry rang from the far eastern end of the rubble. Trevin, weary and sore, wove his way to Jarrod and Catellus.

"We found Lady Jayde's knife." Jarrod handed him a thin, needle-sharp blade.

Trevin's heart sank. "The lady had her knife with her when she escaped. This is Dwin's."

He attacked the hill of debris with the blade, digging like a madman. The knife hit stone.

"Dwin!" Trevin called, prying at the stone's edge. It didn't move, but he heard a groan. "Dwin!" Furiously he swept rubble from the huge stone.

The rest of the searchers joined him. Together they wedged up the massive stone. As they heaved it aside, they saw a small chamber formed by angled slabs of wall. At the bottom lay Dwin, unmoving.

Trevin climbed into the rift. As he stroked Dwin's dark curls back from his eyes, Dwin groaned, and his swollen face contorted with pain. "You'll be all right, Dwin," said Trevin. "You'll live."

"That's a pity," Dwin whispered.

Catellus climbed down with an armful of cloaks tied end to end, and Trevin slipped the center cloak under Dwin like a sling. Together, the search party eased Dwin out of the rubble.

As they approached the burial grounds, Melaia ran to Trevin, her eyes swollen from crying. "Is he—"

"Alive," said Trevin. "But it will be a while before he bests me at swords."

They laid Dwin on a mat beside Lord Beker, who winced as Hanni bandaged his arm.

Melaia knelt on the other side of Dwin. "Trevin?"

He looked up. Even with dirt streaks across her face and her hair mussed, she was beautiful, her eyes wide and questioning.

"My father is badly wounded," she said softly. "What if—"

Trevin felt her panic. If the king died, she would be queen. He surveyed the grounds. Guards, many of them Angelaeon, stood posted in a perimeter around the field. He had been too distraught to sense them before, but now he felt their light forming a barrier of protection.

"My mind is a pile of rubble," she said. "I can't think."

He helped her up, and they made their way to the king. Serai was bathing his forehead with an herb-scented cloth. "He's sleeping," she said.

"His legs are crushed." Melaia sat beside her father. "And one hand."

"Hanni says the king will live," said Serai. "He may regain strength in his hand, but he'll not have the use of his legs."

Melaia wiped tears from her eyes and held the king's good hand.

Trevin felt completely useless. Melaia needed his comfort, but he needed hers. He left her with the king and was wandering toward where Ollena's body was laid out when he noticed Catellus under a tree, bowed over the comains' shields. Trevin moved to Catellus and placed a hand on his back.

Everyone needed comfort, and strangely enough, that thought was comforting.

～✲～

The Full Sail was crowded that night. The king occupied the largest room upstairs with Melaia. Hanni and her girls took a room nearby, as did Lord Beker. Jarrod, Serai, and Livia remained with the injured and dead outside the ruins of Alta-Qan.

Trevin, Catellus, and Pym carried Dwin and the shields into the cellar, where Cilla set out ointment, poultices, and a potion of painkiller, thoroughly instructing Trevin in their use. During the night every time Dwin moaned, Trevin awoke and shifted a poultice or gave Dwin a sip of the potion.

And every time Trevin returned to his mat and closed his eyes, he saw Ollena wielding her sword, shooting an arrow, watching him from the landing at the Navian inn or on the deck of the ship or on horseback on the road. He wondered what he could have done differently. How could he have saved her?

After Cilla brought breakfast the next morning, a puffy-eyed Caepio arrived to fetch the shield of his brother Vardamis. Since Dwin was sleeping soundly, Trevin joined Caepio, Catellus, and Pym over the shields.

"You're certain the comains are melded to their shields?" asked Caepio.

"I'm sure," said Catellus.

Trevin was sure too. Like the flower on Melaia's chair and the cave paintings, the comains were flattened, imaged as their chosen emblem of valor in their shields. Undrian the protective bear. Gremel the defending ram. Brevian the furtive rock badger. Vardamis the swift osprey. Solivius the elusive partridge. Catellus's son as his father's strong white stag.

As Trevin scanned the shields, his hands tingled with heat.

Catellus shook his head. "I know no way of releasing them. Maybe Varic did, but he's gone."

Trevin's hands blazed as if Flametender were touching them. *Seed of wind, heir of fire, born to free.* He rubbed his palms together. *Born to free. Born to free.*

"I know how it's done," he said, heading for the stairs. "Bring the shields to the corner of the temple at Alta-Qan."

After asking Hanni and the girls to look after Dwin, Trevin sprinted to the ruins of the temple, praying he would find the net. Jarrod's quarters were buried under rubble, but Trevin knew exactly where the net should be. He started digging, his hands hot as fire.

As the others climbed over the rubble with the shields, Trevin called to them, "We're looking for Varic's net. It was under a stool in this corner."

Catellus, Pym, and Caepio dug like mad dogs at the debris and soon reached the stool. It had broken, but the silver net still lay underneath.

Trevin drew out the net and unfolded it, marveling at how wide it spread. He draped it over Catellus's shield, then pressed his hands to it.

His palms felt molten. *Seed of wind, heir of fire, born to free.* Sweat dripped from his forehead and sizzled on the net, which began to rise and bulge and push against him. Trevin eased back but kept his hands on the net until he felt the full form of a crouching boy underneath. When he slipped off the net, a lad with big ears looked around, dumbstruck. Catellus had the boy in his arms before Trevin could rise.

"Great stars!" Caepio gaped at Trevin. "How did you do that?"

"Flametender's gift." Trevin stared at his hands. "She touched me with her fire in Eldarra, but I didn't know why."

"A better gift I never knew." Pym solemnly laid Undrian's shield in Trevin's hands. "Freeing what's bound."

Trevin bent to his task once more, this time releasing Main Undrian, a tall, thin man with feathery white hair.

Caepio handed over the next shield, and soon his brother Vardamis emerged, a dashing nobleman smoothing his tunic as he rose with his close-shaven armsman. Bulky Main Gremel and his ruddy-cheeked aide came next. Then paunchy, bald Main Brevian and fair-haired Main Solivius, each with a young armsman at his side.

Trevin's hands remained hot until all had been restored. Then he leaned against the wall, feeling as dazed as the comains and their armsmen looked.

Caepio and Pym ran for water and wagons to carry the comains to the Full Sail. As the wagons rattled down the road, Trevin made his way through the rubble to Jarrod, who was supervising the digging of graves.

Trevin scanned the shrouded bodies. "Ollena?" he asked.

Jarrod pointed to one figure set apart, covered with the king's cloak. "Melaia wants her buried in the royal plot."

Trevin's throat was too tight to reply. He simply trudged to the body, knelt, and bowed his head.

◦❦◦

That night over food and drink in the common room, the comains took turns describing their ordeals. Cilla had given Dwin permission to lie on a mat and listen, and Trevin sat on a bench nearby, leaning forward to hear the details.

In each case an urgent message stamped with King Laetham's seal had summoned them to come immediately to the king's aid at the citadel in Qanreef. On the way each comain had been ambushed by Varic, trapped by a great net of silver mesh. Some said the net made them feel as if the sun was drying them like a raisin, leaving them with nothing but their life force. Others described the sensation of a wasting disease draining their strength and leaving them powerless.

Having survived a net in the Dregmoors, Trevin understood at least part of the feeling. A living death. He shuddered. Trapped within their own shields, the comains and their armsmen had been able to see and think but could not speak or move. They had been helpless when Varic scattered their shields throughout the kingdom to confuse searchers.

The lamps burned low, Cilla cleared tables, and Paullus topped off mugs. The comains began to reminisce, swapping stories of their travels.

Melaia returned from caring for the king upstairs and sank onto the bench next to Trevin. "My father will recover," she said, "but his winter palace is rubble."

"We'll have to stay the winter at Redcliff," said Trevin.

She rubbed her arms. "Redcliff is cold in the winter."

"I'll keep you warm." Trevin put his arm around her.

She laid her head on his shoulder. "In that case I may enjoy winter after all."

Dwin cleared his throat, and Trevin scowled at him. Having a spy for a brother held definite disadvantages.

⟨꧞⟩

One more task loomed ahead of Trevin: confessing to Jarrod about Dreia's death. He tried to tell himself Jarrod didn't need to know and busied himself caring for Dwin, clearing rubble, and mending cracks around the Full Sail.

But each day he avoided the matter, the bigger it grew and the more tainted he felt. He couldn't help thinking of the malevolents, whose aura always seemed corrupted. Rusty, moldy, impure. He wondered if that was because of guilt or shame or self-deceit.

At last Trevin grew weary of fighting it and asked Jarrod to join him on an evening stroll along the wharf.

As they set out, the sea sparkled gold in the setting sun. Fishermen pulled in nets and sorted their catches. Boatmen secured their vessels, and sailors headed to taverns.

Trevin strode tensely along the sea walk. "I've a confession," he said.

"No need," said Jarrod. "I don't hold you responsible for the quake."

"That's good to know," said Trevin, "but my confession has to do with Dreia."

Jarrod looked askance at him.

Trevin kicked a rock toward the skeletal remains of Alta-Qan jutting up from the chalk cliff. "I was involved in Dreia's death."

As dusk settled around them, he explained his past to Jarrod as he had to Benasin and Melaia.

Torchlighters passed, making their rounds. Jarrod kept a measured stride, staring ahead silently, his jaw clenched. Trevin felt the distance between them.

Jarrod stopped at the base of the climb to Alta-Qan and sat on a large stone that had tumbled down the hill. Shoulders slumped, he studied his clasped hands. "You're no more at fault than I," he said. "I was at Aubendahl when Dreia came for the harp. I knew she meant to take it to her child who had come of age, 'breath of angel, blood of man.'"

"Melaia," said Trevin.

"I thought the child was a son," said Jarrod. "I was jealous, convinced I should have been that child. But I intended to go with Dreia. I was in the middle of copying a scroll and asked her to wait for me so I could accompany her, but she left without telling me. She was always doing that. I was so exasperated with her,

I didn't follow. Until the message came that her caravan was under attack. I arrived too late." He picked up a rock and flung it into the moonlit sea.

Trevin scooped up a handful of rocks and threw them one after the other as hard as he could. Jarrod threw his handful all at once. They peppered the water with stones until they were panting and sweating.

For a moment Jarrod stared out into the dark waves. Then he started back toward the Full Sail.

Trevin watched him walk away. No doubt Jarrod would never speak to him again. He grabbed the largest stone he could hold and hurled it at the ruins of Alta-Qan.

"Come on," called Jarrod. "Life is best lived forward."

Trevin turned to see the warrior angel waiting for him.

Jarrod raised his eyebrows. "I happen to know where Paullus keeps a fine aged southern isles wine."

Trevin grinned and loped to Jarrod. Shoulder to shoulder they headed down the torchlit sea walk.

⚜

After the palace fell, the court stayed a fortnight in Qanreef. Then they returned to Redcliff, accompanied by the six comains and their armsmen. As the group traveled north, they found that the earthquake had closed the rifts. But gash had damaged fields and farmlands, and only a few families were on the roads venturing back home.

The day after arriving at Redcliff, Trevin climbed the stairs to the top of the highest tower of the palace. From the parapet he watched a group of settlers journey east across the valley. The weather was sunny and windless but cold, and he drew his heavy cloak tight.

Walking the skies with Windweaver, circling Redcliff, he had sensed that the royal city was the hub of a great wheel. Now he sensed the spokes of that wheel as he paced the square roof, gazing over the walls in each direction. One spoke stretched north to Eldarra, one west to the Durenwoods, one south to Qanreef, and one east. To the Dregmoors.

He stared at the eastern horizon, his shoulders tense. In the depths of his being, he knew he was destined to go back to that land of cliffs and caves.

"I've found you." Melaia stepped out of the stairwell. "You're at the top of the world today."

Trevin took her hand. "Not until you arrived."

She looked toward the valley. "While you were up north, I came here often, thinking of you, hoping for your safe return."

"I did return one day. With Windweaver. We stood in this very place, and I heard you play your harp."

"It wasn't my imagination, then. I heard a question on the wind: *What do you seek?*"

Trevin chuckled. "That was Windweaver talking to me."

"What did you answer?"

"I didn't. I didn't know what to say. Not until later."

The wind gusted, and Melaia pulled her cloak snug. "What did you answer later?"

"I told Windweaver I sought myself."

"Have you found yourself?"

"I have." Trevin drew her into the folds of his cloak. He thought of his image in the eye of the sword. "I'm competent, reliable, persistent, confident, and hopeful." He grinned at her. "Also quite attractive."

"And terribly humble," said Melaia.

"I'm working on that part," said Trevin.

Melaia gave a mock sigh. "How can I hope to ever be worthy of your affections?"

"It's I who have been striving to be worthy of you."

"You know my vow about you still stands now that Varic is gone. My father may not approve of me pledging myself to anyone except royalty, but—"

"Perhaps your father is right."

Melaia pulled away. "What?"

"You deserve only the best. I think you should pledge yourself to someone who is an heir of not one but two thrones."

She stood there, shivering. "Trevin! You can't mean it!"

He drew her back into his cloak. "Take me for example. I'm the son of the warrior angel Arelin, also known as the Asp."

Her jaw dropped. "Son of the Asp? An angel? So you *are* Nephili, just as Livia suspected."

"I may be rather like Jarrod."

"How?"

"My mother is an immortal. Stalia."

Melaia's eyes widened.

He held her astonished gaze, trusting she would understand that he felt as appalled as she did. "Stalia called me *son,* and my memories tell me she's right."

Melaia studied his face. "But that means Lord Rejius is your grandfather. Benasin is your great-uncle—which makes you related to Jarrod!"

"Which will delight him to no end."

Melaia laughed, then bit her lip and paled. "Varic."

Trevin's stomach knotted. "My brother."

"But Varic was not an angel," said Melaia. "No one sensed him."

"I suspect he was a half brother, maybe adopted. But he knew who I was. Remember on the temple roof? He said, 'I shall have the throne. Not you.' I thought he meant the throne of Camrithia, which he would gain by marrying you and denying me the privilege. But he meant the throne of the Dregmoors."

"So that's why he was so intent on destroying you," said Melaia. "He wanted to be heir in the Dregmoors. But *you* are."

"I'm also heir of the Eldarran throne."

Melaia frowned. "*That* doesn't make sense at all."

"It's a long story," said Trevin.

"In that case you should start it now. Maybe you'll be done before we freeze."

Trevin began the story atop the tower, but by the time he finished, they were seated on cushions before the hearth fire in Melaia's apartment. Trevin studied her, smiling. He could be in the most frigid wastes of the north without cloak or fire, and as long as Melaia was with him, he would be warm.

She took his hand. "Two kingdoms will be rightfully yours someday. Eldarra and the Dregmoors."

"We're both heirs." Trevin knelt before her and kissed her soft, scented hands. "Shall we unite our kingdoms, my lady? We don't have to wait until we're crowned."

Melaia knelt facing him. "I have only two harps, Trevin. You know where the third is. I can't settle. Not yet."

Trevin searched her dark eyes. "Have you changed your mind about me?"

Melaia slipped her finger beneath the cord that held his harp pendant and eased it out from under his tunic. She matched it to her own, making a heart.

Trevin wrapped his hands around hers as she clasped the heart.

She leaned closer, her eyes holding his. "I've not changed my mind. Help me unite the harps. Then I'm yours, body, soul, and spirit."

He leaned into her clean lavender scent. "Promise," he said.

"I promise," she said.

"Again."

"I promise."

"Again," he breathed.

"I—"

His mouth found hers. Silver and gold.

The past lay behind. He was the man in the eye of the sword. And he held his future in his arms.

ACKNOWLEDGMENTS

I've never achieved anything without the help and support of friends and family. Many thanks to

friends and faculty of the Vermont College of Fine Arts;

my insightful critique partners,
Helen Hemphill and Wilmoth Foreman;

my husband, Ralph, for his patience;

my agent, Cheryl Pientka,
for believing in my imagined world;

my editor, Jessica Barnes,
who traveled my fantasy world with me and understood.

ABOUT THE AUTHOR

KARYN HENLEY grew up on myths, fairy tales, and spiritual stories and began writing because she loved to read. She is now an award-winning author with more than one hundred titles to her credit, including books for children, parents, and teachers, as well as CDs and DVDs of original music. She received an MFA in writing for children and young adults from the Vermont College of Fine Arts and has traveled worldwide as an educational speaker and children's entertainer. She lives in Nashville, Tennessee, with her husband, a jazz drummer. Visit her at www.breathofangel.com.